I0777756

THE HONEYMOON TRAP CONFESSIONS

CHRISTINA HOVLAND

This book is a work of fiction. Names, characters, places, and incidents are the product of the author's imagination or are used fictitiously. Any resemblance to actual events, locales, or persons, living or dead, is coincidental.

The Honeymoon Trap original copyright 2018 by Christina Hovland.

Revised version, The Honeymoon Trap Confessions, copyright 2024 by Christina Hovland.

All rights reserved, including the right to reproduce, distribute, or transmit in any form or by any means.

For rights information, please contact:
Prospect Agency
551 Valley Road, PMB 377
Upper Montclair, NJ 07043
(718) 788-3217

Cover Illustrations: Enroc Illustration
Cover Design: Christina Hovland

Portions of this book were originally published as
The Honeymoon Trap in 2018.

For L.A. Mitchell, writing coach extraordinaire.

Because she believed in me.

AUTHOR'S NOTE

The Honeymoon Trap Confessions was the very first novel I ever wrote. It's the book I wrote to see if I could write a book. It was eventually published as The Honeymoon Trap with a substantially different second half.

At the time I wrote the original version, I loved reading romantic comedy with some suspense elements. But, for many reasons, the suspense elements didn't make that final cut in The Honeymoon Trap.

Now, in 2024, when I went back through to re-release the book, I added in everything that I wanted to keep. Including those suspense elements.

I hope you love William and Lucy as much as I do.

xoxo
Christina

CHAPTER
ONE

William Covington desperately needed a beer and a place to crash. Most of all, he needed a damn rooster to speak. Sweat beaded along his hairline from the sweltering July heat. Dust particles swirled through the air of the dirt parking lot where the KDVX live truck was stationed. The muffled sounds of a banjo from the bluegrass band on the main stage played in the distance.

He urged the man in the bulky costume to look into the camera and say something. Anything.

"What does Magic Mike mean to the people of Confluence?" William stepped closer and nudged the guy with his elbow, his arm sinking into the mass of feathers.

The director's monotone voice buzzed in his earpiece. "Miracle Mike, not Magic Mike. The rooster's not a stripper."

"Miracle Mike," William corrected.

And he was interviewing a chicken. Rooster. Whatever.

He held the mic closer to his guest's glossy orange beak.

Although the oversize mascot had chatted like a pro before the interview, he now remained silent. Rooster Man apparently took his performance art seriously because he pecked at the air and shuffled silently in place. Festival onlookers shifted backward as the costumed man bobbed his head in the hypnotic way of a chicken.

A fluff piece about the annual Miracle Mike Headless Chicken Festival was fast becoming William's journalistic downfall. Years of working his way up through larger and more exclusive news markets should have prepared him for a situation like this. He had investigated Wall Street scandals, extracted information from whistleblowers, and mastered the man-on-the-street interview. Now, in his debut appearance in the smallest television market he had ever worked, he couldn't get a man in a rooster suit to cough up a sentence. Not even a word. Low-level reporting at the station was meant to introduce him to operations at his family's television station, not humiliate him in front of the whole damn town.

In the years he'd been gone, not much had changed in Confluence. The citizens still thrived on all things nutty— especially the legendary bird. A headless Miracle Mike costume, the mayor had decided, might chase off tourists and didn't leave much breathing room for a full-size man. So the people of Confluence chose to celebrate the Mike of his youth with his head firmly attached. The tourists ate it up.

The roving rooster made a show of pecking his way through the crowd and flapping his wings. Clearly the bird had his own agenda.

William scrambled after him, the cameraman following.

The director buzzed again in his ear. "Get him to talk, Cronkite."

Yeah.

"Will you be running the marathon tomorrow?" William flashed a grin at the camera. He refused to be broken by an oversize cock.

The rooster paused his movement and stood stiff.

Unresponsive.

William held his permanent smile while jockeying to get a response. "I saw you crossing the road earlier. I'm sure our viewers are curious to know why?"

"Bwaak," screeched the rooster.

William's hands itched to choke the chicken.

"Keep it serious," the director said, low and threatening.

William tossed his best what-do-you-want-me-to-do look at the camera.

Rooster man inexplicably burst into a rendition of the funky chicken dance.

William moved out of the way, but the bird bobbed left when his oversize costume feet stepped right, and without even a cluck, he fell face-first onto William.

Feathers, wings, red chicken feet, and William blended into one dusty jumble. He grunted as he reached for a wing, only to get a handful of feathers. They tumbled to the ground, William doing his best to break the fall for Rooster Man.

It worked and the guy now sprawled over him—the top half of a William chicken sandwich.

"There's the money shot." The director chuckled. "Cut back to the studio so these two can have some privacy."

William stifled his groan. He'd never live this down.

The man yanked his costume head free, and perspiration soaked his red face.

With a little help from William, the guy managed to roll off and sit up to brush the dirt from his feathers. "Didn't expect that to happen."

"Makes two of us." William stood and helped him to his huge feet. "What was that all about, anyway?"

Rooster dude wobbled as he stood, tugging the costume head back on. "Method acting, man. Chickens don't talk."

"Gotcha. Well, dedication to the craft. Can't deny that," William said.

William picked up his microphone and shook the dust off the KDVX station flag wrapped around it.

Just like that, he had added one more tick-mark to his father's list of Things William Managed to Screw Up. If he couldn't handle a simple interview, how the hell would he prove he had the grit to run the family company? His father still hadn't forgiven the debacle William's foray into reality television caused, and that was a decade ago.

It didn't need to be so complicated.

Move back to hometown? Check.

Smooth the way to inherit family broadcasting company on upcoming thirtieth birthday? Check.

Interview an uncooperative man in a rooster suit? Nope. Not in the plan.

William rolled the sleeves of his collared shirt to his elbows. His jeans were covered in dirt from the fall, and his whole body seemed to itch in the stale summer air. Parched breaths filled his lungs as he helped the crew pack up cameras and load bags of equipment into the news van.

"Thanks for helping out today," said Al, the cameraman, as he collapsed a leg on the tripod. "You're a lifesaver."

William shrugged. Lifesaver? No. "Only a little teamwork."

The reporter scheduled for the interview hadn't shown so William helped out when the crew was in a pinch.

"Hey, you see Parker yet?" William tossed the microphone into an open bag. Over an hour had come and gone since he planned to meet his oldest, best friend here. Parker was his last shot at a place to crash tonight.

The cameraman grunted and pointed toward the crowd surrounding the news van.

Parker emerged with a smirk. "That is one baked chicken."

In his overpriced suit, Parker had to be roasting. Unlike William, no sign of sweat appeared anywhere. Always dressed his best, Parker exuded Ivy League authority as the station manager.

"About tonight." William squirmed a bit.

"Man, I told you, out by five," Parker said. "I hate to do it, but I have to. Your dad's clear on this, and right now *he's* my boss."

"I can't believe you're on his side. He has his hooks in the whole town. I searched everywhere for a place to live today. I couldn't even get a room at the Pillow Talk Motel." William scraped a hand over his hair.

Parker held up his palms and backed away, frustration etched in the lines around his mouth. "I'm Switzerland here. Neutral. I need my job. Talk to him."

William ground out the words, "Not happening."

"Your call." Parker shrugged. "See you Monday at the station."

Over a decade of friendship, and that's all William got. He didn't want to add his family drama to Parker's plate, but was it so wrong to want a little backup?

It seemed that everyone in town had received a don't-rent-to-my-long-lost-son decree from his father. Joe Covington always got what he wanted, and now he wanted to keep tabs on his son by forcing him to move back under his roof. Hell, it wasn't William's fault his mother left Crestone Broadcasting to him instead of his father.

William massaged the ache in his temples as his last option drifted away. Whatever pride he had packed when he moved to Confluence vanished.

He walked the three blocks to Love's Travel Stop where he'd left his truck. He lowered the tailgate and sat. Forget about proving to everyone he could run his mother's company. At this point, he couldn't even find a place to live. His only option at the moment was a two-hour commute from a hotel in the next county over, but he wouldn't be surprised if his dad's influence reached across the state to Denver.

Nearby, a kid messed around with rocks and a slingshot on the small grassy area bordering the convenience store. A large dog dripping slobber barked and bounded around the boy's feet. The mutt appeared to be the unfortunate offspring of a one-night stand between Sasquatch and a grimy kitchen mop. At the release of the slingshot, he chased the rock across the patch of lawn.

Something near the gas pumps caught the mutt's attention. His ears perked, and he barked once.

William glanced across the lot.

A pretty brunette climbed from a yellow Ford sedan and slammed the door. Her long red skirt caught when it closed. Tethered, she engaged in a mesmerizing "Flight of the Bumblebee" dance until she wrestled the fabric free.

William grinned, disappointed the cloth had surrendered. He wouldn't have given in so easily.

She sauntered past him while pulling her long hair up into a clip, exposing the soft white skin of her neck. This woman wasn't department store pretty, plastered with product and buffed to a shine. No, she didn't need any help. She was naturally beautiful. Her full lips tipped into an utterly kissable pout, and the way her hips swayed when she moved—gorgeous. He followed her with his gaze until she disappeared inside the convenience store.

A golf-ball-sized rock whizzed past him to ding off his truck bed.

He glanced to the boy and raised a questioning brow.

The boy shrugged before he turned to toss rocks toward the creek.

William thumbed through his contacts on his cell phone. Surely, he knew someone with connections for an apartment, a house… even floor space for a sleeping bag. He glanced up again when the brunette came out of the convenience store. She held a massive fountain drink in one hand while she fumbled with her keys at her car door.

A loud bang echoed across the lot. Glass fell from the car window, the small pieces falling in chunks to the pavement. A scream ripped from her lungs, and she flung herself to the ground.

His heart stuttered. He ran to her side and crouched, heaving a hard, fast exhale. "You okay?"

Blood seeped from a gash where her bare knee had collided with the asphalt. Sticky orange soda and little pieces of gravel littered her clothes. She pushed herself up. The woman was naturally pale, but at the moment, her skin had gone white.

She gripped his offered hand to help her sit. Her pulse raced under his thumb.

She leaned against him as he helped her to her feet.

"What was that?" She scanned the parking lot.

He jerked his chin at the boy. "Kid over there is shooting rocks with a slingshot."

The young kid stood with his mouth gaping. His dog's tail thumped the grass.

"A kid? You're kidding." The woman blinked hard and pushed

hair from her eyes. A scent of orange soda mixed with coconut drifted from her. The women he usually dated preferred designer perfume from pricey department stores, not a siren song of the tropics. Her vulnerable chestnut-colored eyes moved to him, and right then he decided his favorite color was brown.

"What's your name?"

"Lu-Lucy—" She stopped and bit at her lower lip. "Just Lucy."

A flicker of recognition sparked in her eyes. Being identified as a TV personality was part of the on-air gig for William, but as a new journalist in Confluence, this was the first time he caught that flash of awareness here.

He introduced himself as they walked to a picnic table on the grass.

She slumped to the bench.

The kid moped to where Lucy sat.

William knew what it was like to be a kid who messed up, so he kept his words as kind as possible. "Did you have something you wanted to say to her?"

"I—I—" the boy began. "I didn't mean to break your window. It was just a rock."

William nodded and glanced around. "Where are your parents?"

The boy lifted a shoulder. "Don't got a mom. Dad's in the store."

William blew out a long breath.

As if on cue, a brawny police officer emerged from inside the gas station. He stalked toward them with the authority of a sheriff in an old-time western movie. The dog let out a deep *wrrrooof*.

"Dad," the boy whispered, his eyes wide.

The officer glanced at Lucy, the slingshot, and over to the shattered window. His mouth dropped in an exact replica of the boy's. "What happened, Simon?"

Tears spilled down the boy's face. "It was my rock."

The towering cop briefly closed his eyes. "Apologies for my son. I'm Jeff Lawson, Chief of Police here in Confluence."

"Chief Lawson, I'm William," he said. "This is Lucy."

"Call me Jeff."

Lucy sat taller. "It's my car."

"Ma'am." Jeff bowed his head slightly and surveyed her oozing knee. "I'll see to the window repair, and that knee may need stitches. Real sorry for my boy."

"I'll be fine. It's just a small cut. But my window…" She waved her hand toward the car.

"I know a guy who'll replace it." He pulled out a cell phone and tapped in a few numbers. With only a few words, he arranged for an on-site fix and then shoved it in his pocket. "He's on his way. I'll deal with my son and be right back." He snatched the slingshot with one hand and the back of Simon's collar with the other. "C'mon."

Simon mouthed "Sorry" over his shoulder and tripped along beside his father. The dog trotted after them, cheerful and oblivious. While Simon climbed in the front seat, Jeff opened the back for the dog and slammed the door before climbing into the driver's side.

William eyed Lucy and sat beside her as the cop drove away.

"I can't believe a kid broke my window." She bit at her thumbnail.

"Is there someone we can call for you?" he asked.

"No one." Something a whole lot like disappointment flickered across her face.

"Then I'll stick around. I don't mind." Not like he had anywhere else to be at the moment, given his lack of housing prospects. Besides, he was a moth to her flame, or some craziness like that.

She glanced to him, her gaze flicking to his lips, and the air around them went heavy. The blood in his veins pulsed uneven.

"Thank you," she said.

The moment broken, she dug through her purse and tugged free a makeup compact. A giant black smudge of asphalt darkened her cheek. The clip had dislodged from her pinned-up hair so loose waves fell down her back. He liked it better down.

A glance in the mirror, and she grimaced.

She went back to rummaging through her purse and a small note fell beside his arm. He reached for the paper and began to hand it back when he caught the words and paused.

Camelot Garden Estates
First left at the Confluence exit...

Funny, he had been all over town today and hadn't thought of Camelot Gardens. That rundown neighborhood still existed? The lady who owned a bunch of property there used to drive his father crazy during his years on the city council, opposing him on everything. If she was still around, maybe she held a grudge?

Lucy wiped the cut on her knee, removed the tabs from a Band-Aid, and stuck it on.

"Do you know someone who lives at Camelot Gardens?" he asked.

Her features turned guarded, and she paused longer than necessary. "I have a friend who used to live there."

"Yeah? So do I."

Camelot Gardens was so rundown, it was an awful idea for him to stay there.

Then again, this idea was better than no idea.

God, *God*, William had aged well. Lucy Campbell's whole body had tingled when he helped her up, but damned if she was going *there*. All these years later, and his presence still managed to override all her brain circuits dedicated to reason. The ones that turned her into a stammering idiot, high on lusty intoxication, were still on alert.

Sure, it was only a broken window. And a bruised knee. With a side of throwing-herself-on-the-ground embarrassment. The years melted away, the clock struck twelve, her coach fizzled into a pumpkin, and she turned back into the mess-of-a-girl Lulu. On cue, her stomach somersaulted and begged for a bag of potato chips. She ignored the plea.

True to his word, Chief Lawson had arranged for a replacement window. It had taken hours, and she was exhausted.

She clicked on the speakerphone and drove away from the gas station.

Her best friend Katie chirped at her. "Lulu, where the hell are you?"

"A kid threw a rock at my car. I had to get my window fixed."

"Omigosh, are you okay?"

"I'll be fine."

"Are you at the house yet?"

"Nope, headed there now."

"Okay, I'm glad I caught you before you got there." Best friends since they were roommates in college, Katie Edwards was the only person in the world Lucy trusted. Katie had left Confluence two weeks ago when she received a promotion to Denver. She arranged for Lucy's transfer to KDVX, the local television station, and promised the house she'd arranged for Lucy would be perfect.

Lucy was done taking handouts from her parents. Done with relying on them. They had the best intentions. Wanted her to realize her dreams without the struggle, but she was ready to do things on her own. They'd encouraged her to rent a luxury three-bedroom condo on their dime. She'd decided to rent a place she could afford instead—baby steps to releasing herself from their grip.

"Listen, promise me you'll give the place a chance," Katie continued.

"Why wouldn't I? It's a place to live," Lucy said.

"It's just not your usual *house*. But the people are great, and you'll be safe there."

The town provided a refuge for Lucy until the police caught the creep who had hurt her, but she should be anchoring the evening news in Cleveland, her next step to the national stage, not driving into a phony life in Nowhere, Colorado.

Lucy resolved to stop ruminating over the turn her life had taken. She gripped the steering wheel. "I hate hiding."

More than that, she hated giving up her dream of being a national news reporter.

The minute she stepped into her first journalism class; a spark had lit inside her. She was born to expose the truth.

"You'll never guess who I saw." Heck, she couldn't even believe she'd seen William again after all of these years.

"Who?"

"William. The 'next, please' guy from Florida."

That was the thing he used to say for the cameras in Florida. When they showed a clip of him in a lip-lock they'd cut to his interview where he always said, "Next, please."

"Get. Ouuut." Katie's words were filled with disbelief. "Did he remember you?"

"Nope." And why would he? The last time she saw William, she'd been a gawky, uncomfortable seventeen-year-old with horrible acne, braces, and ridiculously thick eyebrows that merged together. He'd known Lulu, intern on the *Beach Nights* reality show.

Eight years had been plenty of time for her to transform into who she dreamed of becoming. She now sported clear skin, straight teeth, and two distinct well-groomed brows.

"Did he grow warts all over and turn into a toad?" Katie asked.

"Not even a little bit of a toad."

"Damn."

"Actually, he was really sweet. He even stuck around with me while we waited for the guy to come fix my window."

The same golden eagle eyes and crumpled L.L. Bean charm had melted her like an ice cream cone dropped on a hot sidewalk. Rich brown hair trimmed short but long enough to have a smidge fall to his forehead. He was tall, at least six foot, likely more. Two delicious dimples popped when he smiled, and crinkles fanned from the sides of his eyes. Those hadn't been there all those years ago when she'd crushed on him in Florida.

In her summer internship with that film company, she pretty much did all the jobs that no one else wanted to do and ran errands for the cast and crew. Which, at the time, included William.

One day he disappeared, and she never saw him again... until today.

What the heck was he doing in a small town like Confluence, anyway?

"It's good he didn't remember. I can't be known as Lulu."

No. Now she was Lucy. She had worked hard to shed her former self. She wouldn't go back to the girl she had been.

"There is nothing wrong with Lulu. I liked her. I still do." Katie's voice went soft. "As I recall, he wasn't very nice."

"He just didn't know I existed." There was a difference. "If he's going to be in Confluence, I'll avoid him." She didn't need a reminder of the person she used to be. The person everyone made fun of. "It'll be best."

"Or maybe you won't have to avoid him because he'll 'next, please' himself right out of town," Katie replied cheerfully.

Gravel crackled against the car's undercarriage when Lucy turned into the drive. "I'm here."

A dilapidated sign, white with yellowed edging, announced the neighborhood as Camelot. The *o* and *t* were slightly crooked so at first glance it simply read *Camel*. Instead of a neighborhood, Camelot Estates was a series of squat, one-story buildings that had likely been an extended-stay motel, last remodeled in 1963.

"Oh my God, Katie. What have you done?" Lucy asked.

"Just give the place a chance." The line went dead before Lucy could respond.

No, no, no. Lucy parked the car and climbed out, squinting into the setting sun.

Perhaps being dependent on her parents wasn't such a bad idea after all? If she'd known this was all she could afford then she might've reconsidered handling her living arrangements on her own.

But…no. She could handle this.

An elderly woman emerged from the yellow unit at the end. The woman's personality and clothing bloomed as colorful as the plastic blue, pink, and purple flowers in the window boxes attached next to each doorway. She reminded Lucy of an exotic bird that had flown too close to a lightning storm. Once beautiful, that was clear. Now she had that look of someone who went through hell and lived to tell about it. Singed around the edges with a few fried circuits.

"You'll be Lucy, Katie's friend?" she asked in a sweet-tea Southern accent. Her smile revealed yellowed teeth to match the Camelot sign. "I'm Dixie, your landlady."

The idea of living in a honest-to-goodness motel triggered a burst of anxiety. The suffocating weight of worry she always carried squeezed tighter. "Is this the house you're renting me?"

Lucy waved a hand toward the door where Dixie had emerged.

"Oh, golly, no," Dixie assured her. Lucy let out a breath.

"This is mine. That 'uns yours." Dixie gestured to the unit next door.

Crap on a croissant.

"Um, Dixie?" She smoothed her skirt with sweaty hands. "This can't be right. Katie told me the house is, well, a *house.*"

Dixie's sweet tea manners soured. "That's a house if I ever saw one. And the lease is signed, so no backin' out now. Here's your key." Dixie produced a glittering rhinestone Elvis keychain from her worn cardigan.

Lucy swallowed hard and pasted a grin on her face. She struggled for words. "Thank you," she said finally.

She squeezed the King in her hand as Dixie padded along in front of her.

The thin metal door opened to a room with dark wood paneling, lime green shag carpet, and an orange floral couch. A bouquet of bleach and industrial-strength Mr. Clean pierced the air inside.

Double crap on a croissant. If she clicked her heels together three times, maybe a tornado would whisk her away.

Dixie buzzed about the room, flicking on lights and opening thick, polyester curtains. "We all share the washer and dryer up at the community room. You'll find the Coke machine there, too."

Lucy quietly tapped her sling-back heels together.

Click.

Click. Click.

Nothing.

"Wow, there's a bit more space in here than I expected," Lucy said, grasping for something, anything, to compliment. "And it's… clean."

Dixie frowned. "Katie didn't give us any problems. I expect the same from you."

Lucy never caused problems, but lately, her life hadn't gotten the memo.

"Katie told me what happened to you in California with that man followin' you and all."

The savage pressure inside Lucy's chest escalated. "No one is supposed to know about that."

"Well, I'm no busybody, so I won't be flappin' my mouth."

"No, of course not."

Dixie moved through the room, fluffing the pillows on the couch. "That'll be the kitchen, and over there's your room. Bathroom is on the other side. Now, you'll have to remember the air conditioner is a bit iffy sometimes. Call me. I'll send my Jeff over to fix it."

Lucy attempted to keep up. "Jeff?"

"My son lives across the way. He'll come help with your bags."

The apartment was small, simple, clean…and ugly.

Dixie headed for the kitchen and made herself comfortable in a metal chair at the Formica table. Boomerang designs stenciled in vibrant orange and yellow decorated the surface of both the chairs and the table. She retrieved a full pack of worn and crinkled cigarettes from her pocket, tapped one out, looked at it warily, and then slipped it back in. "Will you be on TV like Katie?"

"No, I'm behind the camera this time. Producing."

"Whatever that means," Dixie said blandly. "We sure were proud watching Katie on the TV each night. Made us feel like royalty having a real-life television star next door."

Lucy tried for courtesy. "It's hard to stay hidden when you're on television."

"I suppose." Dixie made a face at Lucy's beat-up appearance. "You'll want to clean up, I'm sure."

Her hot pink fingernails scrolled across the screen of her cell phone, and she lifted it to her ear. "Jeff, it's your mother. Come help the new girl unload her bags." She clicked the off button without waiting for a response.

"Thank you." Lucy inched toward the bathroom to clean up.

Dixie hauled herself to her feet and headed for the door.

The whole wall rattled when she closed it behind her.

Lucy turned on the bath faucet and balanced on the edge of the tub. Warm water swirled at her feet as she peeled away the Band-

Aid on her knee. With her skirt hiked to her thighs, she angled her body to rinse the debris free. Water poured down her leg, and a hiss formed on her lips. Her swollen knee looked as if a colorful plum had sprouted there. Glass had punctured her outer calf, and bits of skin had scraped off her shin. She wiped away the grime, refusing to focus on her deeply crushed pride.

The tub drained while she patted her legs dry with a rough towel. With a resolution that the rest of the night would get better, she pinched color into her cheeks, ran a hand through her hair, and stepped out of the bathroom just as the chief of police she'd met at the gas station brought in the last of her bags. He caught her eye and grimaced.

"*You're* the handyman?" Lucy asked, dumbfounded.

"I suppose so, yes. Although, I've never thought of myself like that." He lifted the bags to the sofa. "I didn't realize you were Katie's friend."

The room appeared to be two sizes too small for him. The ceiling loomed an inch above his head, like Alice in Wonderland after the *Eat Me* cake.

"I'll just…unpack," she said, ready to be by herself.

"Katie told me about what happened to you," he said with unvarnished authority.

"Does everyone in town know what happened to me?" Because that was not going to work.

"No. Promised I'd keep an eye on you. I've got a connection at the department in Humboldt County. He filled me in on the details. If you think of anything new, you'll be sure to tell me? Even if it doesn't seem important. Small details crack cases."

Lucy began to reply when the door opened, and the full force of Dixie erupted into the room. "Everyone's settled," she said to Jeff before turning to Lucy. "Lizzie, our neighbor right next to you, died a week ago. She was only ninety-eight. Bless her heart. And I mean that in the *southern* way." Dixie's eyes glittered as if letting Lucy in on her private joke. "So we got a new tenant there, too. Been a busy day 'round here."

"I'll head over and meet her," Jeff said.

"Him," Dixie corrected.

"I'll go welcome *him* to the neighborhood." Jeff gave a curt nod to Lucy as he hunched to fit through the doorframe.

"He's handsome." Dixie crossed her arms over her chest.

"Excuse me?"

"Your neighbor."

"Well, that's"—Lucy paused, searching for the right word—"nice."

"I know what happens when a good-lookin' man and a woman live close together. I'm a God-fearing Christian lady, so no for-ni-ca-tion in my houses." She finished with a withering stare.

"I, uh, promise not to…fornicate." The last word caught uncomfortably on Lucy's lips.

Dixie held her head high when she rambled from the house. She slammed the door, shaking the very foundation. Lucy moved a box to the kitchen where a breeze blew through the curtains above the stove. She opened a bag of trail mix and stuffed a handful in her mouth, sliding open the door to the tiny patio and stepping outside. Apparently, she shared the space with her neighbor—a very male neighbor with his own door wide open.

He faced the opposite direction, which provided Lucy the opportunity to appreciate everything his gray sweatpants *didn't* cover. She didn't know a back could be ripped like that. The waistband of his pants hung low on defined hips that led down to a set of tight glutes worthy of Adonis. Right then, Lucy didn't mind living in a tiny motel-apartment, and she should probably send Katie a formal thank-you card.

He turned around, but her eyes stayed planted. Lucy didn't frequent bars, but she knew abs like those played a key role in the invention of tequila body shots.

"Hey, neighbor," he said in a deep baritone.

Her gaze moved up the length of his torso in a slow-motion scan and settled on his face. William.

Just like that she was Lulu again, and this was Florida, and *oh boy* was she crushing on him.

The trail mix she had swallowed stuck sideways in her throat. She pounded on her ribs with a fist to free the constriction and drew a stunted breath. Her belly did a little flip. She tried to say something but nothing came out.

His expression faltered. "Are you okay? Do you need—"

"You live here?" Her voice had an odd, high-pitched quality. Her heart rate kicked up, too, not helping the situation.

"Yup. I think I'm gonna barbecue tonight. Want to light up the grill later? A little welcome to the neighborhood for both of us?" His smile, the way he directed it right at her? Well, it was everything her little teenage heart had wanted.

Also, holy crap, had William just asked her to sit at his table with him?

For sure, yes, yes, she did want to pull up a chair. But, no. No, she wouldn't. She was avoiding him. "Uh…"

"Burgers or brats?" He moved closer to the patio. "I'm good with whatever you like."

She stepped back and shook her head. "Sorry, no. I have to unpack."

"Suit yourself. Jeff and Dixie are coming over if you change your mind."

"Thank you, no. I have other plans." *With a pint of frozen yogurt and a cold shower.*

"Bummer, maybe next time." The gentle way he said the words and his clear disappointment was real.

"Okee dokee then. Have fun." Warmth flooded her cheeks. She didn't need a mirror to tell her they'd become bright red beacons of embarrassment.

"I'll do that." The edges of his lips lifted slightly.

Lucy yanked the sliding door closed before he said anything more.

She leaned against the glass, head in her hands. Avoiding William Covington had become exponentially more complicated.

CHAPTER
THREE

Lucy entered the tallest building in the downtown block and headed to the KDVX studio in the basement. The elevator slid open, and she hit the switch to the hallway lights. Florescent bulbs flickered like something from a B-grade horror movie.

She gritted her teeth. First one here.

Of course she was the first one there. She had intentionally arrived thirty minutes before the morning shift to ensure she'd be ready for the show. Still, being the only one in the huge building chafed her perpetually raw nerves.

The corridor loomed ahead as she hustled along. Dark hallways and corridors were not her friend.

She swiped her keycard against the security panel. When the yellow light flashed to green, she pushed the door open from the hallway to the brightly lit reception area.

"You're early," a man's voice said.

She sealed her lips closed against a scream. Her purse fell from her grip, and her knees froze in place.

"Whoa." A handsome guy about her age with dreadlocks emerged from around the corner.

Not every man is out to hurt you.

"Didn't mean to scare you. Figured I'd get here first. Show you around." He tucked a pen in the pocket of his designer jeans.

Her heart rate continued to run a half-marathon on its own. Someday it would return to a normal pace, but probably not today.

He dropped some papers on the reception desk and retrieved her purse from the floor. "I really am sorry I scared you, Lucille."

"Lucy. Everyone calls me Lucy. Well, not everyone. Most people." She took her bag from him and slipped the strap over her shoulder.

His kind eyes studied her. "You okay, Lucy?"

No. I am not okay. I'm on the run, hiding in a job I don't want, nearly screaming at random men, and living in a make-shift motel room! Not okay. Not at all.

"I'm fine. Sorry about that. I figured I was the first one here."

"Don't sweat it. I'm Reid, your director this morning and official KDVX tour guide." He gestured for her to follow and held open another door for her to pass through. "Corporate offices are on the fifth floor. We operate independently so they mostly keep to themselves unless we screw up."

She hurried to keep pace with him. "Do we screw up often?"

"Often enough." He led her to a darkened control room consisting of a small auditorium and three sets of risers. "This is our temple. A shrine to the goddess of news." He made an elaborate gesture to the top platform. "Producer desk is up there. I'll be down here. We've got a good staff for mornings, so it should be easy. Newsroom is this way." He jerked his thumb toward an open door on the other side of the room. "Police busted a meth ring a few hours ago. We've got a reporter on it now. Should have video in time for the morning show."

"Lucky us." Lucy flashed him an attempt at a smile as they entered the bullpen of cubicles. "Which desk is mine?"

"Against the wall over there. Night producer left you video to go through and a few things came through last night." He pulled her chair out for her.

"Thanks," she replied as she settled in at her desk. "Really. Thank you."

"Good to have you here. Holler if you need me." Reid waved as he disappeared back to the control room.

She resolved she wouldn't ask for help. Not after the Nervous Nelly blip from earlier. Nope, she would do her job and do it well. Within minutes, Lucy lost herself in news stories, scripts, and segues.

By the time everyone was in place for the news two hours later, the sludge of fatigue tugged at her. She swallowed a yawn. The dead weight of fear Robbie would track her down again kept her up at night. Freaking psychopath Robbie. The ridiculously early wake-up call for her first day of work didn't help her fatigue.

"Three minutes, boys and girls," Reid said from the director's desk. "Let's see if Anderson can go a whole hour without sticking his finger in his nose. Who's up for that wager?"

Anderson, one of the morning news anchors, flipped him the bird.

"C'mon guys. I only need you to behave for an hour," Lucy chimed in.

"Listen to the lady in charge, Anderson." Reid punched at a couple of buttons on the control panel in front of him. "Sorry, Lucy. We're not used to a real producer keeping us in line."

"What do you think my odds are of getting Lucy to go to dinner with me tonight?" Anderson asked.

"Slim to none," Reid replied. "She's out of your league."

Lucy smiled at him and swiped a highlighter across the top of her script, color-coding the times she'd need to track. "Two minutes."

Reid leaned back in his chair, his fingers threaded behind his head.

The milk from the bowl of cereal she had forced herself to eat curdled in her stomach. Maybe this whole experience of hiding in a small town could turn into a good thing. Maybe if she said it enough, she'd believe it. Confluence would simply be a brief stop on her flight to the big leagues. A layover weaved into the journey of her life.

Layovers weren't always awful. You could meet new people, have a drink at the airport lounge, and maybe even buy a souvenir mug in the gift shop. Most of all, Confluence was the place where she could work off-camera in a town few people knew existed. Keep her head down and her past concealed—and stay away from William. The award for avoiding attractive neighbors definitely went to Lucy. She'd managed to keep away from him so far.

"Any words of wisdom you'd like to impart?" Reid pierced the silence through her headset. He turned from the director's seat in front of her perch and peered up.

Blood thrummed in her temples as Lucy glanced at the stack of papers comprising the hour-long news script.

The headset crackled when she pulled the microphone to her mouth. "I think as long as Anderson doesn't go knuckle deep in his nostrils we'll be fine."

The staff erupted in laughter.

"Thirty seconds," Reid said through a husky chuckle. He turned back to the bank of monitors against the wall, leaving her with a view of his thick dreadlocks. "She's a keeper."

The anchors moved onto the lead-in for the meth story, and Lucy's smile faded. The intense craving to be a reporter again took hold. What wouldn't she give to go back in time, to be behind the anchor desk again, fighting for the truth. Anywhere but in the dark control room, in a small station, where no one would ever know she existed.

———

Anderson finished reading the kicker, and the national morning theme song played over the monitors. Lucy slipped off her headset.

"Lucy's in charge of the coffee run today," Reid announced. "I'll get you a list. Shop's up the street."

"Because I'm the new girl?" She stretched her arms over her head.

"Initiation." He winked.

Whatever. She wasn't above playing coffee gofer.

Lucy grabbed her jacket and headed through the lobby to the street. Daylight crept along the mesas, sandstone canyons, and desert mountain rock formations surrounding the Confluence valley, but the early morning sunrise had not quite erased the shadows of night. She made her way through the quiet town square. Her high heels tapped an increasing clickety-clack on the pavement as she hurried.

She glanced over her shoulder every few seconds—phantom footsteps always chasing her. With two more blocks to the coffee house, a coil of anxiety squeezed her chest.

Nearly there.

Her shoulders slumped when she entered the sanctuary of the little shop. Rich coffee, cinnamon, and fresh-from-the-oven bread permeated the air. The tiny café had room for the barista, a bakery case, and a few stools along a window bar.

A young woman in a maroon apron stood behind the counter.

"Hi, I'm Lucy from KDVX. I have a list—"

"Same list every morning," The woman's mouth curved into a smile as she steamed milk, poured chocolate syrup, dripped espresso, and sloshed froth into the cups. "I memorized it months ago. Haven't seen you before. What can I add for you?"

"Small coffee with room for cream, thanks."

"What do you do at the station?"

Lucy adjusted her hand-me-down tan Gucci wool blazer to cover the raised scar along her neck. God, she loathed Robbie for what he did to her. "I'm the weekday morning news producer."

"News producer." The barista arched an eyebrow. "I pegged you for talent. You're dressed like an anchor."

"Nope, just the producer." Lucy frowned. She should be talent… but, no. Not anymore.

The barista sang under her breath as she finished the order and packed the drinks into cardboard carriers. She carefully placed them into a large paper sack and flashed a smile to Lucy. "It's easier than trying to balance them the whole way back."

Lucy held the heavy bag against her chest with both arms. The awkward set-up slowed her momentum on the trek back to KDVX. She hurried anyway. An elderly woman walked a small dog across the street. The sun was up and people dotted the square. Even so, Lucy's fingers itched to grab her can of pepper spray.

In the lobby, she reached for the elevator button, careful to keep the bag balanced against her chest. A loud ping echoed through the empty room to announce the elevator. A man rushed out—slamming right into Lucy.

Scorching liquid burned her chest. She cursed and the sack slipped from her grip. It dropped between them, sending steaming coffee to splatter everywhere. She teetered on her high heels, but didn't go down.

"I'm so sorry. Really. I'm so sorry," the man said, over and over.

No way. Impossible.

With a groan, her eyes met William's gaze. She wasn't getting that medal for avoiding him after all.

"Lucy." He glanced at her press pass that detailed her name and credentials. Shock registered on his face, and then his gaze softened.

Her body responded with goose bumps. For a moment his eyes met hers and it was as though someone pressed the pause button on reality. She was a teenager again with a crush on a boy she could never have. Except the way he looked at her made her sort of think that wasn't true.

But guys like him didn't go for girls like her. They went for beauty pageant winners with tiaras and sashes that read Queen of the Chicken Festival.

And she definitely didn't go for guys like him. Playboy rich kids were not on her to-do list.

"You work here?" he asked.

"Producer." Her coffee-splattered jacket was drenched. She

yanked it off and draped it over her arm. Why was she always covered with sticky beverages when he was around?

William glanced around for something to clean up the mess.

Her blouse was ruined. Brown splotches covered both her breasts and coffee dripped from the silk. William tugged off his navy suit jacket and began patting it against her…breasts.

"William?" she asked carefully. "You're touching my boobs."

His hand stalled mid-wipe. "Shit." He dropped the cloth to the ground like it was a ball of fire. "I didn't mean—"

His gaze rested on the dripping coffee falling from her chest.

"It's fine," she muttered.

They both reached for his jacket at the same time, his forehead colliding with hers. The impact knocked her backward into the puddle on the floor. A very unladylike oomph escaped her lips. Stunned, she lay still for a moment, studying the vaulted ceiling and skylights of the lobby.

"Lucy, hell." He came into view over her.

He offered his hand to help her.

"If you keep helping me, I'm going to wind up in the hospital." She batted him away. "Why are you here at my office?"

He ran a hand over his face. "I work here. Consumer journalist."

Um, what? No, no…no. She'd done her research before she accepted her position at KDVX. William Covington was not listed anywhere as an employee.

She stood. His gaze rested on her face a beat too long before he bent down to collect the scattered cups and lids. Whoever made his jeans should get a substantial bonus for the way they fit against his…thighs. Yup. Thighs. That's what she was looking at.

Lucy kneeled to pick up a cardboard drink tray. When her knuckles accidentally grazed his, she drew a faint breath.

No. She stopped herself and tugged her hand away.

The teenage girl who crushed hard on him no longer existed. That girl had transformed into a strong woman with a career and a plan for her future that absolutely did not include him. Impressions, however, did matter to her. How was she supposed to salvage the beginnings of the reputation that she hoped to have in the news-room when she now wore the coffee she was supposed to bring back?

"I'm sorry. This is my fault." He dumped the dripping mess into the garbage.

She rubbed a hand over her forehead. "I can't show up without coffee."

"I'll get more." He stared at her again for a long moment. Like he saw something there… a memory.

Crap. Had he finally recognized her?

"What?" she asked when he continued to stare.

"You have freckles," he said softly.

She raised her index finger to the bridge of her nose. "Uh-huh."

Oh. The damn goose bumps reappeared. This time with tingles she refused to give a second thought.

He gestured to her cheek. "You have a little coffee there."

Oh. Right. Coffee. Sure.

She wiped it away and held her shoulders a little higher. On that reality show, he had wrestled tongues with more women than there were notches in a belt. Teenage Lulu had desperately wanted to be on the receiving end of a William lip-lock exchange. Adult Lucy would never allow herself such a self-indulgence. Kissing William had no place in her life anymore.

She refused to be the next, "next, please."

This was the guy who had floated pizzas in the swimming pool and built a vodka ice luge on the roof of the Florida frat house where they filmed the show. He had no business making her tingle.

"I like them," he said.

"Like what?"

"Freckles." He shook his head slightly and gestured for her to follow. In a nearby hallway, they found a janitor. William collected the supplies and insisted on cleaning the mess himself. "This'll only take a second, then we'll go get more."

Lucy helped mop up the spill, checking the clock on the wall.

She'd have to be quick about this coffee run. They had a national cut-in soon.

Outside, Main Street stirred as they walked toward the coffee house. The sun was up, shops had opened their doors, and more people milled about on the sidewalk. Lucy strove for a brisk pace, but William seemed in no hurry. Clearly, etiquette in Confluence involved waving and commenting on the weather to complete strangers.

"Hello again. And look, you brought a friend," the cheerful barista chirped when they entered the shop.

"I had a little accident back at the station. I dropped the whole thing. Can you re-make the order?" Lucy asked quickly.

The coffee girl leaned toward William. "Would you like any extra sugar this morning?"

Seriously?

"I'm more of a honey guy." He flashed his dimples. "Table sugar is too sweet."

"And you're not...sweet?" The woman batted her eyelashes at him.

He glanced at Lucy and held her stare. "Suppose I can be in the right circumstance."

Well, huh. She felt those words in a very intimate place. The barista banged a portafilter against the machine.

Lucy snapped back to the situation at hand and dug through her purse for her wallet. "This time make mine a large." She jerked her head toward William. "And he'll have an extra hot Americano with honey and a dash of cream."

He stilled. The shocked expression on his face quickly turned blank.

Ugh. Speaking without thinking was becoming a dangerous habit.

She'd ordered the drink he used to send her to pick up daily for him in Florida. Back then she fetched anything he wanted. Not that she minded—except the blondes. He did have an exceptional fondness for groupies who used too much peroxide on their hair.

"I mean…" Lucy glanced between William and the barista.

He didn't even blink. "Just cream."

"So close." Lucy's smile faltered. "It's a gift. I can look at someone and know how they take their caffeine. I'm a coffee savant."

Coffee savant?

He raised an eyebrow at her as the bell over the door jingled.

A beautiful woman brushed past them. In her fifties by all appearances, except her weary brown eyes suggested she'd been around longer. They reflected a heck of a lot of life, and by the glimmer of worry, not all of it had been good. She wore a conservative blue, paisley dress, straight off Meryl Streep in The Bridges of Madison County. The woman drew a sharp breath.

"William, you're here," she whispered in a thick Italian accent.

"Teresa… You look well. How's Dad?" William said carefully.

The older woman blinked against watery eyes. So maybe Lucy wasn't a coffee savant, but she was decent at reading a room. Vibrations pulsing through the little café were anything but peaceful.

William and Teresa stood there for a time, staring at each other before William turned back to the counter. His Adam's apple bobbed vigorously. Lucy set her credit card on the counter, her eyes drinking in the scene before her. The barista had quieted while she finished the order, stopping to write a phone number on the sleeve of William's cup. She reached for Lucy's credit card, but William slipped his sleek gold card in its place. He slid Lucy's card toward her hand, and his fingertips brushed against hers.

Curls of comforting warmth seeped through the dull ache of loneliness in her chest. She snatched her hand back, shoved the plastic card in her wallet, and reached for the coffee cup that had been placed on the counter for her.

Teresa's longing gaze had never left William. He took the offered bag in one arm and his drink in the other hand. "Your father and I… We would like you to come visit."

She reached for his arm as he opened the door for Lucy.

He shook his head. "Not a good idea. You know where things stand with Dad and me."

Lucy bit her lower lip and scooted past them. What the heck was that all about? She glanced behind her as he exited. One look at his broken face, and it was clear that any mention of Teresa was off-limits.

Lighthearted, superficial William had never carried this intensity.

"The coffee girl gave you her number," she said to lighten the mood.

He shifted the bag of drinks to read the writing. "Not on the market."

"Girlfriend?"

He made a face as though he had eaten a spoonful of used coffee grounds. "No girlfriend."

"Fiancée?"

He flinched. "None of the above. Just not on the market."

The crisp air and a surge of caffeine boosted her confidence. Her mouth took off before she filtered her thoughts. "Born-again virgin? Celibacy isn't only for martyrs. We ran a story at my old station about the whole thing. It's intriguing."

"I'm not a monk, or born-again anything. I'm just not looking right now. You?" He held her stare as he had done in the coffee shop.

The question hung heavy in the air between them.

"I'm not a monk, either," she finally said.

"Ah…one of those born-again things?"

"No. I mean…not attached, either." She tucked a strand of hair behind her ear. "That's such a funny way to say it. Attached. Like stapled to a man. Or handcuffed."

William's eyebrows lifted slightly when she mentioned handcuffs.

She studied the cracks in the sidewalk as they walked in uncomfortable silence. Finally, she asked, "How do you know Dixie?"

"She doesn't like my dad, and he's trying to dictate where I live."

"Why would he care? You're not ten."

Bitterness tainted William's laugh. "My dad is a big deal around here. Huge benefactor to charities, countless years spent as an elected official and, for now, he's the head of Crestone Mountain Media."

She pressed a hand to her lips. Life did that run-her-over thing again. Why did everything in this town have to be so connected?

"We don't talk. He's got it in his head I should move in with him and Teresa so we can be a happy family again," he continued. "Got here a week ago, and he made it impossible for me to find a place to rent."

"Impressively passive aggressive of him. Why would he care, though? You're old enough to take care of yourself."

"Control." He glared ahead at nothing in particular. "It's all about control."

"I take it Teresa back there is connected to your dad?" Lucy gestured down the block from where they came as the automatic doors of their building opened for them.

He moved to the side so she could go ahead. "Yeah. She's his wife."

Oh.

True to form, families never failed to bring on the worst kind of drama. Which is why she avoided hers.

Lucy scooted ahead of him. A Wet Floor sign near the bank of elevators served as a reminder of their collision.

Thanks to the coffee massacre, Lucy entered the newsroom more than an hour after leaving. William passed the bag of drinks to her and sat at what must have been his desk at one of the cubicles.

Reid emerged from a small editing bay near the door. "Don't producers manage time for a living?" He held his watch up and tapped the face. "Whoa. You're supposed to bring the coffee. Not wear it."

Lucy's heart sank.

So much for first impressions.

CHAPTER
FOUR

William thumped his pencil on his notepad as he worked alone from the leather couch in Parker's office. In contrast to the bare-bones newsroom, Parker's office was plush—white walls, straight lines, and not a particleboard to be found. He deserved it. Parker had hustled his way up from the wrong side of the tracks, put himself through college, and worked his ass off to become station manager at KDVX. He hadn't been handed a thing. Ever.

News staff milled around William's cubicle, making it impossible to concentrate. Add in the distraction of Lucy, sitting only two desks down, and he got nothing done out there.

The introduction to the afternoon news promo played on a large television mounted in the corner of the office, directly in line of sight from where he worked. A perky reporter with chin-length blonde hair started the news hour with a story about the humane society and their donation shortage.

Not the best lead-in.

He grabbed the remote and turned up the volume. Overnight, one of the largest methamphetamine drug rings in the state had been taken down near Confluence. That should be the lead. The entire town buzzed about it. Both the morning and midday news had led with *that* story.

William chewed on the end of his pencil when Parker breezed through the door. His assistant scurried behind him with a fistful of message slips.

Parker stilled as the television came into view. Several volunteers paraded across the set with a menagerie of cats, dogs, and rabbits that did not seem to be enjoying their moment in the spotlight. Parker motioned to the screen. "Things are out of hand in the newsroom."

"No kidding," William replied.

"You found a place to live, huh?" Parker waved the assistant out and leaned against the desk, arms folded across his chest.

"Barely, but yeah. I found a place."

"All that time you spent as a kid trying to convince your parents to move away, and you still wind up here. Brilliant." Parker sorted through the message slips.

"I've been around the world. All roads lead back to Confluence, and there's no reason to put people here out of work if I don't have to."

"Still only two things to do in town. Chase tumbleweeds and women." Parker grinned a wry smile.

"You never cared much for tumbleweeds," William said mildly.

"Nope." Parker full on smirked. "Neither did you."

That was a long time ago. William stopped being the "next, please" guy as soon as he grew the hell up. He wasn't that guy now. Not anymore.

On the television feed, a dog barked. A kitten hissed and jumped from the anchor's arms to bolt across the set. Two mutts howled and charged after the cat. The man holding the leashes hurtled off the set behind them.

William shook his head at the screen until someone in the control room finally cut to a commercial break. "You've got a plan for that?"

"I'm working on one." Parker moved to his chair. "The new morning producer's really good. Hopefully she can turn things around."

Lucy.

He'd barely gone ten minutes without her invading his thoughts, since he'd scraped her off the concrete of the gas station and waited with her for the glass repair guy.

"What do you know about Lucy?" William rested his elbow on the edge of the couch and kept his expression neutral.

Parker's face hardened. "Oh no. I've seen that look in your eyes way too many times. Trust me, you don't want to go there with staff."

"Go where?" William played innocent.

Parker pointed at him. "Where you're trying to *go*. She's off-limits."

"She's funny, and pretty." *With freckles. I adore her freckles.* And no way in hell was he going to be dictated to on who was off-limits when it came to his life.

"She's a challenge." Parker stared him down. "Drop whatever this thing is you've got going on in your head about her."

William's phone buzzed. "I've got to take this. My attorney."

"Go for it." Parker's own phone rang.

William stood, turning his back to Parker. "This is William."

"Are you sitting down?" his attorney, Dawn, asked breathlessly. "Because the judge just threw out your father's final appeal. Crestone's yours. No more appeals, no more court dates, this is it. The company transfers on your birthday, like your mother requested."

William gripped the phone tighter. He had won.

Nearly a decade had passed since he'd left Confluence after the reading of his mother's will. He had not returned, choosing instead to spend the next phase of his life proving himself a respectable newsman while attorneys and mediators sorted out the legalities of his inheritance.

And. He. Won.

William had shed tears when he heard his mother had died. He stood by her grave weeks later, numb, tired, and cold inside. Over the next years, he'd fought the image that damn reality show had created. The persona they'd created for him followed him everywhere. Confluence media had a heyday with it. His father had to deal with his reckless son's behavior, when he should have been mourning his wife. And the whole time, William felt...nothing. Like he'd been the one who died.

Right now? The frigid vise gripping his heart started to melt.

"You there?" Dawn asked.

William swallowed the intense emotion threatening to spill. "Yeah, great news. Thank you. Really. Thank you."

"I'll be in touch with paperwork," she replied. "Congratulations."

William turned toward Parker, unable to keep his grin at bay. "I've got news."

Parker dropped his phone in the cradle. "I heard. Your dad called."

An ominous feeling crept up in William's chest. "You talked to my dad?"

Parker shifted uncomfortably. "I did. You need to meet with him. The Colorado Springs merger is precarious. This is the worst possible time for you to take over."

What the hell?

That was certainly not the vote of confidence William had expected. "Worst possible time? Sorry my dead mother's plans and my birthday don't work for your calendar."

"That's not what I meant, man. You know that. Your dad's *pissed*."

Yeah, probably. His dad spent most of his time furious with his wife for dying and leaving her family company to William instead of him. Years fighting her last wishes had left his father bitter.

"He's been working on this merger for years. He wants to meet with you. Hash everything out."

Absolutely. Succession plan preparation should happen soon. First, William needed to do his own research before any meetings so he would go in prepared.

"I'm putting *that* meeting off as long as possible." He rubbed against the pressure in his chest he experienced whenever his father's name came up.

"You need to go visit him. Now."

"Nope." Now that things were going his way, he would do this on his own terms. In his own time.

Parker cursed. "Don't be a jackass."

"Seriously, when did you become his lackey?" William set his hands low on his hips.

Parker glanced away.

"Why the hell have you been working with my dad?"

"He's my boss. I talk to him." Parker sifted uneasily through the message slips on his desk. "If you're not meeting with him, then what's your plan?"

William glared at him. "We need to announce to management soon but, for now, I'm only a consumer reporter. That's all anyone needs to know. And as far as my dad's concerned, I'm still the screw-up who embarrassed the family on national television. I need a solid strategy. With the big Colorado Springs acquisition you're so concerned about, I have to be prepared. I'm not walking blind into any meetings."

Parker pressed his lips together. "Don't screw up the merger, William. It's got to happen."

"What's it to you, anyway? Your job here's secure with or without it." Unless. William's whole body went wired. "He promised you a Colorado Springs job, didn't he?"

Parker glanced down at the carpet. "Vice President of Operations."

William's last girlfriend always said he had major trust issues. Right here. This illustrated why he struggled having faith in anyone. If you couldn't rely on your friends to have your back, who could you count on?

"When you kicked me out of your apartment, you weren't worried about your job here. You were aiming for a promotion."

"After the merger, your dad plans to move all the offices to the Springs. You haven't been around. You have no idea what this company needs. The merger needs to happen so we can move everything there."

Never. His mother set the offices in Confluence because she loved this town. "I'm keeping the offices in Confluence."

The door burst open, revealing Parker's flustered assistant.

"I'm sorry to interrupt. Mr. Covington." She glanced at William. "The other Mr. Covington is here to see you."

Looked like that meeting with his dad wouldn't wait after all.

"Son."

One word, and everyone paused. William couldn't breathe. Air wouldn't come. His father's presence erased everything William had worked toward. He was a twenty-two-year-old brat again, ruining the family name.

The perplexed assistant scooted aside to let his father pass.

"Dad." William clenched his fingers against his palms. He would not go back in time. He would not allow his father that control. He would not be that kid again.

"I suppose congratulations are in order." Dad had aged over their time apart. Oh, he still owned the room when he entered, but his hair was whiter and the lines on his face deeper. "It's been a long time. We've got some work to do to get this transition moving. Best get on that."

He turned in the direction of the conference room without any other words. He didn't need them. People followed Joe Covington wherever he led.

"Best get on that." Parker jerked his head to where William's father had stood moments before.

"We're not done." William pointed a finger at Parker and headed the opposite direction of the conference room.

He refused to come when called.

William was on edge. A string of tense meetings with his father over the past two weeks had been punctuated with uncomfortable, over-the-top civility. Twice his father had broached the subject of William staying at the family house. Twice, William declined. Politely. Through gritted teeth.

Better to live in a rundown place he called his own than move back to the altar of broken dreams, otherwise known as the family home where his father and stepmother lived.

Parker had tried to contact him a few times. William had avoided the calls and sidestepped him at the station.

But his father's endless persistence, and Parker's two-faced friendship, weren't the only reasons he couldn't sleep. The yowling outside had become unbearable. He yanked a thin bubblegum-colored blanket over his head.

Two a.m. and a first-class pain-in-the-ass cat would not shut up. William groaned.

Even without the cat, a person could not sleep in a house drenched in the color palette of Pepto-Bismol.

He was a successful reporter. A goddamned heir to an empire. All of that sounded great, but his life was like a late-night infomercial. Looked amazing on television, but once you got it, you realized it was total shit and the return shipping wasn't worth the effort.

The bellowing outside grew louder, several short meows and a long, high-pitched cry.

He rolled off the bed, stood, and stubbed his toe on the dresser.

"Fuck," he said, under his breath as he rubbed the injured digit.

Barefoot, shirtless, and without any pride, he limped through his living room in only his boxers. Not like anyone was outside to see him or his damaged dignity. Clearly, he was the only one awake in the neighborhood. Aside from the cat.

He grabbed a pastel pink laundry basket from the sofa and stepped outside the patio door. His bare feet hit the chilled metal steps. He shivered. Clouds covered the moon, so the only light came from a streetlamp at the end of the building. Not even the stars were out tonight.

Step one, catch the cat.

Step two, feed the cat.

Step three, no idea. He'd figure that one out after some sleep.

The yowling continued from around Lucy's side of the patio. William stepped with care across the AstroTurf lawn, hopping away from jagged gravel to avoid the legion of pink flamingos he'd inherited with the place.

Yes, he'd been flocked.

His breath came in thin, foggy bursts.

He was a predator hunting a…Puddy Tat.

Quoting *Looney Tunes* to himself while tracking a cat around a compound of sketchy apartments? Yeah, he needed sleep.

He slipped along the length of Lucy's unit. The feline in question bellowed and scratched at the metal siding below Lucy's window.

A branch snapped under the pad of William's foot. The cat stopped howling and stared him down. If he was quick, William could grab him. Or maybe he should try calling the mini-beast—it might come.

He cleared his throat quietly, not quite believing he was doing this. "Here kitty, kitty," he sang off-key. "Kitty, kitty, kitty. Here kitty."

A violent hiss erupted from the cat's mouth. William nearly laughed when the cat bared its fangs. Fang. The decrepit marmalade, long-haired cat was missing a tooth. Clumps of fur were gone, too, and the creature appeared as though it had been on the receiving end of a late-night bar brawl.

Sympathy stirred inside him. He'd definitely give an extra serving of late-night supper to the dude.

"Here kitty, kitty…" he sang again. Gravel crunched behind him.

He spun around.

Lucy wielded a baseball bat at him like a maniac. When she raised the bat higher, her nightgown crept up to her thighs.

When he should've been concerned about the possibility of a concussion, his body instead responded to that small bit of bare skin like a twenty-year-old kid at a strip club.

"What are you doing?" he whispered.

"Seeing who is outside my window." Her hair was tousled and, damn, did he want to run his fingers through the mess of it.

She lowered the bat. "What are *you* doing?"

Checking out the pretty neighbor and making an ass out of myself.

Clearly, she had no idea what her presence did to him.

"Trying to help the cat." That sounded much better than trying to figure out how to get her to agree to an impromptu roll on the AstroTurf.

"You scared me." Her lip trembled, just a little.

He reached his hand out to comfort her, but she stepped away.

She nodded toward the ball of fur. "What's the deal?"

The cat stopped bellowing.

"No idea," he said. "Figure I'll take him to the Humane Society so he can find his family."

The cat stalked closer and hissed again. It turned to Lucy and… smiled.

She set the bat down and kneeled in the fake grass, wriggling her fingers toward the cat. "Aw, how sweet is he?"

The cat strutted to her opened fingers, tail held high, and sniffed. She massaged its chin and turned the tags on the collar over to read them.

She glanced at William. "Her name is Mitzy. It lists your apartment number."

The dead former-occupant-lady had a pet?

Lucy let the mini-beast on her lap. Her nightgown rose higher on her thigh as she comforted her.

William stifled a groan. She killed him without even touching him. The nightgown wasn't even that short or sexy. Except on her, it was both of those things. Cotton, not silk, with a picture of a panda bear eating a cupcake with the cherry right at her... No, he was not going to examine the cherry and the position it held right over her breast.

"Hey there." She rubbed her hand over the tufts of fur. "It's okay. I'm here."

A deep purr vibrated through the dark night, and Lucy beamed. "She likes me. I like you, too, Mitzy."

The distinctive click of the hammer being pulled back on a gun sounded through the darkness. Then a shot rang through the night.

William instinctively stepped in front of Lucy and Mitzy.

"Who's there?" Dixie shouted.

He glanced to where the gunshot had come from.

Dixie held the rifle in question.

"It's us. William and Lucy," he shouted back.

Lucy had the cat wedged against her side. The hissing, pissed-off cat apparently didn't appreciate being squished against Lucy's armpit since the pissed-off hissing continued with new vigor. He glanced to Lucy. The whites of her round eyes were huge.

"Are you okay?" He asked.

She nodded, holding the cat by the scruff of the neck tight against her chest.

"It's the middle of the night." Dixie's tone was firm. "What the devil are you doin' out here?"

"Cat hunting." William gestured with his head to Lucy and Mitzy.

"Well, I'll be a monkey's unc—" Dixie started.

"Mom?" Jeff hollered from across the road.

"Oh, good, it's a party." William dropped his hands to his waist.

"She's over here, Jeff," Lucy said, her voice sharp.

Jeff trudged around the corner in a pair of plaid pajamas. His eyes grew wide when he saw his mother pointing the rifle at William. His gaze followed the barrel of the gun, landing on William's crotch. Jeff coughed into his hand and glanced away. William adjusted his hands to cover the bulge. Jeff whispered something in Dixie's ear before he patted her on the shoulder and moved her gun into his hand.

"Everything okay?" Jeff asked.

"Depends on your definition of okay." William jerked his chin at Lucy. "Your mom shot at us. We caught a cat."

"Warnin' shot," Dixie chimed in. "If I'da meant to hit 'em, I woulda."

"Mom, we've discussed this. No warning shots." Jeff glanced up to the starless sky. "No shots at all."

"Protectin' the place is my job. Is that Mitzy?" Dixie asked. "Thought she up 'n died, too."

Lucy held the cat tight against her.

Mitzy rewarded her with a crazy cat smile.

"Can I keep her?" Lucy asked Dixie.

Dixie scowled. "I s'pose you ken keep the cat."

Jeff rested a hand on his mother's shoulder. "Let's get you home, Mom."

"Where's your clothes?" Dixie jerked her chin at William before she shot an accusing glance at Lucy.

At least the present conversation had killed the punch of lust he experienced earlier. "I was sleeping."

Dixie pointed at his crotch. "Syphilis is a reality. You'd best remember that."

Jeff coughed again. William rolled his eyes to heaven. The

awkward moment lingered until Dixie harrumphed, turned on her heel, and marched back into the darkness. Jeff followed.

The fur ball purred louder as William walked Lucy silently to the porch.

Her cheeks burned red in the porch light as she opened the door. "Need something?"

"No. Just… uh… enjoy your cat." He reached to pet Mitzy, but she nipped at his outstretched fingers. He jerked his hand back.

Lucy held her hand on the doorknob. "I will."

"Good night, then." He stepped backward and cleared his throat.

The door closed only inches from his nose, and the lock clicked into place.

He trudged into his own apartment, climbed into bed, and tunneled his face into a pillow. When he closed his eyes, visions of Lucy in that ridiculous shirt swam in the darkness. He was hyper-aware of her presence just next door.

Yeah, he definitely knew she existed. Certain areas of his body reminded him constantly. But on paper, Lucy Campbell didn't show up anywhere. William dug up stories better than most of his colleagues, and he still couldn't find anything on her.

He needed to convince his body what his head already knew. The insane desire he experienced around Lucy was a simple case of lust.

He grumbled to himself, rolled over, and willed sleep to find him.

CHAPTER
SIX

Ten minutes late for her first assignment meeting. Great.

"Thanks," Lucy said to Parker when he held the door to the conference room for her.

The pit of self-doubt she carried with her weighed heavier as she entered the small, crowded space. The conference room had a long rectangular table with mismatched black leather chairs haphazardly placed around it, one door, and no windows. Confidence. She needed a bucket load.

Unfortunately, demanding she be confident never seemed to work.

Staff talked over each other, bantering about their plans for the weekend. Some sat at the table, a few were perched on the table, and a couple leaned against the wall. William had claimed one of the leather chairs. He tossed a worn baseball into the air, caught it, and threw it again. He intercepted her gaze and flashed his dimples. He was literally everywhere. Their shared porch, the coin-operated laundry room at the apartment building, the newsroom, and the coffee shop…everywhere.

Hello, Dimples. Tingles that had no place at work tickled along each lusty nerve in her body.

Bridgett, the afternoon producer, laughed at something he said.

Everyone quieted when Parker spoke. "Lucy is taking over as assignment editor. She'll still produce, but she'll also head up the weekly assignment meetings for the immediate future. Listen to her. Do what she says." He lifted his chin to Lucy. "Good luck."

Without anything further, he left.

How hard could it be to run an assignment meeting? As a reporter in California, she'd sat through countless meetings just like this one.

She snatched a white board marker and fiddled with the cap. "Shows need content. Let's get through this quickly"— Lucy bit at her bottom lip and waved a hand toward the room— "and you can go back to work. I realize I haven't been here long." Lucy scrawled the words *Story Ideas* across the white board. "But let's be honest. Things are messy in the newsroom. We can do better."

A general rumble of dissent rolled through the room.

Lucy ignored it. "We've had multiple reporters show up for the same story three times in the past week. The Rivers Edge newspaper has scooped us on four interviews. We need better coordination. If we work as a team, we can report some real news."

The room went silent.

Lucy met the daggers directed at her, head on. "Just because we get a press release on the pet rescue's lack of donations doesn't mean we need to turn the story into a three-part series urging our viewers to open their checkbooks."

"What you're saying is you advocate the extermination of kittens?" Anderson mumbled.

Lucy opened her mouth to respond.

"Knock it off, Anderson." Bridgett glared his way. Lucy gave her a smile of solidarity.

"I happen to know Lucy adores cats," William said like it was an inside joke between the two of them.

Why did Lucy like that so much, dammit?

"Why didn't anyone ask why donations are down? Anyone know the rate of euthanasia? How does it compare nationally? It's not our job to raise funds for kittens. Our job is to share actual news.

The Edge ran a story about domestic violence rates in Confluence and how they're at a five-year high. Where were you?" she asked instead.

No one spoke. Apparently, they had no idea where they'd been.

Lucy wasn't giving up. She addressed the room at large. "What story ideas are everyone working on?"

The group fidgeted with their pens and notepads, but no one looked at her. Finally, she caught Anderson's gaze. "C'mon, you have to be working on something?"

"Trying to convince you to have dinner with me. Not going well so far." Anderson's thousand-watt smile likely had women throwing their panties at him regularly.

It didn't work on Lucy. She preferred her panties on, *thankyouverymuch.*

"Work related, Anderson." Lucy leaned forward on the table. "Not—"

"I'm considering an investigation into Twin Lakes Resorts." William sliced through her reply. "They're based in Denver, but the chain includes three hotels within hours of Confluence. They do these big honeymoon retreats. It's wedding season, and we've been getting complaints about couples on their honeymoon being up-charged for things they didn't order, pre-paid rooms being unavailable, and personal items going missing."

"Great story." Lucy scrawled Honeymoons from Hell at the top of the whiteboard.

Bridgett turned to William. "You'll need to go undercover? Pretend you're on your honeymoon? I like it."

He shrugged. "Something like that. I'm working on the details."

"That's why we're here. To help you work out specifics." Lucy underlined the words on the white board. Twice, for good measure.

Within minutes, the team was throwing ideas back and forth. Lucy shook out the cramp forming in her hand from keeping up. This was good. Exactly what they needed in the newsroom.

"When William goes undercover, he'll need a wife." Bridgett was all business.

"Who wants to be William's wife?" Lucy asked offhand.

"It can't be a reporter anyone will recognize," Bridgett pointed out. "Someone behind the scenes makes the most sense."

"Lucy," William interjected. "You're behind the scenes. Looks like you're the one."

Nope. That was a bad idea. Her hormones were already all out of whack when he was around. But, if he took someone like, say, Bridgett, then they'd both be out of her hair for a while. Win-win or whatever.

"Actually"—Lucy capped her marker—"I think you should take Bridgett. I don't mind covering her shifts."

The lines around William's mouth hardened. The look shouldn't have been sexy, but it was.

Bridgett grinned. "This is so fun. I'll get a dress and a ring—just like the real thing without all the messy paperwork when it's over."

By the time the meeting finished, everyone had solid assignments. Lucy rubbed her wrist and organized the markers she had used to color code the board. She turned to leave. William had stayed behind and was leaning against the closed door.

"Please, don't do that again." He shoved his hands in his pockets.

"Excuse me?"

"I prefer to pick my own wives."

The way he made that declaration made her feel like she was seventeen again. Her heart thumped quick in her chest.

Pick me. Pick me!

She mentally instructed her heart to shut up.

"Ah." She moved to put the table between them. "I'm sorry. I thought I was helping."

"I'd just prefer if you didn't send me away for a honeymoon with someone else." His announcement hung heavy between them.

"I'm sure you'll have a lovely time though." She looked down to her notepad and collected her things.

"Lucy."

She glanced up.

The space between them practically disintegrated with the way he held her stare. She couldn't look away. Could hardly catch her breath.

"I like you, Lucy. You're doing a good job here." He turned on his heel and disappeared down the hallway.

His words hung in the air like a promise.

———

Lucy's phone rang at six o'clock the next Saturday. It wasn't her morning to be at the station, and absolutely everything else could wait until she woke up. She reached over to her rickety nightstand and clicked off the ringer.

At six thirty, she couldn't ignore the knocking at her front door. It continued as she threw her feet over the side of the bed and made her way through the cramped living room. She tossed back the orange curtain on her front door. William stood there on the porch, his gaze directed down. His right hand lay relaxed on the top of the doorjamb, and the tight tee he wore showed the ripples of muscle on his biceps.

"*Mrrrrrrrrrow.*" Mitzy sauntered into the room.

"No. Kidding," Lucy replied, under her breath.

When he glanced up and caught her gaze, little spikes of desire pulsed in her veins. She dropped the polyester curtain.

Mrrrow indeed.

The scruff on his face announced he hadn't shaved in days. Lucy was apparently into shaggy men, as of right that moment.

Way too early for this.

More knocking. "Saw you. Know you're in there, Lucy."

She drew the curtain back again.

He pointed to the handle and mouthed, "Open? Please?"

She opened the door a crack.

"Lucy, I need to talk to you," he said through the thin opening.

"It's way too early for conversation." She ran a hand over her obnoxious morning hair.

He'd probably start talking about how he liked her again, and then she'd get all confused again, and her hormones would get wonky. It'd be a whole thing.

"I need your help. Bridgett's sick," he said.

A knot formed in Lucy's belly. She released the safety chain and opened the door. "What happened?"

"We're supposed to leave for Twin Lakes today, but she ate something with peaches, and apparently she's allergic. I just came from seeing her. She's all puffed up."

Peaches? That sounded awful.

"Will she be okay?"

"They say she'll be fine, but she needs to rest. I really need you to be my wife."

The knot in her belly tightened, and she stepped backward into the living room. "It is way too early to discuss marriage, William."

He followed her inside. His gaze traveled over her, and the edges of his lips ticked up. "Please, Lucy. I need a favor. And you look like you need caffeine. Where do you keep the coffee?"

She crossed her arms across her chest. "At Starbucks."

He tossed her an annoyed look.

"Kitchen," she said, tilting her head that direction. "And this is me saying fine to the coffee. Not the marriage." She followed him into her kitchen where he snagged the tin of blonde roast off the counter.

"Coffee liners?" he asked.

She grumbled under her breath where he could find them in the cupboard.

"I'll tell you what. You go do whatever you do to wake up." He turned and stepped toward her. He didn't even have to touch her to leave a trail of goose bumps along her skin.

Unable to move, she shivered.

He stood there all sexy stubble and man in *her* kitchen. "I'll make coffee."

His gaze rested on her mouth, which at some point had parted against her will. She promptly shut it.

"Then we can talk about a trip to Twin Lakes," he said.

Full-bodied with an extra shot of persistence was apparently on her menu this morning. "I have to work, I've got a cat, and there are three thousand other reasons I can't get away."

"Let's talk after you resurrect Happy Lucy. Meditate, whatever you usually do…then coffee." He returned to the coffee pot.

The universe seriously had a messed up sense of humor.

She stared at him, scruffy, delicious, and in her kitchen. "Shower. I usually shower first thing."

"You…uh…getting that shower going or are you waiting for me to take one with you?" he asked without turning around.

She scowled at his ridiculously attractive back for a beat.

It wasn't fair that even his back was sexy. Her gaze traveled lower to his shorts. Over his ass. His legs. His calves.

He cleared his throat. She glanced up quickly to meet his… dimples.

"I'll come, too, then?" He was clearly joking, but as his lips formed the husky words, they practically hypnotized her.

He took a step toward her, the tin of coffee still in his grip.

She froze, certain the look on her face must've mirrored an early-morning deer meeting the headlights of a Ferrari. Like, if she was gonna get hit by a car, might as well be a good one.

Oh boy, was she about to get run over.

She licked at her lips.

His gaze fell to them, mouth parted, eyes flared.

Next, please.

She noped right out of there. Turned and bolted for the bathroom, ensuring the lock on the door clicked behind her.

Head in her hands, she slumped against the thin wood panel on the wall beside the cracked tub.

She was officially hiding from William in her bathroom. She needed to wake up. Her hair needed shampoo. And she had lusty irritation to rinse down the drain.

By the time the hot water ran out, the aroma of coffee, eggs, and bacon filled the kitchen.

Lucy emerged from the bathroom with wet hair and a fresh outlook, but forgiveness for the early wake-up would cost a lot more than breakfast.

William waited at the table, newspaper in hand with his ankle propped across his knee. He'd set two plates of food and mugs of coffee for them.

"Aw, you waited for me," she said, her mood definitely improved by the hot water and the scent of coffee.

"Cream or sugar?" He held up her Wonder Woman coffee mug without moving his gaze from the paper.

"Lots of both." She dropped into the chair across from him and meticulously lined up the silverware he'd set. She placed her napkin delicately on her lap. The scene was too domestic, with a side of comfort she refused to acknowledge.

She sipped from her mug. It turned out William made a decent cup of coffee.

"So…" He unceremoniously folded the newspaper. "Will you marry me?"

The slice of bacon she had raised to her mouth stopped just short of her lips. "I hope you do dishes, too. I don't do dishes this early in the morning."

"Did you hear me?" He ran his hand over the delicious stubble on his chin. "I really need a wife here, Lucy."

"And I need sleep. Oh, look." She gestured between them with her fork. "We both have needs. Unfulfilled needs."

Molten gold eyes bored through her. "Tell me more about your unfulfilled needs."

She couldn't help the puff of a laugh that came out at his comment. "Sleep. Only sleep. That's the only thing I need right now."

Though her resolve cracked a bit with the way he stared.

"Sleep?" The intensity of his expression didn't change with the question.

"That's what I said, right? The only thing I need from you is a little time with my mattress."

Oh my God. She wanted to scoop those words up and shove them back in her mouth.

"Your mattress," he confirmed, and this time it was his turn to chuckle.

The man was unnerving and ridiculous and the idea of him with her on her mattress sounded nicer than she'd ever want to admit.

She drove an icicle stake through the thought. "Alone. Alone with my… You know what? Never mind."

"Bridgett isn't available, and I need help." The puppy dog eyes he tossed her way were entirely unfair. "Please?"

"There is literally no one else you could marry?" No other *next, please*?

Apparently, not all the bristle got washed off in the shower.

"You are a behind-the-scenes employee at the station. A female employee, unmarried, with no plans for the next few days." More puppy dog eyes.

"How do you know I don't have plans?" At least the man had a way with eggs. What could she say? They were fluffy and perfect.

He gestured at her with his fork. "Do you have plans?"

"I mean I have to work. I'm covering for Bridgett, plus my shifts."

"Handled," he assured.

"It can't just be handled. It's my job."

"Parker's taking care of it."

The persistence. Dear heavens, the persistence.

She firmed her resolve. "What if I would rather have a colonoscopy on national television than parade around as your wife?"

Those puppy dog eyes darkened. "Lucy, do you know how many stations my family owns?"

She didn't answer.

"Enough of them so that if it's true, and you'd like to have a colonoscopy on national television, I could make it happen for you. Your choice isn't really that hard. You're either my wife for the next few days, or you could be backside up under a curtain on Good Morning America by Monday."

She bit into her bacon, but now it tasted like ash. "Fine," she muttered. "Let's get married."

He grinned brighter than the sun coming through the window. "It'll be great."

Hours later, Lucy lugged her bag through the newsroom, ready for her fake honeymoon in Twin Lakes. William had told her to wear something post-wedding appropriate, so she had tugged on a cream-colored business suit and packed a bag.

As always, the reporters on duty stood gabbing in the corner of the room. They turned collectively to gawk at Lucy.

Anderson let out a catcall and began a slow applause. "Congratulations on your wedding."

"Don't even start." Lucy jerked at the hem of her jacket.

William emerged from one of the editing bays with a case of equipment. The black tuxedo he wore fit him entirely too well, amplifying his muscles and encouraging Lucy's daydream of being a glorified bridal Barbie about to marry a real-life Ken.

His lazy gaze wandered over her. "You look pretty."

"Thanks," she whispered, ignoring the way her cheeks heated at his comment.

"What all did you pack?" He glanced to her oversize suitcase and humor flashed in his eyes.

"Just what I need for a few days."

"Uh-huh." He didn't sound at all like he believed her.

"What does that mean? Uh-huh?"

He stacked her bags near the equipment cases. "It means, sure."

"You say 'uh-huh,' but your tone implies something else." She smoothed the fabric of her skirt.

"Remind me never, ever to wake you up early again." He said this like he had every intention of waking her up early.

"I can't believe I agreed to marry you," she huffed.

"The wedding's barely over, and you two are already bickering like an old married couple. Need me to show you how to handle her?" Anderson asked.

William grinned. "Nah. I got this. C'mon, Snookums."

"Pet names? Really?" Lucy checked her phone.

"I couldn't get ahold of Jeff to watch Mitzy."

"Dixie and Simon will stop in and take care of her while you're gone. I arranged it while you were in the shower this morning."

"That was a little presumptuous, don't you think, *Snookums*?" Lucy asked.

"Probably, but it worked out anyway."

"Did anyone talk to Bridgett? She didn't respond to my texts." Lucy pushed her phone into her purse.

"Stopped by to see her on the way here. She's on the mend." He reached into the pocket of his slacks and tossed Lucy a ring box. "To make it official."

"We don't need to be so old-fashioned. Forget the ring. I'm a woman of the new millennium and all that."

He shook his head. "Oh c'mon. My wife wears a ring."

"Hey, Dimples. We're not really married. You get that, right?"

She glanced to his left hand. He already wore a gold band.

Lucy removed the lid, revealing pear-shaped sapphires surrounding a massive diamond.

"I can't wear this." She held it up. Light bounced off the diamond. "It has to be three carats."

"Nah, it's a fake." He took the box from her, removed the band from the velvet lining, and pushed the ring gently up to her knuckle.

It slid right off.

He pushed the ring gently onto her finger again.

It dropped back into his hand.

"Shucks, it doesn't fit. I'm not your Cinderella."

"It has to." He pressed it up to her knuckle and squeezed the band, so the flimsy metal molded to her finger.

"Classy. I see you spared no expense." Sarcasm came in handy at that moment.

His fingers trailed across her hand before he shoved the little box back into his jacket.

Lucy followed him out the door, staring at the ring.

In what reality did she wear a fakey-fake engagement ring to go on a honeymoon with William?

He hoisted the bags and equipment boxes filled with cameras and various gadgets into the back of the old red truck he'd driven the first day she met him, hurrying around to the passenger side just in time to open Lucy's door.

His hand rested against her elbow for a moment. A flash of light caught the metal of the gold band on his left hand, taunting an impossible reality. Her blood pressure spiked; her breath turned ragged.

The scent of him swirled in the air—spice, citrus, and the forest at dusk.

"Relax," he said against her ear.

For the briefest of seconds, she thought he might nip at the soft skin of her earlobe where his lips brushed. A shiver slinked around her, over her, straight through her.

His grin broke the spell.

"What's with the not shaving thing?" Lucy climbed inside.

He glanced at the hem of her dress where it slipped up on her thigh, for about four beats too long. She cleared her throat and tilted her head to the side.

"It's my cover." He closed her door.

Cover?

He moved his hand over the hood as he jogged around the front of the truck. Once he climbed inside, her nerves did that purring thing they were so fond of when he was around.

"Do people recognize you a lot?" she asked.

"Not here in Confluence. But why take the risk?" He backed out of the parking lot. "It helps that people see what they want to see. What they expect to see. They don't expect to see a reporter, so they don't."

"Kind of like an alter ego. Except instead of spandex and a cape, you grow a beard and drive a truck?"

He smirked, and it spread into a grin. "Yeah, I guess so."

"Well then, you'll need an alter ego name. Maybe I'll call you Willy?"

"Not on your life."

"Can you at least talk with a special accent and low voice like Batman?"

"No," he said as they stopped at a red light.

"C'mon William, you can't be called 'William' all the time when you're on assignment. You need something more fun. What if I just call you Dimples then?"

He gripped the steering wheel and stared ahead for a moment. When he turned to her, the tenderness of his expression nearly did her in. "I'll tell you what, Lucy. You have special permission to call me Will when we're on assignment."

"Superhero Will who grew a beard and drives a truck. Sounds good to me." She toyed with the hem of her skirt. "Tell me more about where we're headed."

He reached over and opened the glove box, grazing her uncovered knee with the back of his hand.

Inappropriate risqué thoughts about what harlot Barbie would like to do to Beach-loving Ken surged through her mind. She sucked in a hot breath as he handed her a brochure.

Get a grip. This is not a real wedding night.

"Fancy," she drawled, flipping through the brochure. "How far is this place anyway?"

"An hour," he replied.

She slid a sideways glance at him. An hour alone in a cramped space with William. She was amazingly awful at keeping her distance from him.

———

Rain from the night before had drenched the abundant potholes scattered along the cracked asphalt. Focused on the road ahead, William jerked the bowtie at his neck loose. Bridgett had decided they would "dress the part."

Lucy hadn't gotten that note. He'd rather not be in a tux, either, but the way Lucy's jaw fell open when she saw him at the station made it worth it. Girls dug a man in a suit—he already knew that. Raise the stakes to a tuxedo and he'd hoped it might put a crack the armor she kept tight around herself.

So far, no luck.

"You're quiet." William briefly slid his gaze from the windshield to her and back to the country road leading to Twin Lakes.

Lucy had been studying that brochure for a while now. By his estimate, she'd read it cover to cover more than a dozen times. He'd intentionally left the radio off; confident she might be feeling chatty. She wasn't.

"Not much to talk about, I guess." She turned to him a little. "Maybe we should figure out our backstory. How we met. All that."

"Where's the fun in a pretend backstory? I'd rather get to know the real Lucy."

He glanced to her again. A breeze from her open window blew strands of her hair loose from where she'd tied it up.

His fingers itched to tuck it behind her ear.

Hands at ten and two, bud. Hands at ten and two.

"No. I promise, I'm not interesting." She frowned.

He begged to differ.

"Not true. If there's one thing I've learned as a journalist—everyone's interesting. Everyone's got a story to tell." In his experience, this was the truth that kept the industry moving. Find the story. Tell the story.

"Oh yeah? What's your story then? The interesting parts?" She grinned his way.

The interesting part involved a ruined reputation and a now defunct reality TV show. Both things he wasn't going to talk about. He'd spent years doing damage control. No way was he bringing it up now.

For a fickle industry without much of a memory, the entertainment machine had held his reputation hostage following the disaster in Florida. No matter how hard he worked, for years someone always brought up the show. Even when he'd finally moved past it, proven himself a decent reporter, the memory of that summer still haunted him.

"I see what you did there." He jerked his chin toward her.

"What did I do?" She feigned innocence.

"Answered a question with another question. Anything else you learn in journalism school?'

She squinted his way. "Oh, tons. What did they teach you?"

"A little of this. A little of that." He chuckled.

"What's your plan when we get to the lakes?" She held up the brochure she'd studied so thoroughly.

"Figured we'd lay out some obvious cash and then some not-so-obvious cash. I snagged a few pieces of jewelry to tuck in our suitcases when we get there, too."

"Hidden cameras. Lay the bait. What else do we need to do while we're there?" She unclipped her hair, ran a hand through it, and tucked it back up.

"Listen, discreetly ask around, but, mostly, lay the trap and see if anyone falls into it. That leaves a lot of time for us to…talk."

God as his witness, before the trip was done he'd squeeze out more about her.

The truck hit a pothole and a boom echoed through the cab of the truck. Lucy screeched. Her body went stiff. She grabbed his thigh.

He hit the brakes and pulled to the shoulder of the road. Shit. He'd blown a damn tire.

If she moved her hand up any farther, he'd blow something else, too.

"What the hell was that?" Her hand squeezed tighter through the fabric of his slacks.

"Pothole. The tire blew." He closed his eyes.

She hadn't moved her hand. *She needed to move her hand.*

"Lucy?" He dropped his head against the headrest.

"What?" Her fingers still held a death grip on his thigh.

"Could you move…your…uh, hand?" He covered her fingers with his own to shift them closer to his knee.

They locked gazes and the cab of the truck shrunk between them. Neither of them moved. Her lips parted. His followed suit.

She jerked her hand off of him. "Oh my God. I'm sorry."

He glanced to her. She'd gone red again.

His lips twitched.

"No worries. Let's just get this fixed."

"Do tow trucks even come out this far?" There wasn't much around them except a great deal of trees, a meadow, and a speed limit sign. A few cars splashed by, but the nearest town would be an hour out.

"I don't need roadside assistance. I've got a jack and a tire iron." He swung open his door and dug behind the seat for his tools. He may have had a privileged childhood, but his dad made sure he knew how to change a tire. One of those life skills that came in handy. Before his mother passed away, his father had actually been a decent guy. Taught him a lot of shit that came in handy, even now.

She scooted out the passenger door and pushed it closed. "How can I help?"

He knelt beside the tire in question and went to work. "Cheer me on?"

She did a little jazz hands number. "Go, Will."

He paused at her use of the nickname. No one called him that anymore. He preferred his full name usually. Coming from Lucy, though, he didn't mind the nickname. Hell, he even enjoyed it. He tugged off the jacket to his tuxedo to lay it across the side of the truck bed.

"That the best you can do?" Sleeves rolled, he put pressure on a tight lug nut.

"I wasn't exactly a cheerleader."

"No?" That's the most information he'd gotten from her so far.

"Ha. No. *Go, Will* is the extent of my—"

A particularly large SUV picked that moment to pass them. A sheet of water from one of the abundant potholes drenched his back.

He looked to Lucy. She was soaked. Shit. Damn.

He was on his feet in a second. The wall of water got them both, but he had his head down by the tire. A full-frontal attack hit her. Head to toe.

He tagged his jacket to wipe at her cheeks.

"Sonofabitch, Lucy. I'm so sorry." The last time he tried to help clean her up—after the whole coffee debacle—he accidentally felt her up. No way was he going to make that mistake again. This time, he kept his attention to the neck up.

She shrugged off her blazer, revealing a sleeveless blouse that exposed the creamy skin of her shoulders and arms.

"I'll grab your suitcase. Get you something to change into." He reached into the bed of the truck and grabbed her bag.

The damn thing was soaked through.

Fake or not, this was not how he meant to start their honeymoon.

Lucy was covered in flakes of mud, dried road water, and William's tuxedo jacket when they pulled into the parking lot at Twin Lakes. Her suitcase was a mushy pile of laundry, so she had nothing else to change into.

The Twin Lakes lodge appeared to sprout out of the side of the mountain. Nestled among pine trees and stunning blue reservoirs, primitive log cabins surrounded the out-of-place hotel. A couple of fishermen cast their lines as they stood perched along the banks of the lake. In the parking lot, a few hikers headed toward a trailhead.

William opened her door and helped her down to the dirt parking lot. His slacks also had mud smeared on them, his shirt was wrinkled, and his hair was a mess. Rolling around in the dirt and sweating while changing a tire suited him. She'd never seen him in anything but put together. Normally he looked good, but messy suited him nicely.

He had the disheveled James Bond thing down *pat*. The dust of stubble on his face and the bow tie tossed over his shoulder bumped his hotness factor up a solid ten degrees. And he did not need that raise.

Lucy handed him his jacket and smoothed her skirt. "This place is amazing."

He slipped on the suit coat in one smooth movement. "Mrs. Monroe?" He held his hand to her.

"Monroe?" Her belly flipped when his fingers gripped hers.

"We're using Parker's last name to check-in."

Lucy and Will Monroe.

"Mrs. Monroe," she said under her breath as they walked across the lot to the lodge entrance. "Got it."

"Ever done undercover reporting before?" William asked, releasing her hand.

She shook her head.

No. Her stories were generally straightforward. She showed up with a cameraman, a script, and her reporter armor—a smart suit with sensible pumps and perfect makeup. Her weapon of choice? A handheld microphone, which she used as a tool of intimidation by pushing it closer when someone got too aggressive or started to twist the truth.

This undercover wedding assignment was new territory. They made it a few steps before he slipped on a pair of black-rimmed glasses. "Smile." He pointed to one side of the rims. "Camera."

He extended a hand to her. She took it.

His hold kept them tethered together as they moved toward the two massive doors at the lodge's entrance. With their fingers tangled, an unfamiliar calmness settled around her.

An inlaid wooden image of an elk in a meadow crossed the double doors of the entryway. He opened the lobby door for her, still not releasing her fingers. The rustic elegance of the reception area screamed luxury. Huge, polished log beams crossed high above on the ceiling. A bank of clear glass windows filled the entire side of the room, giving an impressive view of the forest behind. An elk-horn chandelier hung above a sitting area and fireplace.

How easy it would be to imagine herself cuddled up right there in front of a raging fire stroking hands with someone special. Except it was summer, so there wouldn't be any fires. And she was with William, so stroking was off-limits. Also, she was covered in dried sludge. There was also that.

The rough pad of his thumb brushed her knuckles as she stepped inside.

Or not.

She did her best to ignore his touch, but her body had other ideas.

She couldn't allow any intimacy between them—pretend or not. The honeymoon gig was a front, nothing more. He spelled trouble. A link to a past better forgotten, and he had no place in her future.

He released her hand, and a ridiculous emptiness settled through her, but she had a part to play—doting new wife and all that entailed. She fidgeted with a cup of pens on the front desk while he checked them into the honeymoon suite. A small part of her hoped they'd lost the Monroe reservation, as had happened to so many other couples. The charade would end, and they'd head back to Confluence.

"I hope you'll have a wonderful stay with us." The front desk hostess's gaze ran the length of him. Her black blazer matched her dark hair, and she had a vibe about her that would bring most men to their knees.

"I'm sure we will," he replied, apparently oblivious to being checked-out while being checked-in. "Is there a laundry service available?"

"We have a full-service housekeeping staff available to assist you with laundry. If I can help with anything else, I'll be right here. The library's next to the conference room. There's a wine reception here in the lobby at six. And don't hesitate to reach out if you require anything else." She slid their room keys into a small envelope.

"Darling." Lucy did her best to be the dutiful wife. She rubbed her hand up his arm for effect, channeling Marilyn Monroe even if the word came out sounding like a disjointed Lucille Ball. "I don't think I want to go to a wine reception tonight. I'd rather drink alone." Moths had clearly taken up residence in her brain. "Alone. But with you."

Right.

She bit her lower lip and winked at him for good measure. Peacocking. That's what she was doing, and not well.

Time for the big guns.

The five second flirt: smile your biggest smile for a full five seconds and watch the magic happen. Men turned to putty. Or so Katie had told her. Personally, she'd never tried it before.

Anyway.

Lips tilted up. Appear delighted. Happy.

Pleased. Amused.

Dash of tenderness.

And… The edges of William's lips twitched. He wasn't putty. He was laughing.

Right. Improv flirting. Not her thing. Good to know. Look at that, she'd already learned new things about herself on her first hidden camera honeymoon.

Oh hell.

He was wearing the damn glasses, so it was on camera. He swallowed hard and put the back of his hand against her cheek as if checking for fever, but he did it so cavalier, it must have appeared endearing to their desk clerk audience. "You okay, Luce?"

Nerves purring, moths flying in her brain…and he called her *Luce*. Now who was putty?

"Great." The word came out high-pitched and a teensy bit screechy. She should stop now, get the nerves and the moths under control, and smuggle herself back to Confluence.

But his hand brushed the apple of her cheek, and her knees turned to apricot jelly.

"I'll just…go peek at the brochures," she muttered.

Something a normal bride would do even if for her it meant tucking her outrageous tail feathers and running.

The desk clerk stood with her head tilted to the side. "Please let me know if there is anything I can do for you, too, Mrs. Monroe."

Lucy backed away and did her best not to fall on her face on the way to the wall of brochures about…fly-fishing. No, thank you. She didn't care for large bodies of water.

She browsed a flyer for a local watering hole instead.

"Hey." William's warm whisper teased the hairs at her neck. He rested his palm on her shoulder which, thanks to the mud situation, meant his hand settled mostly on naked skin and a tiny bit of fabric.

Which, of course, meant *putty*.

"All checked in. Did you find anything interesting, *darling*?" He drawled that last part too long, his eyes bright with clear amusement.

He totally had her number when he smiled at her. For a full five seconds.

She wasn't putty anymore. Nope, she was pretty much a goopy mess of Lucy.

He raised his eyebrow and nodded to the brochures she held. "What'd ya find?"

"Fly fishing and bars." She held up the two flyers, one in each hand.

"Sounds like the makings of the best day of my life." His gaze moved over the photos of the fishing brochure. "Babe, we're goin' fishing."

She *so* was not going fishing. "Babe?"

"You didn't seem to care for Snookums. Figured I'd keep trying 'til I find one you like."

She cringed. "You're impossible."

"I've been called many, many worse things."

"I don't fish."

"First time for everything, Honey Pie." He snagged her hand and tugged her along beside him.

He'd called most of the members of his harem in Florida that particular endearment. "I hate that name the most, Dimples."

He paused, everything about him turning abruptly serious. "Then I'll have to keep trying, won't I?"

Crap.

———

The honeymoon suite turned out to be even nicer than the hotel lobby, which said a lot. Lucy kicked off her shoes and curled her toes into the plush carpet. Tonight she would sleep in luxury.

"This place is amazing, Will." She traced a fingertip along one of the ribbons on the pillowcases. "These have to be over a thousand-thread-count. Come here and feel."

He dropped an armful of bags. "I'll feel up the bedding when I get back. One more trip should do it."

"Do you want any help?" She glanced up.

"Nope, enjoy your time with the pillows." He grinned a told-you-you'd-like-it smile and tugged the door closed behind him.

She sorted through the bags of equipment he'd left along the wall.

The oversize picture window framed the wilderness surrounding the lodge. The sound of a keycard in the door knocked her back to reality. The door didn't open.

"Will?" she called.

Nothing.

She peeked through the eyehole. The man on the other side was not William.

"Can I help you?" Lucy squinted into the small fisheye hole that made everything outside look wonky.

Tall and built like one of those heavy-duty trucks, he shoved the keycard in once more. The reader buzzed and clunked, but the door wouldn't open.

He paused, key still inserted and flipped over the envelope in his hand. "Sorry. I think they gave us the wrong room number."

William had said the resort had a reputation for double booking rooms.

They had all been given the same room. Simple. This was the reason he had come with cameras on a secret consumer news mission.

"Hold on." Lucy rummaged through the equipment bags to find a camera. "Just a second."

With no time to do anything but set it on the dresser, she flicked the thing on. The angle would be crap, but maybe she'd get something usable.

She peeked through the door into the hall again. A sandy-haired woman with huge doll-like eyes stepped into view, and the man slung his arm around her shoulder.

Lucy pushed back the bolt and opened the door a sliver. "Hi. I think the lodge made a mistake. My husband will be right back. I'm sure he won't mind walking to the front desk with you to sort this out."

William picked that moment to step around the corner with the bags.

"What's going on, Sugar Lips?" He did that drawl again. The teasing should have pissed her off, but damn it was kind of cute. He moved forward and kissed her on the forehead as he stepped through the entry.

Jelly. Not just her knees this time. Her whole body whimpered.

"Looks like they gave us the same room." The other man waited in the hallway with his wife.

William dropped the bags beside the bed. Two beats, and he held out his hand confidently to the Mack-truck dude. "William."

The man shook it. "Max."

"What do you say we head to the front desk and find out what's going on, yeah?" William asked the guy.

Without waiting for a response, William moved, and they followed. A magnet. He drew people to him, with him, beside him. As he closed the door, his eyes caught hers, and he said softly, "B-roll, babe. We need raw footage of everything."

"You're so bossy." She settled her hands on her waist, her elbows flared. "And seriously, Sugar Lips?"

He glanced to her mud-soaked shirt. "I'll grab you something to wear from the gift shop." A wink and he slipped on the glasses.

The door closed, and Lucy stood alone in the big room with all the bags and a big bed she'd likely not get to sleep in after all.

CHAPTER
EIGHT

William and Lucy got demoted to Cabin Number Six—down by the lake.

Of course they wouldn't kick a real couple out of the honeymoon suite on their actual honeymoon. Simple and private—that's what the front desk clerk assured William when he offered to move out of the suite. The suite Lucy had seemed really into. And since he was really into Lucy, the last thing he wanted was to disappoint her. It's not like she'd been excited to tag along on this little excursion anyway.

While the cabin wasn't the luxury of the suite, it wasn't awful.

William had re-loaded the bags, sent Lucy's clothes to be cleaned, and waited while she changed into the only clothes he could find in the gift shop. The pajama bottoms had *Princess* stamped across her ass. They fit snugly around the aforementioned backside, the waistband resting just below her navel. She filled out the word *Princess* perfectly.

Honestly, he could get behind whatever declarations she wanted to display on her ass at any point during their trip.

The simple cabin had a living and bedroom combo that made up the majority of the large room with a fireplace on one side and a kitchenette on the other. A giant bed crafted from logs faced the doorway. The bathroom only had a shower, but they could live with that. No television, though. That would be harder to live with.

He and Lucy went to work, taping footage of the space before he moved in their bags.

William itched to get out of the monkey suit he'd had on since they left KDVX. In the bathroom, he changed into jeans and a plaid button-down shirt. Before he hung up the suit coat, he retrieved the worn envelope he carried with him all the time. He ran his finger along the edge and tapped it on the counter before closing his eyes and leaning his forehead on the mirror. His future was secure in Confluence. That's what mattered. It's what his mom had worked so hard for, and he swore to himself he wouldn't let her down again. This would be his last story as a reporter, and he'd make it a good one. Then he'd run her company just as she would have.

He leaned away from his reflection and took a deep breath before opening his eyes and slipping the envelope back into his pocket.

"You want to check my footage before I put everything away?" Lucy asked as he emerged from the bathroom.

"I need to?" He dumped his clothes on a chair.

"Nope."

"Then no, I trust you."

She frowned slightly. Like he was a puzzle she tried to solve, but a piece was missing.

The curtains on the window near the small sofa revealed a picture window framing the lake.

"You swim?" he asked.

"No."

"Not at all?"

"Not at all," she replied.

"Why?" he asked.

"Sharks."

William banked the smile that tugged at his mouth. He gestured to the window. "Not too many sharks in a freshwater lake."

"I don't swim." She shook her head, her hair tumbling in a wave over her shoulders. "Not my thing."

"Because of sharks?" His fingertips prickled with the desire to run through her hair. Touch her and make a connection.

"Originally, yeah."

"More, Luce," he said.

Her eyes warmed, and her mouth went slack. He had noted she did that whenever he called her Luce.

That was better than the frown from before.

"I lived by the ocean growing up. Lots of sharks. They scared me, so I never learned to swim." She shrugged.

Since that first day at the truck stop, this was possibly the most she had ever shared with him.

"You lived by the ocean?" He dropped to the bed and propped himself up on an elbow.

"Uh…yup." She started unpacking the remnants of her bag into one of the dresser drawers, and her shirt lifted just enough to expose the small of her back as she bent over.

His gaze lingered. "Your parents didn't teach you to swim even with a giant body of water right outside the door?" Living next to the ocean and not learning to swim was ludicrous—like being from Colorado and never going skiing. Sacrilege.

"Nope." She rubbed her hands together, clearly pleased with her unpacking skills.

"I'll teach you to swim." He leaned toward her. "At the lake. It'll be fun."

"No."

"Why?"

"Sharks."

William grinned. She was adorable.

"We need food. I haven't eaten in hours." She obviously angled to change the subject.

"Right, I forgot." He removed the spa voucher from his wallet and handed it to her.

She glanced at it. "What's this?"

"Spa voucher. Compliments of the resort for making us move. I'm not into pedicures, and I figured you'd enjoy it."

"I say, 'I need food' and you hand me a coupon for a pedicure?" She studied the slip of paper.

"They also comped our meals while we're here, so we can head to dinner whenever. Or they said they'd deliver something tonight if we want since it was their screw up."

"I need food," she said again.

"You want to order?" He snagged a menu from the nightstand.

"I hoped if I said it again, you might pull a manicure from your wallet next." She grinned now, and if he didn't know better, he'd say she was flirting. Damn, she had a killer smile when she used it— which wasn't often enough.

"You're cute." He tossed her the menu.

She caught it in one hand.

"It'll probably take a bit for delivery. I'm going exploring. Order me a burger, babe." He stood from the bed.

"Stop calling me 'babe.'"

"Stop being adorable."

Her eyes moved from the menu to stare at him with a disbelieving gleam. "I'm not adorable."

"Uh-huh." He slipped on his shoes.

"I can't believe you're leaving me alone on our honeymoon," she huffed.

"As you pointed out, Princess, it's not a real one." He'd prefer to go exploring with her, but he needed to return calls. Taking over a broadcast empire the size of Crestone entailed a lot of meetings, phone calls, and paperwork. The attorneys handled the majority of the paperwork, but he still had to attend an obscene number of meetings. Every time he checked his phone, five or ten more voicemails needed attention. Most of the calls came from the attorneys, sometimes from his father, occasionally from Parker.

"Later, Princess." He didn't turn around as he left the cabin, but he knew her eyes never left his back.

Exploring for William meant arguing with his father, and hoping his chest wouldn't implode from lack of oxygen, while sitting on the beach near the lodge. By the time he finished, he was hungry, tired, and as grumpy as Lucy in the morning. He'd expected once the judgment came through, his father would quit jerking him around. Turned out the verdict only ignited his father's anger, and Dad was on a mission to continue running not only the company, but also William's life.

When he finally got back to the cabin, he found Lucy sprawled on the bed, asleep, and the table near the kitchenette set with two trays. One tray was picked over while the silver room service cover remained fitted on the other. He lifted it and took a bite of tepid hamburger.

After he finished eating, he cased the cabin. Room service had delivered a six-pack of beer with dinner, a bottle of wine, and a *Thank You* note from the manager.

All he wanted right now was to sit and watch a game. Any game. He'd even take a soccer game or NASCAR if it meant a break from the lunacy going on in his head about his dad, his company, and Lucy spread eagle on the bed. And he hated soccer and NASCAR. Now, Lucy spread eagle…that he could get used to.

Her mouth moved as if she carried on an important conversation even in sleep. It was probably creepy that he enjoyed watching her this much. He didn't particularly care because, well, he *did* enjoy watching her. At least asleep she didn't seem angry with him for dragging her along on his assignment.

He needed to find something to do.

The closet next to the bathroom held extra linens and pillows, a handful of paperback novels, and a stack of board games. He sifted through the novels—mainly mysteries he had already read and a few Stephen King books. The board games were pretty standard. Monopoly was his game. He could wipe the floor with anyone when he played, so it wasn't fair to Lucy. Dirty Jenga. Now, that one held promise. The last game was called *Confessions: The Ultimate Game of Getting to Know You.*

He'd found a winner.

Lucy squirmed on the bed. He guessed she'd be awake soon, so he cleared the trays from the table, popped the top on a beer, and set up *Confessions.*

The instructions were easy enough. It worked similar to poker. William was counting chips when Lucy sat up in bed, stretched her arms over her head, and yawned.

"Hey." She swung her legs over the edge of the bed and headed to the table. "What's this?"

"We're playing *Confessions.*" He gestured to the chair across from him and resumed his counting.

"What's *Confessions*?"

"A board game. Damn, we're short." He glanced around the room.

"What're you looking for?" Lucy's eyes were still hazy with sleep.

"Something to use as chips. We're short ten."

"What kind of chips?" She stretched again, clearly trying to test the limits of his sanity.

"Like this." He held up a couple of the poker chips.

Lucy glanced at the table before heading back to the bed. She opened the nightstand and rummaged around for a minute before emerging with a purple box. Her hips swayed as she moved toward him to toss the box on the table. "These'll work."

"These are condoms." He shook the box, so it rattled.

She squinted at the box of condoms on the table.

"They're the right size, aren't they?"

He glanced down at his at-attention crotch. Uh. Yes, she was definitely testing the limits of his mental health.

She absolutely could not be propositioning him. He wouldn't say no, of course, but this felt like a trap.

If it looked like a trap, smelled like a trap, and had a big ol' latex lock on it, it was probably a trap. He lifted his eyes to meet hers.

A blush crept up her neck. "Oh my God. I meant the size of the chips! Not..."

Her face was full crimson now as she glanced at his inseam.

"Why do you have condoms?" he asked slowly.

She'd brought condoms with her. A whole, unopened box.

"I don't have condoms." She was wide-awake now. Her eyes were huge, and her shocked expression was as if she'd licked a bacon-flavored sucker when she expected grape.

"You gave me a box of condoms." He held up the box.

"They came with the room. I saw them when I put the menu away."

Okay, so she hadn't packed condoms for their hidden camera honeymoon. He wasn't sure if he was disappointed or relieved.

Disappointed. No question, really. "And they're on the kitchen table because...?"

Lucy pressed her hands against her temples. "Someone tell me I'm still asleep."

"Still waitin' for that answer, Princess."

"They're the same size as the chip thingies you need." Just when he thought her face couldn't get redder, there it went. "And I cannot be responsible for the things I do when I first wake up."

"So, we're playing *Confessions* with condoms?"

"I'm not playing a game called *Confessions* with you." She sat in the chair he'd offered a few minutes ago and dropped her head to her hands.

"You just threw condoms at me. Pretty sure we're playing this out."

"This isn't happening. I'm dreaming. None of this is happening." She glanced up briefly before dropping her forehead to her palms.

"Adorable."

"Am not." She shook her head, still in her hands.

"It's cool. I'm down with condom *Confessions*." He lifted an eyebrow. "Unless, you want to use them for a different game."

Lucy looked up just as he ripped open the box.

CHAPTER
NINE

Lucy stared at the question on the card she held, a pile of condoms stacked in front of her. Her face burned with a combination of embarrassment and something she couldn't quite put her finger on.

She'd been groggy when she had agreed to play a get-to-know-you game with the one guy she didn't want to get to know. Once again, proving to herself she should not make grown-up decisions right after waking up.

Geez, she hadn't slept that soundly in months.

Strange that sleep would be simpler in the cabin. All kinds of sleep existed in Lucy's post-stalked life: fitful, tearful, angry—yes, angry sleep happened—but never deep and never without taking something to knock her out. She blamed the sleep for her current predicament. There was no other explanation.

Why couldn't they play Monopoly—a simple game with no personal sharing or latex?

Lucy was awful at playing *Confessions*. She didn't want to share anything, so she passed on all the questions. She learned William's favorite color was brown, he grew up in Confluence, and his first kiss happened when he was ten, outside the Go-fer Food store.

First of all, who chose brown as a favorite color? Second, how had she missed that he'd been raised in Confluence and his father ran Crestone *before* she'd made the plans to come here? Furthermore, who got their first kiss at age ten? No wonder he'd been such an esteemed tonsil-hockey player when she met him in Florida. With all those years of practice, he had already gone pro by the time he turned twenty.

"I'm losing you." William sliced through the silence. She squinted to focus on the question on the card.

"What is the most important part of friendship?"

He tossed a chip into the center of the table. "I'd like to hear your answer here."

Lucy tossed a chip as well. "You first. I'm calling."

"Honesty and loyalty." He took a slug of beer.

"You didn't start with 'I confess.'" She picked at the label on her barely-touched beer.

"I *confess* honesty and loyalty are the most important part of any relationship."

"You sure?" Her heart skipped a beat as she waited for his reply.

Honesty and loyalty hadn't exactly been part of any of the relationships she'd witnessed him having in Florida.

He cocked his head and narrowed his eyes.

"Absolutely. You should match the confession." He sucked down a gulp of beer.

Unfortunately, her streak of not sharing couldn't go on much longer.

Lucy twisted the hair. "I confess I know a lot of people."

She glanced down at the table. "But I only have one real friend. She's there when I need her, and I return the favor. So, to me, the most important part of friendship is being there when you're needed."

From the moment Lucy had moved into the freshman dorm at college, Katie had stepped up to be her friend. When Lucy struggled, Katie was there for her. She'd helped Lucy buy in-style clothes that fit, and introduced her to the painful reality of an eyebrow wax.

William stared at her for a few beats. "Only one real friend?"

"Honesty and loyalty are really your thing?" Lucy raised her eyebrow at him.

Back when she'd known him before, she lived in a world of make-believe and hoped she was important to him. She had daydreamed of the day he would realize she was more than the awkward production assistant, and he'd give her some of that attention he'd reserved exclusively for the other women on set. Yep, she had crushed hard on him. Her heart broke that summer when he left, and she swore the next time she met a guy like William, he wouldn't forget about her.

He sat forward on his chair, leaning his arms on the table. "Did I do something to upset you?"

Fine. So she was being a total grouch and scratching at old wounds to ensure they wouldn't close. Eight years had passed. The statute of limitations on judgment for his past indiscretions was over. She wasn't that insecure, shy girl anymore. Her past no longer defined her. He didn't remember her, and it was better this way. Time to let it go and start fresh. "Sorry, no. Next question."

William read the next card. "If you could change anything about the way you were raised, what would it be and why?"

She sucked in a breath. Her parents weren't the kind you talked about openly. No, they were the kind who left you with enough issues to fund the vacations of future therapists.

"You go first this time." William nudged her shin with his toe.

"You didn't add any chips," she pointed out.

"Let's just answer the questions. We'll get to know each other better. It'll make the time here easier." His dimples swept away her resolve.

"I confess I would've liked parents who kept me around." Where did that come from? Sheesh, yeah, it was true. But it wasn't something she shared with anyone.

"Your parents didn't want you around?" Abruptly aware of his proximity, she glanced down to where his hand rested only an inch away from hers.

"Mom and Dad are different." She heard herself speak, but

remained unclear which synapses were giving direction at the moment. "When they're together, they want me around, when they're in the midst of one of a thousand breakups, they pretend I don't exist. They toss money at me. I stay away. A few months ago, they broke up again." She'd refused to take anything from them this time around. This time around she decided to do things herself. Which is what landed her in Camelot. "We've only emailed a few times since. Last I heard, it's looking promising they might reconcile soon."

Not that it mattered to her. Not really. She was done with that part of her life.

"Siblings?" The slightest of movements brought his fingers even closer to hers, and the desire to trace the line of his gold wedding band nearly overpowered her.

"No." Thankfully, some part of her brain wasn't focused on his proximity and continued to play the game. "You?"

"No siblings." He frowned. "Always wanted a big family, but that didn't happen. Mom got sick when I was a kid. Cancer. She beat it. Couldn't have more kids, so she threw herself into her work at Crestone. Cancer came back. She died. Dad married the housekeeper."

Whoa. "That's awful."

"You have no idea." His face went totally blank.

"I met her at the coffee shop. Teresa, right?" Lucy asked.

"Yeah." He rolled his beer bottle between his palms.

Right. Moving on. Lucy grabbed another card. "What's the most embarrassing thing that's ever happened to you?"

William lifted his bottle to his lips.

"You first," Lucy said quickly.

His face turned thoughtful. "I confess I was on a reality show once."

Lucy's heart stammered. Of course she knew that. "Yeah?"

The word came out breathy.

"A *Real World*, *Big Brother* type show. They made me look like an idiot. I was a kid, and I was naive, so I didn't think. But I needed the cash, and it seemed like a good idea at the time. In hindsight, it was a bad decision that led to years of embarrassment." Sadness oozed through his words, and he had the look of a man banished to Confession-induced purgatory.

"I thought you were loaded. Why'd you need money?"

The question apparently caught him off guard. "My parents shut off my trust fund. My mom was pissed at how I blew through cash. She was right. I get that now. I was stuck in Florida with Parker, and he had to get home for work. I got the casting call, took an advance, and sent him home with my payout. My mom got sick when we were filming. She died, and I missed her funeral because I didn't get home in time."

William cleared his throat.

"Then your dad married the housekeeper…Teresa," she whispered. The beautifully sad Italian woman from the coffee shop Lucy's first day at KDVX. She could relate to that type of thing… That's the type of thing that tore her own parents apart again and again.

"A slime-ball producer spliced together video of me that implied I screwed half of the female population of Florida, aired it on national television, caused a rift between my dad and I, and *then* my dad married Teresa." He tipped his beer toward her. "Now, the production company is trying to convince me to do a reunion episode."

Lucy had apparently missed that invitation. But, then, why would they invite a lowly production assistant anyway? "Maybe you should do it?"

"No way in hell am I opening myself up to that kind of embarrassment again."

"Will, hey, this is supposed to be fun." She reached for his hand to give what she hoped was an innocent squeeze. She tried to tug her fingers away, but he held tight.

"I confess Teresa wasn't just the housekeeper." His hollow words echoed through the cabin.

"I think—"

"When I was a kid, she was my nanny. She helped raise me… She was never just the housekeeper." The pain of his father's betrayal to his family flickered in William's eyes.

Silence stretched between them, but he still didn't let her hand go. Lucy used to make him laugh in Florida and had prided herself on being exceptionally good at it. Right then, she wanted nothing more than to help him find his way back from whatever dark place had sucked him in.

"I confess that this one time, on assignment, I threw a box of condoms at my colleague. That was pretty mortifying." She rolled her eyes, hoping to diffuse the tension and lighten the heavy atmosphere.

He slid his hand away and opened another beer for himself, tossing the cap into the trash bin. "That was pretty awesome."

"Wrong word. Humiliating is more accurate," she corrected.

"Luce, it was spectacular. And they're multi-purpose for all kinds of fun games" His eyes moved over her in a way that was anything but innocent.

Her resolve disintegrated on the spot, but she kept on. "I confess this other time I reported on location and totally rocked it. When I say rocked it, I mean I. Was. On. Fire. It's such a rush being on live television." She peeled off the rest of the label from her beer bottle. "And then a fly flew right into my mouth. I gagged and couldn't finish. Somewhere, I'm on a Best of Bloopers reel, gagging and coughing up an insect on live television. I didn't have a rooster collapse on me, but it was still holy-crap embarrassing."

"You heard about the rooster, Luce?" he asked.

"Everyone's heard about the rooster."

That got her the dimples.

"Next question." She grabbed a card. He would not be getting her all mushy with the Luce business again. "Wild card. Ask any question."

"Sounds fun. I like to be wild." Wasn't that the truth?

She snorted. "What were you really doing when you left earlier?"

"I confess I had business to deal with."

"Two-part question." She tossed the card on the table.

"You've got to say that first."

"That's not in the rules." Not that she'd actually read the rules. But she was pretty sure it wasn't there.

More dimples.

"What business exactly? Is it a news story?" she asked.

He leaned forward so their hands nearly touched. "If I confess something to you, can you keep it to yourself?"

She cocked her head to the side. "Did you do something illegal?"

"No."

"That's too bad. Your confession would be more interesting." She tossed another piece of label into the pile littering the table.

"Would you keep a secret if I did something illegal?" he asked.

"That depends." The small pile of shredded label grew alongside the stack of condoms in front of her.

"On what?" When he tipped back his beer, the shirt he wore stretched taut across his upper body, giving her a view of the definition underneath.

She parted her lips. He tossed her a questioning look. "What exactly you did. Hypothetically, of course," she finally replied.

His grin widened. "What illegal activities would you keep a secret?"

"Let's say you beat up a guy because he threatened a kid or a puppy. That's you being a decent human being. So, I'd keep that secret. Now, if you unalived someone, I'd be forced to call the police."

Dear Lord, just when she thought his grin was at its sexiest, it got bigger, teeth and dimples and all.

"This is confidential. I trust you'll respect the bonds of *Confessions*?"

She nodded, mesmerized by all that was him.

He leaned closer, and the heat from his golden eyes hypnotized her. Or maybe it was the heat from thoughts of how they could use the substitute game pieces. Either way.

"I turn thirty in a few weeks. I confess that when that happens, I'll inherit Crestone Broadcasting. The transfer of ownership involves a lot of phone calls and paperwork. I dealt with that today—the phone calls part."

Well, that wasn't so big. Not murder big, anyway. Still, though, not small.

Okay, crapola. This was huge.

William would be her boss—a boss with access to her personnel file. A boss with the ability to call the shots with her career. She absolutely wouldn't get involved with him. No way.

"That makes you my boss."

"Not yet. Right now, I'm still a reporter on assignment with an adorable producer, which makes *you* kind of my boss."

"If I'm the boss, then why are you always so bossy? Huh?"

He tangled his fingers with hers and stroked the sensitive spot between her thumb and pointer finger.

He's going to be your boss. He's going to be your boss. He's going to be your boss.

Her breath hitched. "Three-part question," she whispered.

"Got a feeling no matter what I say, you're asking anyway. Shoot." He untangled his grasp.

"Why do you call me Princess? Before you were messing around with the other names, but this one's stuck. Why?"

His eyes danced. "Luce, it's on your ass."

She blinked hard. "Come again?"

"The writing on your pants says '*Princess*' right across your... ahem...backside." He gestured to her nether regions.

"I cannot believe you were reading my ass."

He opened his mouth to speak, but she got there first–"Watch your words carefully."

"You walk around with words stamped on your pants, men are gonna look."

"They're not my pants." Well, they weren't. It's not like she'd chosen them.

"Not your pants?" he asked.

"That's what I said." Her heart beat faster with the knowledge he had checked her out.

"Luce. You gave the same defense of every crackhead who gets arrested with blow in his pocket. Gotta be honest, the logic doesn't fly. You're wearing them, they're your pants. End of story."

"Are you always this difficult?" She shuffled the cards again.

"You've got a couple of days to find out." She let out a deep breath. "My guess is yes."

"Your guess is probably right. My turn. Honesty this time. Why are you so afraid of water?"

She opened her mouth, but he cut her off. "Don't say sharks."

Ugh. She didn't like doing personal, and they'd been getting very personal.

"I confess I do pools fine. Anywhere I can see the bottom and know I can touch. When I can't see the bottom I get panicky about what's down there. Add to that, drowning would be the worst way to go. So I avoid the possibility." She set the stack of cards in front of her.

"Drowning wouldn't be so bad," he said with confidence.

"Uh, yeah it would be awful. Your lungs burning up when you're unable to get to the surface. The panic. Ugh. No. But, seriously, thank you for ensuring I won't sleep tonight."

"I'll distract you later. You'll forget." He tipped his bottle to his lips and winked at her.

Warmth flooded her cheeks. She studied the wood grain of the table as though it held the answer to the meaning of life.

"Eyes on me."

So bossy.

She didn't want to, but she did.

He was all seriousness. "You're under the water, and you panic. After the panic, you accept the end, and there's only a brief fear before you breathe in the water. Peace fills your lungs, and you float to wherever you go when it's over. They say drowning is... tranquil."

"Tranquil?" she repeated. He was certifiable. No one thought drowning was anything but awful. "Who says? Because this isn't something you come back from and say 'Hey, guess what? Not so bad. This is the way to go. Totally pick drowning.'"

"Freaking adorable. You get that, right?"

"Stop." She said it but her heart wasn't in it.

"No."

Damn.

"Seriously," he continued. "One of the networks I worked at did a special about people who got brought back after a near-drowning, and they all said it wasn't so bad. Drowning wouldn't be fantastic, but it wouldn't be like dying in a fire. Fire is not the way to go. Or a guillotine. Avoid both of those."

"I guess I'm not sleeping tonight." She spoke under her breath.

He raised an eyebrow, and a fissure of yearning skittered through her as he gave her another body scan. "Don't mind staying up."

"Can we play something else for a while?"

"Absolutely." He grinned wider than the devil himself, and she knew exactly what game he wanted to play.

She stood. "I think I'll go to sleep."

"Not thinkin' so. Drowning, fire, and guillotine will have you back here in five. Don't mind waiting, though, if you want to try the sleep thing."

Of course he was right. She flopped on the chair. "I need another beer. Mine's warm."

"You sure? You've got more label to shred on that one." He pointed to the stack in front of her.

"Next question." She gave a one-handed flutter of a wave.

He popped the top off another beer and slid it across the table. "Tomorrow night, there's a barn dance near the lodge. You coming with me?"

"A barn dance? Which century are we in?"

"C'mon, Princess. It'll be fun. We'll take some video and call it research. You won't let me teach you to swim. At least let me teach you to two-step."

He was William, and if she wasn't mistaken, he'd asked her on a sort-of date. Her inner-teenager was breakdancing at the idea. "Fine. I'll go. But I don't know how to dance."

His finger traced the ring on her hand. "Luce, the thing you're not getting is I'm an exceptional teacher. And I know how to do all kinds of fun things."

She bet he did, especially since he had spent a summer practicing with half the female population of Florida.

———

Two more beers and several more rounds of *Confessions* erased all of the gruesome ways to die from her memory. He had rolled a sleeping bag on the floor, and she burrowed under the covers on the bed. The dark cabin was eerily quiet without any city noise.

"Will?" she called.

"Yeah, Luce?" His voice was relaxed, throaty.

"I had fun tonight," she said in his direction.

"Me, too." It sounded like he punched at his pillow.

She bunched the blankets at her chest. "How's the floor?"

"Smells like dog piss. How's the bed?"

"Smells like clean sheets." Not thousand-thread-count sheets, but they weren't awful. She adjusted her own pillow.

He sneezed.

She stared at the ceiling, willing sleep to come. What had she gotten herself into? What did a guy like him wear to bed? Was he a boxers kind of guy or a nothing kind of guy? Her belly fluttered with a craving not even chocolate cake would fix.

He sneezed again. "You okay, Will?"

"Allergic to dogs. Given the smell down here, whoever owns this rental brings their dog along when they visit."

"Will? How do you feel about a pillow line?" She sat up and leaned over the bed, her eyes finally adjusting.

"A what?" He faced the ceiling, his hands resting on his chest.

"You know, a pillow line? I let you come up here, but you can't cross the pillow line."

Didn't everyone know about the pillow line?

"Is that a thing?" It was dark, but she could practically see the devil's-smile he must've had.

"It's an Amish thing."

"It's not an Amish thing." He rubbed his hand over his eyes, and the sleeping bag rustled as he sat up.

"Fine, you're right. It's a Lucy thing." She tossed the covers back and scooted to the other side of the bed.

"To be clear, you're inviting me into your bed?" he asked.

She sucked in a heated breath, and not even double-fudge chocolate cake would overpower her craving now.

He sneezed again.

She sighed. "Yeah. I guess I am." She set up a pillow down the center as he slipped underneath the covers.

"Luce?" he asked.

"Yeah?"

"Knew I liked you."

"Go to sleep, Will."

Sometime during the night, the pillow line blurred, and William's arm snaked around her waist. In the depths of sleep, she had snuggled against him and settled her head under his chin. He smelled of sleep and safety. When she came to, she tried to tug herself away, but his arm tightened, and his breath evened. It was then, when she knew he was asleep, he mumbled her name. Oh God, the way it sounded on his lips. This time, instead of wriggling away, she burrowed deeper into his embrace. She wasn't asleep. And she'd hate herself tomorrow.

Probably.

CHAPTER
TEN

Lucy pressed her foot into something hard. She nudged it with her toe. Hard and warm and human. She jolted up on the bed. A warm hand pressed the tender spot above her ankle. A warm, male hand.

"If you wanted a foot rub, all you had to do was ask. No need to kick." William sat at the bottom of the bed in his plaid, lumberjack-inspired shirt. His attention was currently on the bare foot she'd shoved against him, his thumb giving some deep tissue attention to the arch.

"I didn't want a— Oh. That's nice."

He hit some kind of trigger point. She moaned. Yup. She did. Right there in bed with William. The yearning from the night before pulsed through her again like warm honey.

"Luce, I have to go take care of some stuff. You're on your own today. Can you swing by the lodge, ask some questions? I'll follow up when I get back tonight."

What? They were kind of married, and he was rubbing her foot. He couldn't just take off.

"What time is it?" She flicked her hair from her face.

"A little after six. Got something that needs attention."

He covered her foot with the blanket and tucked it in.

What could possibly need attention when he was on his honeymoon?

Cue a Lucy reality check. This wasn't real. Well, the massage had been real, but the rest, definitely not real. All smoke and mirrors and…foot rubs.

And next, please.

"'Kay." She propped herself on an elbow. He had obviously been up awhile. Wet hair curled around the collar of his button-down shirt. What would it be like to unfasten each of those little buttons and run her hands along his chest? Her gaze moved back to his wide-awake face.

Functioning on no sleep was clearly one of his superpowers.

"I'll get some video and chat with the other guests. See if they've had anything stolen."

"Visit the spa. That'll give you lots of time away." He shrugged and then moved his hand in another slow caress of her ankle. Over the comforter, but she'd take it. A little tug between her thighs reminded her that she was a woman, he was a man, and they were on a bed together.

Sweet baby Jesus. She really did make the worst choices right after waking up.

She pulled a pillow over her face.

"Start by de-grumping before you hit the wilderness? I'll be back in time to two-step." He tucked the quilt around her waist before sliding away to shove his wallet in his back pocket and tag his keys off the counter. "Don't forget to turn on the cameras when you head out."

He snagged his cell phone and gave a little two-finger wave as he left.

Through the grog of morning brain, she heard him talking. He didn't sound happy. "What'd he do this time?"

Lucy lay still, trying to convince herself the things happening between them weren't a big deal. Except, somewhere around two a.m., when he had cuddled her close and whispered her name, it had become a big deal. Her breath stayed trapped in her chest at the memory. This time she wasn't an awkward teenager with nothing to offer. No, she was the new and improved Lucille, and somewhere within, a tiny piece of her had hoped William was ready for "more" with the new Lucy. But, no, that didn't work. A fling with her future boss was a bad idea all around.

She blew out a sigh, took a long shower, and dressed in her favorite worn jeans. The sun slanted through the windows as she tugged on a sweatshirt with her father's law firm logo, checked the hidden cameras one last time, and set off on a slow walk to the lodge for breakfast. It was all very forest-y here. Pine needles littering the ground, the scent of…well…*pine* in the air. Little woodland creatures skittered around the trees, making noise as they rustled the leaves. Squirrels maybe? Perhaps chipmunks? Who really knew?

Her plan for the day was to eat, give the staff plenty of time to steal something, and spend the rest of the day getting raw footage of the lodge for William's story. Absolutely no thinking about the night before.

She arrived at the sleepy lodge and made a beeline for the restaurant.

A party of one at a table for two, she ordered eggs and toast with a full pot of coffee.

She flipped through a magazine and sipped from her mug as the waitress set her breakfast down in a flutter to get to the other tables.

Lucy barely finished buttering her toast— "I'm Sarah."

Lucy glanced up, mid-bite. The honeymooner who got the suite stood at the edge of the table. She wore a button-down pastel-blue blouse, slacks, and entirely too sensible sneakers. She also appeared exceptionally well rested. Not a dark circle to be found under her eyes. Not really unexpected, given the quality of the sheets she got to sleep on. Lucy wasn't jealous since she got to sleep on Will—

"I wanted to thank you for moving out of the honeymoon suite for us." Sarah fidgeted with her purse.

"Lucy." She spoke through a mouth full of food. "My name, I mean. I'm Lucy."

"Everything worked out okay for you?" Sarah asked, concern written across her face.

"Yep. Everything's great. They found us a cabin. How's the, uh, suite?" Lucy asked, knowing damn well the suite was ah-mazing.

Sarah's face lit up. "Great. They sent me spa coupons since they screwed up our reservation. What a mess. It felt so weird when the front desk lady asked Max for incentive to move us in there."

Wait. What? Lucy's reporter radar perked to attention. She set her coffee aside.

"I'm sorry. She asked for incentive?"

"Not directly, no. But you know how these things work."

Sarah waved her hand as though Lucy should know.

Lucy didn't know, but she was getting the idea. "What exactly did she say?"

"She told Max that they'd made a mistake and since you were already in the room, there wasn't much she could do. She emphasized the word, much. It just felt funny to us. But your husband talked to her manager, and they'd already arranged for you to move. So it didn't matter anyway."

Except it mattered a lot.

"What do you think *much* meant?" Lucy pressed.

"I think it was pretty clear, if we wanted the room, we needed to grease the way a little with an extra tip." Sarah's expression was of total distaste. "The whole thing was odd."

"You want to sit down?" Lucy's desire to dig deeper won out over any latent annoyance with Sarah for sleeping on thousand-thread-count sheets.

"That'd be great." Sarah slumped in the chair across from her. "I came down for breakfast. Max isn't an early riser, and he can be amazingly grouchy in the morning." She laughed. "I figured I'd slip out. I'm so glad I did because I love making new friends."

Apparently, Lucy had received a promotion from William's "honeymoon prop" to Sarah's "new friend." That probably meant her day was looking up.

Lucy really wanted some time alone to process last night's

confessions and the two a.m. cuddle, but this was more important. The woman seemed desperate to talk to someone, and really, Lucy was happy to be that someone.

Lucy took a stab at small talk. "How long have you been married?"

"Eight months. We finally had a chance to get away. Max is a doctor, so his schedule is crazy. What does your husband do?" Sarah asked.

"He's a landscaper." *Liar.*

"Max is a doctor."

Yeah, she had mentioned that. "A doctor in the family must come in handy."

"You have no idea. He's a specialist, so I get referred to a colleague when I'm sick. It's okay, though. I know how busy he is. Do you work?"

Uh…

"I work with him at the landscape company. I'm his reception-ist." *Lies, all lies.*

"That's so romantic." Sarah's eyes got dreamy. "What are your plans for the day?"

Now that she had a lead, she needed to coordinate with her missing reporter. Wherever he'd gone.

"Will had to go deal with business. I'm on my own." Lucy lifted a shoulder.

"Then I declare today a spa day." Sarah clapped her hands together softly.

In Sarah-world, apparently that was that. She had proclaimed the day a spa day, and so it would be. Since nothing had been going to plan anyway, and Lucy's schedule was clear until Will returned, she might as well hang with Sarah at the spa and ask questions there.

———

Facedown on the massage table, Lucy was awkwardly covered with only a thin, white sheet as Rebecca, the massage therapist, kneaded out a kink in her neck.

Sarah had persuaded her to get a couple's massage because "it would be so relaxing." In hindsight, nothing was calming about being naked while Sarah—also facedown on the next table over—chatted about everything from the weather to her desire to breed designer Chihuahua puppies.

"What are you doing tonight? Come to dinner with Max and me so the boys can get to know each other, too."

"We have plans. Some kind of dance Will is taking me to this evening."

"The barn dance! I saw the flyer. Oh fun, *fun*. I'll talk Max into going, too. We can double. Oh! And tomorrow I signed us up for that honeymoon therapy thing with the guru. You guys should come."

"We're only here a couple more days. It's a short honeymoon. William will want to spend time alone tomorrow."

Perhaps.

"Well, darn. I guess since we're going to the dance, we should get our hair done. Makeup, too." Sarah gave a sly smile. Apparently, she didn't do spa days halfway. "Do you own cowboy boots? Every girl needs a pair if she goes to a barn dance. I wonder if the gift shop sells them?"

"Um…" Lucy wasn't so sure about cowboy boots.

"Girl, I'll show you how it's done."

No doubt she would.

For once Sarah was quiet longer than it took to take a breath. Rebecca found a tight spot in Lucy's arm and did a pinch and roll combination that was surprisingly uncomfortable and relaxing at the same time.

"Lucy?" Sarah asked.

"Uh-huh." The knot of muscle relaxed under Rebecca's brilliant hands.

"Have you two been together awhile?" Sarah continued.

"Uh…yeah." Kind of.

"How do you keep things fresh with Will? In the bedroom, I mean."

Rebecca's hands stilled before pinching, rolling, and pressing against a new muscle Lucy had no idea existed in her arm.

"Um…" This was not what Lucy had signed up for when she agreed to the massage. "I'm not really comfortable talking about this."

"If you can't talk with your girlfriends, who can you talk to?"

True, but that rule was probably meant for girlfriends who had been in her life longer than five minutes.

"Will and I aren't intimate." Damn. Seriously, Lucy should never say the first thing that came to mind. She burrowed her face into the headrest at the end of the table.

"Ever?" Sarah sounded shocked.

"No, he and I…we…uh…the thing is…" Lucy licked her top lip. What was she supposed to say? "He's not able to… you know. Major performance anxiety."

Damn. That was so *not* what she should have said. She glanced to Sarah.

"What happened?" Sarah's Precious Moment's eyes got huge.

"It started with the syphilis. It was a whole thing." Lucy swallowed and dug her forehead into the headrest of the massage table. *Stop talking, stop talking, stop talking.*

"Syphilis? Like what killed Al Capone?" Sarah darted her hand out across the space between their tables to squeeze Lucy's. "I am so sorry."

"He…uh…got treated. It was after he met me. Before. I mean before. Before he met me. The thing is…" Lucy's pulse quickstepped, and she tried to calm herself down with deep breaths.

"All done." Rebecca moved the sheet back up along Lucy's shoulders. "Take your time getting up and be sure to drink lots of water today."

Rebecca and Sarah's therapist made a hasty exit. Lucy lay perfectly still.

"You love him anyway, so you stuck with him. Oh, girl, you are a God's honest blessing to that man," Sarah said, all dreamy.

Lucy cringed. William was going to kill her. "Please, you can't tell anyone. You have to promise."

"Girlfriend's honor. I'm so sorry you have it so hard. My church group will add you to our prayer chain."

"No, no. Please, you cannot tell anyone." Lucy bit at her bottom lip. William could not know what she'd said. Ever.

"Promise," Sarah agreed, but Lucy wasn't convinced.

Seriously, where was a Bible when you needed someone to swear on one? The Gideons apparently hadn't visited Twin Lakes yet. This was the only hotel she'd ever stayed at that stocked condoms instead of Bibles in the nightstand.

CHAPTER
ELEVEN

Carbonated bubbles popped along the surface of Lucy's third Diet Coke. She sat alone at a wooden table in a large barn near the edge of Twin Lakes' small, town square. Sheesh, she thought Confluence was small. Twin Lakes had a lodge, a bar, a post office, and a gas station that doubled as a general store. And a big 'ol barn.

The barn was primitive, the planks weathered from decades of nature's abuse. Someone had taken a great deal of time to deck the vast room with twinkling strands of white lights hanging haphazardly from the rafters. A raised stage across the room contained a bluegrass band with fiddles and banjos, along with a performer in full drag impersonating Dolly Parton.

It was long past time to two-step, and William still hadn't arrived. Sure, he had texted he was running late, and she should go on ahead, he would be right behind her. But that was hours ago.

Her phone buzzed with another William text.

Uh-huh. If "nearly there" meant what it did thirty minutes ago, then he'd arrive somewhere around nine a.m. tomorrow morning.

She'd already worked the barn for hidden camera footage and chatted with the other guests to find out how their experiences had gone.

If she wasn't stuck in a pretend marriage without a ride back to the cabin, she would have called it quits and evacuated. Since Sarah and Max had driven her there and then hit up the dance floor, she was stranded.

Alone.

In a barn.

Like a cliché country song.

Even with the chilly evening breeze through the open windows, it had warmed inside by the time Dolly announced a break. The swarm of people shifted, and an energy she didn't understand pulled Lucy's gaze intuitively toward the door. William stood there, his jaw tight, glancing around the room. Her whole body tingled with awareness when he caught her gaze, relaxed his shoulders, and stalked forward. Lucy studied her drink for a few beats, glancing up just as he reached her. He leaned in to plant a kiss on her forehead. Her body buzzed with inappropriate anticipation clear to her toes.

"Luce. I'm so sorry. That took longer than it should have." His gaze moved over her. "You're beautiful."

Of course she looked beautiful, *thankyouverymuch*.

Sarah had done an exceptional job with her. The gift shop at the lodge was lacking, so Sarah insisted they visit the outlet stores in the next town over. The denim button-down shirt she bought was tucked into a gauzy, cream skirt that hit right above her knee. She finished with an oversize brown leather belt and rhinestone cowgirl boots. Sarah tried to convince her she needed a cowboy hat as well, but the woman at the salon had painstakingly curled Lucy's hair. Lucy loved the curls entirely too much to even consider smashing them with a hat. Even the kickass one Sarah had found.

"Where'd you go?" she asked.

"Had an emergency. My attorney called. We had papers to sign, and some Crestone stuff came up she needed to talk to me about. I'm sorry it interfered with everything." He sat next to her and pulled her against his side.

In that moment, Lucy didn't particularly care where he'd been because something about the familiar touch drove her slightly crazy.

"It's remarkably hard to stay pissy at you," she huffed.

He squeezed her hand. "Yeah?"

"Yeah." She tucked a curl behind her ear.

"How'd things go today?" His finger tapped along with the country song coming over the speakers.

"Well… I'm glad you asked. I met a lovely family with two kids who had a watch go missing from their room the other day. They were kayaking at the time."

The watch turned out to be fairly expensive and had been left in their suitcase—a gift from his grandfather.

The music blared louder. Will leaned closer. "Any leads?"

"They said they told the front desk, but I couldn't find a police report or anything." She had to yell over the music. "Front desk said if it wasn't in the safe, there's nothing they can do. I asked around at the spa, too, to see if anyone there had similar stories. Nothing on that front. But I got my massage." She shrugged. "So not a total loss."

He grinned her way.

"Oh, and Sarah and Max were asked to give a little incentive to the front desk in order to transfer our suite to them." She dropped the bomb and twirled a curl with her finger like what she'd said was no big deal.

His mouth dropped. "That's amazing. Looks like we have a story." His expression softened. "You're amazing."

Dolly began singing about why someone would come in here lookin' like that. William tugged at Lucy's hand.

"Spent the day cleaning up messes. Now, I've got a promise to keep." He pulled her to the side of the dance floor. Lifting her hand in his, he adjusted her palm on his shoulder before running his hand along her back to her waist. Traces of cedar and the earthy smell of straw hay bales amplified the woodsy scent that was his alone.

He nudged her backward, "Relax and follow me, yeah?"

She stepped on his foot.

"Sorry," she muttered.

"It's fine. Relax. I'll do the work." He stepped forward as she stepped forward, knocking into him.

"Sorry," she repeated. Geez, this is exactly why she never went to dances in high school. This, and the fact no one ever asked her.

"Take a breath. Watch my eyes, go backward, and don't worry about your feet. They'll follow."

She couldn't meet his gaze, not plastered this close against him. His thigh brushed intimately against hers, the movement pushing her along, his hand at her back to guide her.

Counting as he moved with her, she wouldn't meet his eyes. He moved his mouth to her ear and whispered, "I confess my day got a whole lot better when I walked into a barn in the middle of nowhere to find you all dressed up."

The barn was warm, but she shivered. He tucked her closer.

Nice.

"A natural," he whispered.

She leaned her head back and grinned. He traced a hand along the curve of her back as one song blended into another, and another. Damn. Maybe she should have found someone to take her to a dance in high school. She clearly had no idea what she'd missed out on. He held her tight, her cheek resting against his chest.

For the first time in a long time, she found peace. Peace that had come in a loud, drafty barn filled to the brim with what appeared to be the entire population of Twin Lakes.

The music stopped, but she didn't release her hold.

"Princess, song's over." His voice was husky, like it had been the night before when he climbed into bed at the cabin.

Right.

She started to step away, but he caught her and pulled her back to his chest so they both faced the stage. He settled his hand at her hip in what appeared to be a gesture of possession—a gesture that sent a stampede of butterflies straight through her.

"Ladies and gentlemen, tonight we have a very special couple with us celebrating their honeymoon at Twin Lakes," Dolly boomed over the speakers.

William's fingers tightened. Lucy's heart dropped. She glanced around, her gaze landing on Sarah near the bar. She gave Lucy two thumbs-up and a wink.

Oh no.

The room plunged into darkness. Lucy squinted as a spotlight focused where she stood with William. Dolly clanged a spoon against an empty wine glass. "What d'ya say? A kiss from the newlyweds?"

"Crap," Lucy said to no one in particular.

Everyone watched. Lucy's stomach felt like someone had danced right over it.

Okay. Not a big deal. It wasn't like it was her first kiss or anything. And she'd only fantasized about this moment with William for, like, her entire teenage existence, so doing it in front of a room of strangers wasn't a big thing.

Nope, it was a huge thing. Massive.

"Luce, breathe," William whispered in her ear as the crowd began to clap.

He turned her so she fit in his arms face-to-face. His sharp, golden eyes softened. She curved her hand around the edge of his collar as he moved to erase the final millimeters separating them.

The applause on the dance floor increased, and with the added boot stomps, the whole barn moved. Or maybe it was just Lucy's world tilting on its axis. She sucked in a shallow breath. And then, because she was clearly in an alternate reality, he tilted his head and the rest of the space separating them disappeared.

Holy. Crap.

On that note, her eyes drifted closed.

He tasted like spearmint gum as his lips moved gently against hers before settling deeper, demanding more, the bristle of his stubble a tempting contrast to smooth lips.

He could kiss. Not just kiss, but *kiss*.

He had to be the one to break the bond since she wasn't remotely coherent enough to do it herself. If it were up to her, they would have stayed lip-locked for hours, days even. No need for food, water, shelter, or air or *anything*, because the only thing she needed for survival was him.

The glow filling her slipped abruptly away when he dropped her hands. She slid her eyelids open, and the spotlight clicked off. Cheers died off, and the crowd pressed around them as the music kicked up.

William's face was an unreadable mask as the mass of people forced him farther from her, deserting her on the rough wooden planks of the dance floor. She should've expected that he'd desert her again. But stupid, she'd dropped her guard.

A large male body bumped hers along, transporting her through the swirling crowd of people.

The pungent scent of heavy tobacco smoke, whiskey, and cloying-sweet cologne scorched her nostrils. Familiar in the worst way. It was the invasive scent of Robbie—of the man who had attacked her.

No.

Desperate to find the source, she jerked her head around, shoving frantically as she was pushed through the barn. Her heart thumped erratically. Her vision tunneled, and her mouth went dry as anxiety chewed at her. She scanned for an exit route. What had the psychiatrist said about breathing? Something about it being important. But she couldn't remember his words. Couldn't remember anything but fear.

She scanned for an exit route and shoved through the door to the parking lot.

Frigid mountain air filled her lungs. Her body began shaking, and her teeth chattered. She was sixteen again. Unwanted. Not good enough.

In a failed attempt to control the tremors, she wrapped her arms around herself.

Alone again.

CHAPTER
TWELVE

What did he say to the woman who rocked his world with a kiss?

Nothing. William had said nothing to Lucy.

The two of them had enough chemistry to split thousands of damn atoms and make them dance a happy, merry jig.

True to form, he had screwed it up. Life wasn't a goddamned fairy tale. It wasn't his fault he hadn't anticipated that insane kiss.

Insanely good. In a really *not* good, totally threw-him-off-his-game kind of way. Insane in that his mind had stopped working, and he'd slipped into some kind of earthquake of confusion when he let her go. The crowd had moved in, and she had disappeared.

Vanished.

He rubbed an exhausted hand over his face at the memory. It was all his fault.

He had found Lucy leaning against his truck in the parking lot. She had been distant when she asked him to take her to the cabin. When they returned, she had immediately changed into her *Princess* pants and collapsed into bed.

Now, he sat across the room as she slept. Even in sleep, she was stunning. More than that, being with her was generally, well… fun. He missed having fun.

From habit, he slid the worn envelope from his pocket and

tapped it against his chin. What advice would his mother have given him about Lucy?

Mom would've loved Lucy's fierce independence and work ethic. Not just because Lucy was a good producer, but because she was real. And a kick to be around.

Right now, though, his time was currently divided between masquerading as a consumer reporter, handling the Crestone acquisition, the Colorado Springs merger, and proving he was up to the task of running the multi-million-dollar company.

Which meant he didn't have time for a serious relationship. More than that, he didn't deserve her. He wasn't an idiot. Lucy was too good. Him? Not so much. He'd never earn the right to lay claim to someone like her.

Lucy as short-term enjoyment? Yeah, that was fine, but the woman behind that lip-lock wasn't for temporary entertainment. No, that liaison was charged with the undercurrent of a whole lifetime of responsibility.

Lucy shifted on the bed and pushed herself up. Her gaze moved across the room, searching.

For him? His gut clenched.

"What're you doing?" The just-awake-middle-of-the-night tone she used was ten steps past sexy.

"Couldn't sleep." He sat on the end of the bed and placed the envelope on the nightstand. He set a hand on her ankle, like he had when she kicked him that morning.

"You won't get to sleep sitting up." The warmth was missing from her brown eyes tonight. They drifted closed, and she laid her head on the pillow.

She had a point.

He climbed into bed and rested his hands on his chest.

Her breathing evened out in the telltale beat of slumber.

There was no way he could take whatever this thing was between them further. He'd start setting his own boundaries and respecting hers.

Sleep had nearly found him when she shifted to rest her head in the crook of his shoulder. Without waking, she curled into him as if it was the most natural thing in the world.

Now what the hell was he supposed to do? He swallowed hard.

Little sounds and half-coherent words occasionally slipped from her mouth. His chin brushed against her hair, and he inhaled the scent of coconut shampoo. So Lucy. All real.

But not his.

After a while, he closed his eyes, savoring for a moment the woman he wouldn't allow himself to pursue.

William woke early and disentangled himself from Lucy. She didn't wake when he rose from the bed and left to grab video and talk up the staff. So far their hidden cameras in the cabin showed nothing.

They were close, though. He could feel it. Two more days to snoop around, ask questions, and tie up the story. Two more days. He could keep his distance from Lucy that long. Hell, he'd just give her the space she'd been pursuing herself. When the story was finished, he'd let her continue on her path of avoiding him. Encourage it even.

A few hours and a hike to and from the lodge later, he returned with an entire Thermos of dark roast. Lucy was up, the bed made. In snug fitting jeans and a Twin Lakes T-shirt, she dried her wet hair with a towel. Her bag lay open on the bed, and she rummaged through it with her other hand.

His gaze drifted to her ass-cupping jeans.

"Hey. You brought me coffee?" she asked, more than a little shock in her voice.

"Cream and sugar, too." He set the coffee on the table and snagged two enamel camp-style mugs from the counter.

"Will?" She settled at the table.

"Yes?"

"Thanks." She raised her mug in a semi-salute before sipping.

She toyed with the handle. Neither of them said anything more. Best to address the awkwardness head on.

He moved the chair next to her and sat. "What happened yesterday at the barn—"

She held a hand up in the universal sign for him to stop, not up for discussion. "Nothing happened."

He pressed his lips together. He certainly didn't expect his heart to shrink at the declaration. "You want to play it this way?"

"It's not a game." She gripped her cup between her hands.

"Fine. Nothing happened," he clipped. Except, everything had happened.

"What's on the agenda today?"

"Didn't get that far. Figured you'd need caffeine before any communication, so I got on that."

"I'm up for whatever. What can we do at the lodge to give the staff lots of time to come in and out?" She twirled a piece of hair with her finger.

He couldn't seem to jerk his gaze from that strand of hair. Like some trick of the mind, he just stared at it. "I'm glad you asked. Today is group therapy for the honeymooners."

Her jaw slipped open. "You're joking."

"Nope. It's part of the whole honeymoon retreat experience." He held his mug wide in mock enthusiasm. Therapy sounded about as much fun as ripping out his own toenails with a salad fork.

She gave him a look that would wither a lesser man's balls.

He ignored it. Not like he was particularly looking forward to dodging questions in a group setting, but if they didn't show up it might raise questions. The group sessions were part of the entire Twin Lakes honeymoon experience. "It won't be that bad. We'll tell them we're private people."

"You think that's going to work?"

He didn't have a lot of experience with therapists, but he had a feeling there was no way in hell his plan was going to work. "Nope."

"We should get our stories straight then. I told Sarah you're a landscaper and I'm your receptionist." She kept her eyes on her coffee.

Landscaper? He couldn't keep a potted plant alive. He had, however, once managed to keep a cactus from decomposing for about six months. "You told her I'm a landscaper?"

"You know, lawn installation and stuff." She shrugged. The neck of her T-shirt slipped down her shoulder the barest of centimeters. Still, it was enough to make his pulse beat louder in his ears.

"Luce, I know what a landscaper does. Why on earth wouldn't you tell her I'm a businessman?"

She bit at her bottom lip, her teeth dipping into the flesh there. "I was working on the fly. We really should've discussed this before we got here."

He placed his mug on the table. "First rule of telling lies, keep them as close to the truth as possible. That way they're easier to keep track of. But, for now, fine. I'm a landscaper. You're my receptionist. How many pretend future kids do you want?"

She gave him some serious side eye. "Uh…none."

"None? At all?" His foot dropped to the floor. The small thud matching the way his heart plunked to the bottom of his ribs.

"Nope."

"That's not going to work for me. We've got to have at least one."

"Fine. I'll have *one* pretend child with you."

"You sure you don't want two? Being an only pretend kid isn't any fun."

She thinned her lips and shook her head. "I'm putting my pretend foot down."

"Alrighty then. We have professions. Family aspirations. Anything else?"

"How long have we known each other?" she asked.

"Five years." Seemed like a reasonable amount of time.

Not that he had much of a track record to go from.

"That's kind of a long time." Her forehead pinched, and his fingertips itched to smooth those lines.

"Five months?" he countered.

She grimaced. "You think that's long enough?"

"If we tell them five months then at least it'll make sense when we don't know anything about each other," he pointed out, scooting his chair closer to hers so their knees nearly bumped.

"Five months ago, you hired me at your landscaping business."

"And then you were all over me."

She sat taller and crossed her legs, bumping his knee with her own and quickly pulling back. "I was not."

"Okay. I was all over you. It was love at first sight." Not far from the truth—not that he was in love with her. Serious lust, maybe.

She trailed her finger around the edge of her mug. "You can't believe in that."

"Lust at first sight then?" he asked.

"Seriously, Will? Fine. Love at pretend first sight."

"Fair enough. We figured, why wait? Our whirlwind romance led to us getting married and ending up here at Twin Lakes."

She pulled out a thin reporter's notebook and began scribbling. Why did he find that charming? Maybe he did need to get his head examined. "Where are we from?"

"Confluence."

Her pen stalled. "Confluence is too close. What if one of the other guests is also from Confluence? Then they'll know we're lying."

"Fine. Nebraska."

"Nebraska?"

"Yeah."

"Why Nebraska?"

He took a sip from his cup. "Why not?"

"It's just that if we're going to keep this as 'real' as possible—so we can keep things straight—we should probably pick a place we've both been."

"Good call. Maryland?"

"Nope. California?"

"Not since I was a kid."

"I suppose Nebraska it is, then." She tossed him a smile that didn't quite make it to her eyes. "Hopefully, someone will steal something, and we'll get a video. I'd hate for this whole thing to be a waste."

His resolve not to pursue her weakened. Dancing, making out, and waking up next to her? Not a waste.

"Can I ask you a question?" she asked.

A warning bell clanged in his mind. "Confession time is over, but I suppose it depends on the question. Shoot."

"Why is confession time over? Shouldn't it always be confession time?" She tilted her head to the side slightly.

Funny, she hadn't been gung-ho to play Confessions the other night.

"Last I checked, I'm a reporter, not a priest. This means confession time has limits. What do you want to ask?"

"What's in the envelope on the nightstand?" Oh. He'd forgotten to take it with him.

"Don't answer. None of my business." She shook her head and poured more coffee for herself. "I was just curious because I've seen you mess with it a few times."

"Okay, I'll play. But you agree to match the confession, yeah? What're you putting on the line?"

"I already agreed to have pretend children, isn't that enough for one day?"

He leaned forward, so they sat knee to knee, and spoke slowly. "I confess in the envelope is a...letter."

She pulled her knees against her chest. "Right, Sherlock. I got that part. Who is the letter from?"

He backed away from her. "My mother."

Shock registered on her face. "Seriously?" she whispered.

"Seriously. Got it at the reading of her will." He crossed his ankle over his knee and shifted in the chair. "I keep it with me. Keeps me grounded."

"What's it say? The letter, I mean."

"As you pointed out, it's unopened. Which indicates, Watson, that I don't know what it says."

She glanced up then. "Why haven't you opened it?"

"Don't want to know what it says."

He leaned back, dangling his arm across the back of the chair on the other side of him.

"Why?" Her brown eyes were genuinely curious.

"Doesn't matter what the letter says. Most likely it's a final diatribe of how I screwed up my life. Mom kicked me out, and I didn't see her for over a year before she passed. The last thing she said to me on the phone was that I needed to quit pissing my life away. Not in those exact words, but you get the idea. The conversation involved a lot of yelling. I don't need a written reminder of how disappointing I was to her."

"Why do you keep it with you?" Those eyes. Hell.

"That's a good question. It's also the third part to your original one-part question, which you didn't declare when you originally asked," he deflected.

"You answering it?"

"I'll answer if I get the next question. And you actually have to answer. No dodging this time."

She nodded.

He shrugged. "I confess it says what I need it to say."

She scrunched up her nose. "Huh?"

"I keep the letter with me so when something happens, and I can use some advice, the letter says whatever I need it to say. It stays with me, so she stays with me. I didn't get to say goodbye, and I don't want to. The letter keeps things open."

"Will. She's gone. She wanted to tell you something. Don't you think you owe it to her to read it?"

"She's gone. She said all she needed to say when she was alive. Some things are best left alone. I was a disappointment as a son, and I don't need that in my life now. I've worked hard to put that guy behind me."

"You should open it," she insisted.

"Let it go. You wanted to know. Now you know."

"You were never a bad person." She was doing the quiet thing again.

"You'll never know who I was. Thank God for that."

Her face changed. It was soft before, but it gentled further, and she opened her mouth to say something.

He, however, was done with this conversation. "My turn. Why'd you disappear at the barn last night?"

Her gaze drifted to her coffee. "I confess…I needed air."

He rested his elbows on his knees. "That's the best you can come up with?"

"We got separated, and I needed air."

He locked his gaze on hers. "Seriously, that's the best you can come up with?"

"Stop saying that." She tucked a hunk of hair behind her ear.

"Stop lying." His words came out harsher than he meant.

Her expression turned to ice. "I'm not lying."

He leaned even closer into her space. "Being untruthful breaks the bond of *Confessions*. You don't kiss someone like *that* and then vanish."

"I thought we agreed it didn't happen?" she reminded him.

She had him there.

"For the next few minutes, it happened. Then it can go back to not happening."

"I needed air," she repeated. "Sticking with that?"

She tossed her hands up, a splash of coffee sloshing over the side of her mug. "You're impossible."

"Mm-hmm." He handed her a napkin. "You kissed me, not the other way around."

"I did kiss you. And you kissed me back. Then you disappeared," he pointed out.

"You stepped back. Last night." Hurt filled her eyes. "Maybe we should both step back this time."

She landed a direct blow by agreeing with him. A perfect way out. No risk of failure for either of them.

Except. A way out was the last thing he wanted. He could split his time between work and Lucy. Hell, having her on his team sounded pretty great right about now. They'd had a connection from the moment he helped her at the gas station. Pursuing her might not be the best idea, but he couldn't help being drawn to her. Until that kiss, he figured they'd just enjoy whatever they had until it burned out. It always burned out.

Even the couple of times he'd felt like things might progress into something, the spark always faded.

This time was different.

"What if I said I want to see where this takes us?" He rose from his chair, scooted it back with his foot, and crouched in front of her. He took her hands in his. They trembled, but she didn't move away. He pressed his forehead gently against hers so their breaths mingled.

"Not for pretend?" she asked.

Risk everything and hope it didn't end with him alone— he was going to do this. "Nothing I'm feeling right now is pretend."

He was a bastard because she deserved more than him. But he didn't care. "You're scared. I'm giving you time to get to know me, see that you're into me as much as I'm into you. Today that involves a pretend couple's therapy session. When you're ready, it involves a whole hell of a lot more." He ran the back of his knuckles along the apple of her cheek.

"You stepped back." Her fingers lay limp against his.

"Won't happen again." He traced a thumb across her jaw and then rested his lips against her forehead.

Then he let her go.

Lucy's existence was already complicated. Now William was into her? What did that even mean? The best course of action would be to pretend his declaration never happened and move ahead. To couple's counseling.

William's palm grazed the back of her shirt when they walked through to the therapy room—apparently also used for spin classes, given the bikes along the mirrored wall, and yoga, given the mats laid out in a semi-circle. The room had the same rustic-chic feel as the rest of the lodge, but huge amounts of mountain sunshine speared through the high windows.

"Hello!" A woman dressed in black khakis and a polo shirt with *Twin Lakes* embroidered across the pocket emerged from the small equipment closet.

Lucy jolted. Rebecca.

Her massage therapist.

Damn. Damn. Dammit.

"Lucy, it's so good to see you." Rebecca's cheeks must've hurt from smiling so wide. "I'm so glad you're here."

"Hi." Instinct took over and Lucy stepped backward— directly into William.

His hand settled just above Lucy's waistband. The nerve endings there warmed in response. Little traitors. He must've known her intent to run because he smoothly scooted her forward toward Rebecca.

"This must be your husband?" Rebecca gestured to William.

"William." He dropped his hand to shake Rebecca's.

"Rebecca," she replied. "It's so nice to meet you. I've heard so much about you." She did the wide cheek smile thing again.

Heat spread through Lucy. William was going to find out what she'd said, then he'd kill her in the middle of the woods where there would be no witnesses. He'd probably shove her off a cliff or something.

And she deserved it.

If he wouldn't even go to the *Beach Nights Reunion* show because he couldn't stand the possibility of embarrassment, he was definitely going to hate this.

Her throat started to close. She swallowed hard. "What are you doing here?"

"I'm the leader of the couples counseling and group therapy." Rebecca waved toward the yoga mats scattered over the floor. "Since you're first, pick any mat you'd like."

"But you're a massage therapist." Lucy's feet seemed to have planted themselves on the hardwood floor and sprouted roots. They would not move.

"I do it all." Rebecca laughed—the sound something like wind chimes would make on a breezy day. "I don't even have to change my name tag."

Lucy's eyes shifted to the tag above the *Twin Lakes* writing. Sure enough, it read *Rebecca, Therapist*.

"Your other friend signed up, too." Rebecca unrolled her own mat and plopped down in the center, crisscross applesauce.

William took a step toward one of the mats, reaching for Lucy and tugging her along. Reluctantly, she followed. He settled down on the thin rubber mat and pulled her along with him so her back settled against his front.

"In any case, I'm glad you're here a little early so we can chat.

I've been thinking about your little *issue*." Rebecca made air quotes with her fingers around the word—making it seem much bigger than it needed to be.

Oh no. Discussion of that *issue* was a horrible idea.

Epically bad.

"You said Sarah is coming?" Lucy deflected and eyed the door, willing the others to come through.

"What issue?" William asked, his breath against the back of Lucy's neck.

"I know you probably don't want to talk about it in front of everyone, but there are quite a few things you can do that don't involve *actual* intercourse." Rebecca made those damn air quotes again.

Lucy glanced to the door, gauging how quickly she could get up and out of the room before William tackled her.

He cleared his throat a tad too loud. "Come again?"

"It's okay. There's no need to be embarrassed. I know many couples in your situation."

"Situation?" He squeezed Lucy in his arms and whispered the question directly against her earlobe.

She squirmed in reply.

"Lucy, I'm so glad you're here." Sarah saved the moment, bustling into the room.

Rebecca winked at Lucy like they were conspirators in international espionage. "We'll just chat about this after."

"What situation, Luce?" William asked again.

She turned her head, so her cheek was near his lips. "Ignore. I made it up as I went along the other day. Nothing you need to worry about."

Max trailed in after Sarah, and another couple Lucy hadn't seen before followed him.

"Everyone pick a mat. We'll go ahead and get started. We've got a lot to cover this morning." Rebecca took her place back on her mat. "I call this the 'honesty hour.' You have to promise your partner complete honesty for this type of therapy to be effective. And, trust me, it's harder than it seems."

Lucy just bet it was. She squirmed again with the unfortunate side effect of her bottom rubbing against Will's—you know what? She'd just scoot forward a smidge.

"If everyone could turn and face their partner." Rebecca waved her hand in a circle to illustrate.

Lucy moved around so she faced William. Unfortunately, this meant she could see him—something that severely cracked her resolve to flee. It was the dimples, she was certain.

"Now scooch together a little closer and hold hands."

Lucy studied a scuff on the floor behind her fake husband and offered her hands.

"Look into your partner's eyes and say the first thing that comes to mind."

Lucy shifted her gaze to meet William's and her mind went blank. Totally and utterly blank. Nothing. Nada.

"I'm glad it's you that came with me," he said low enough that no one else would hear.

Her heart did a little fist pump.

"Your turn." The little divots of his dimples flashed uncertain.

"I like your cheeks," she heard herself say.

His forehead pinched together as if to say, "the hell?"

"The dimples, I mean," she clarified.

Oh Lord.

"Thank you," he replied as though it were the most normal thing in the world for her to have said.

The room melted away and it was just the two of them again.

"Fantastic," Rebecca cut through their moment. "Now we're going to talk about intimacy. I'd like you to share with your partner some of your favorite things about being alone together. I'm not just talking about intercourse"—She paused too long on that word, stared too long at Lucy and Will, letting it just hang in the air like an unwelcome rash—"I mean all of the little things that make your relationship special."

"I went first last time," William pointed out, his voice staying low, so his words were for Lucy alone.

She paused, his presence intimidating. "You smell nice."

"I do?" he asked. "What do I smell like?"

"I don't know how to describe it. Just nice."

"How are things going?" Rebecca knelt beside them.

"Lucy was just explaining how nice I smell."

"Oh, that's good!" Rebecca settled in, apparently ready to stick around for a while. "What do you think of Lucy's scent?"

"I think she's amazing. All of her." He held Lucy's stare. "I love her scent. Her eyes. Her kindness. The way she cares about people and wants everyone to be happy. Yeah, I think she's pretty awesome."

Lucy's mouth opened and closed like a fish tossed onto the banks of a lake.

Rebecca laughed like wind chimes again. "Did you know that finding your partner's scent appealing is an indicator that your genetics are compatible for children? Have you two discussed that? The things they can do in a lab these days are pretty intense."

Much like this conversation.

William squeezed Lucy's hand and rubbed at the fleshy spot between her thumb and forefinger. "We'd like two."

"You guys are just butter on-a-roll," Rebecca enunciated each syllable and bounced up. "I'll check back in a bit."

Lucy pulled her hands away and scraped them over her face. "Yay."

"All right everyone." Rebecca clapped her hands together. "Next up. I want you to tell your partner your deepest, darkest fear. If you've already shared this, great, time for a re-share. If not, now's the time. Get it all out there."

"I think we should discuss politics or religion," Lucy said, deadpan.

William chuckled and shifted so his knees were on either side of her hips. "Your deepest, darkest fear is water, right? That's not so bad."

Lucy swallowed over her suddenly dry tongue and sandpaper throat. Large bodies of water weren't her favorite by any stretch. The truth of it, though? In that moment, her biggest fear was William would remember the person she'd been—the high school kid with fake friends who pretended to like her when they needed something. The girl the football players tossed bologna at in the cafeteria while they barked, because their buddies thought it was oh-so-hysterical. The girl who spent a summer helping on a television set and crushed on the resident playboy, only to have him forget everything about her.

If he remembered who she was, he'd never be able to see her for who she'd become.

"Luce?" he asked, concerned.

Right. He'd implied her fear was of water.

"What's yours, then?" she asked, deflecting the truth.

"Failing." He glanced to the purple yoga mat they sat on. "My deepest, darkest fear is of failure at Crestone. Failing my mom."

"You won't." Certainty filled her full up. William would succeed.

He grinned. "I wish I had your confidence."

Somehow, and she wasn't quite sure how, they made it through the rest of the session.

"What should we do now?" Lucy asked as they headed back to the cabin.

"They've got a few groups going fishing. Or we can go hiking?" William suggested.

"Fishing this morning, hiking this afternoon."

"Fishing involves water," he replied.

"No kidding?"

"You okay being on the lake?"

"It's not like we're going swimming. Besides, fear of water is ridiculous. You want to go fishing, and I really should face my fear. I promise not to freak, if you agree not to push."

"I can do that."

Last night's barn freak-out was a prime example of how she'd been living her life. She was tired of being scared. But hopefully the police would soon find Robbie. Her luck couldn't stay this awful.

Robbie hadn't been at the dance last night. His scent was an elaborate trick of her mind. The frantic pressure of all the people had triggered the memory. That was all. When William stepped back all her insecurities rose to the surface, and she got scared.

A trauma response. That's all it was.

The time had come for her to start moving on from the terror one idiot had brought into her life. Living a life of fear, shrinking into the sidelines, was no life to live. Somebody had probably said that once. If not, they should have.

And, really, of all the things that freaked her out, water was the least intense. On her quest to be a new woman, free from crippling fear, she would start her journey by conquering the depths of Twin Lakes. It couldn't be that bad. Not too awful. It's not like people drowned frequently.

Except when they did.

No, she would slay her demons starting today. Along the way, maybe she'd even be able to put her attack behind her. First, water, and then, well…she'd see what happened.

She continued to the cabin while William set out to deal with the rental situation and ask some strategic questions there. She gave herself a pep talk while she re-set the cameras in the room. Her phone rang. Katie's name appeared on the display.

"Hey," Lucy answered.

"You haven't returned my calls," Katie accused.

"Things have happened. Lots of things. I'm in the mountains. An exposé at a resort…" Lucy paused and bit at her lower lip. She decided to go all in. "With William."

"You're *what?*" Katie's screech could've burst a thousand eardrums.

Lucy cringed.

While Lucy told her *nearly* everything, Katie remained silent, listening. When Lucy finished, her friend took a deep breath before speaking. "Do you remember the first time you told me about him?"

Of course she did. That conversation had occurred a year after the whole Florida thing.

"I remember," she replied.

"Then you'll remember telling me about his trail of women. *I* remember the tears you cried over a douchebag guy without a clue. Am I the only one who remembers this? Geez, Lulu, you weren't even a couple, and he broke your heart. He'll do it again, and from everything you've said, this time will be worse."

Katie had a point.

Lucy sat cross-legged on the bed. "Things are different. He grew up. I grew up."

"You also changed your appearance. Now he's all about getting into your pants? As your friend, I don't like that at all."

Lucy pressed a pillow against her chest.

"This guy. This whole situation is messy. He's a colleague. You and I both know it can't go further."

A colleague? Sheesh, it was so much more complicated because he was about to become her boss. Lucy had promised William she wouldn't say a word about his real relationship with Crestone, so she kept that tidbit to herself. "I'm afraid it's already gone past the colleague thing. He kissed me."

The kiss to end all kisses.

"Holy hell, Lulu. Did you kiss him back?"

"Um...yes?"

"Lulu!" Katie shrieked.

Lucy held the phone away from her ear, catching only snippets of Katie's fuming objections. "Could you calm down? It only happened the one time."

The line was silent for a moment before Katie spoke. "People don't change," she said carefully. "I get that you're confused, but with a guy like him, you've got to be straight. Tell him you're flattered, but he's not your type. Clean break."

"Katie, if I had a type, he'd be it." Unfortunately.

It's not like Lucy never dated. She did. But after she put in the blood, sweat, and tears to transform herself, the guys who asked her out started to change…and not always for the better. Dating had never led to much because it wasn't worth it to open herself up to anyone.

But, as Katie pointed out, this couldn't go further.

"I'll talk to him," Lucy promised.

Katie went in for the kill. "William is a right-now kind of guy. He's not about the future, but he is about the past. Don't go back, Lulu. Don't do that to yourself. You've done too much to change and put that girl behind you."

Crap, but she was right. They ended the conversation, and Lucy flopped on the bed. She flung her arm over her face.

William trudged through the door and dropped an armful of tackle gear by the bed.

"The cameras are set. Did you get a boat?" She sat up and twisted her hair, pinning it in place.

"Uh-huh. It's ready." He didn't glance up as he separated two tackle boxes and sorted hooks.

Sheesh. How much stuff did it take to catch a fish?

He finally glanced at her, and his eyebrows shot up. Perhaps she should have evaluated her fishing attire more carefully before settling on the green bikini top and cut-off shorts. His eyes flamed. The way he stared did not bode well—like she was the catch of the day, and he had her on his hook.

"This one's yours." He held up one of the fishing poles and handed it to her. His hand brushed hers briefly when she took it. One tiny brush of his fingertips and her body went wired. This had to stop.

"Nervous about the boat?" he asked.

"Maybe." She inspected the pole and turned the reel thing. Then she clicked a button to release the tension. Easy enough.

"How nervous?"

She glanced up at him. "A little."

"How much is a little?" he asked as though she meant more to him than only a colleague.

"Less than a lot," she replied.

"Lucy." His expression turned serious. "We'll catch some fish. You'll conquer your fear."

Uncertain, she nodded. "I haven't been on a boat in over a decade."

The anxiety she was experiencing at the moment didn't paralyze her, so she had definitely made progress. Yes, a fishing trip to the lake was a step toward her future, a move she found herself ready to make.

"We don't have to do this."

Why did he have to be so nice? Couldn't he be a little bit of a jerk so it'd be easier to stay away?

"I want to." She did. Really, she did. This whole excursion illustrated her commitment to forward momentum. She smiled tentatively.

He reached out to her and tucked a piece of hair behind her ear before the damn dimples dented into his cheeks.

CHAPTER
FOURTEEN

Cameras set once again, cabin secured, Lucy and William evacuated to the lake like the normal honeymooners they were not.

The fish weren't biting at Twin Lakes, but Lucy had gotten into a boat and hadn't had a panic attack. That was huge.

The last time she'd been on a boat was at her tenth birthday party. Her father had rented a large yacht for the day. It would be a year before her parents started the on-again, off-again nonsense that had marked her adolescence.

Lucy was a fourth grader with zero confidence. The other kids were cruel. They called her "Caterpillar" because her thick eyebrows looked a little like caterpillars. Her mother refused to let her tweeze them into submission. Brooke Shields and Audrey Hepburn had eyebrows like Lucy's—that's what her mother insisted. Lucy would bet a tub of hot wax that Brooke and Audrey never got called Caterpillar because of them.

Lucy hated everything. The eyebrows. Her clothes. The nickname.

But nothing could mar her birthday because she wore a gorgeous dress and, for once, the world revolved around *her*. As the children arrived with armloads of gifts, she could feel, absolutely feel, her luck change.

The birthday song was sung, cake distributed, and Lucy sat at the head of the table with Italian buttercream icing smudged on her lips, her feet swinging. The chaperones disappeared to do whatever it was adults did. To her left sat Grant McFarland with freckles and light brown hair.

He scarfed his own slice of cake. Then he ruined everything.

"Caterpillar, don't you think you've had enough? You'll be even *bigger* if you keep eating," he taunted.

Her cheeks heated with embarrassment. Tears stung her eyes.

At the end of the day, as the kids disembarked on the pier, her parents packed up all the party things. Jayden and his crew of boys waited for their parents. Her mother insisted Lucy stay with them, as a good hostess should.

"Caterpillar, climb down that ladder. Betcha can't touch the water." Mischief clouded Evan Powell's eyes when he spoke.

"Can, too," she replied.

"Let's see it then," he challenged.

Lucy gripped the pier and, still in her party dress, climbed down the four rungs to the edge of the water.

"Dip your toe in," Evan commanded.

Lucy dipped the edge of her ballet flat to the surface of the ocean. Then she moved her foot back to the rung, but it snagged the hem of her skirt. Holding on with one arm, she moved her other hand to push the fabric away. Her foot slipped, and she fell backward into the salty darkness. She kicked to the surface, but her leg tangled in some wire, and she couldn't reach.

The water overwhelmed her. Her lungs burned as she held her breath for what felt like forever.

One of the workers on the dock pulled her free. Her parents were livid. The ruined dress clung to her while her father ranted.

"Stupid Caterpillar," Evan had murmured as he walked away.

Stupid Caterpillar reverberated through time and burst into the present, encroaching on this latest excursion. Lucy's reflection from Twin Lakes reassured her the hair and the acne were long gone. The emotional scars?

They remained.

Her stomach pitched a little when the wave from a speedboat rocked the small canoe she shared with William. The muscles in his arms working as he rowed were the highlight of the trip. Her massive neon orange life jacket suffocated her skin, and the dang thing chafed. A lot.

Universal fit. *Not even.*

Finally, she'd had enough of the thing. She unlatched the clasp and tugged the keyhole opening over her head, breathing a sigh of relief as cool air hit the sweaty skin trapped under the polyester-covered foam.

Heaven.

William sat at one end of the boat; his legs sprawled while he twitched his rod every so often. Lucy stayed at the other end, ignoring her line completely.

"Does anyone actually enjoy this?" she asked.

He glanced from the lake to her. "It's peaceful. Don't think. Relax."

That's what he'd said at the barn dance, too. That didn't end so well.

"I can't relax," she muttered.

"What's on your mind then?" He set his fishing pole against his leg and focused on her. "How are you liking Confluence?"

"It's okay." She shrugged. "You know how it is in this business. Don't get too comfortable anywhere because the next opportunity is always going to move you away."

"You're not staying in Confluence?" he asked seriously.

"Not forever." She shook her head. Facing her fears was the first step. But even without that, broadcast journalism was an inherently fickle industry. He had been in the business long enough to know how things worked at this level.

He scowled, rummaging through the tackle box near his feet. "I don't know why everyone wants to leave Confluence. You're an excellent producer, and Parker's happy with the way you're handling the assignment editing. Maybe you should consider sticking around. You could easily make news director in a year."

No. His idea didn't fit into her goal of moving up quickly to the national stage. News directors stood at the top of the food chain in the news department of any station, but that didn't work with her plan. A top-twenty market. Cleveland, maybe, would be next. Then onto Los Angeles or New York.

"What's your end game then?" He twitched his rod again.

For the briefest of moments, she had forgotten she talked to an exceptional reporter with a specialty for digging out information. She didn't want to share more than absolutely necessary so she dodged his question with one of her own. "Why do you do that? The twitching-your-rod thing."

The edges of his lips tugged up. "Twitching my rod?"

"Yeah, the whole jiggling your pole bit."

His shoulders began to shake with laughter. "Jiggling my pole?"

"Oh my God, seriously, Will?"

He began chuckling uncontrollably. "Every time we talk about my rod, your cheeks turn red."

He could not be for real.

"It's the sun," she said, defending herself.

He pulled himself together. "You're the best wife ever, Lucy. I want you to know that. I haven't had this much fun since I was a kid."

"Best *pretend* wife. Seriously, though, what's with the flicking thing?"

"Well, Luce, I flick my *thing* so the fish will think the worm is alive. Try it."

She mimicked what he did. Nothing happened. The story of this fishing trip was summed up in those two words—nothing happened.

Light played across the ripples of the water, and the boat swayed slightly. They'd been drifting for a while when the tip of her fishing rod jerked. She held tight to the pole and glanced at him. He saw it, too, and moved carefully toward her.

"Put a little pressure on it," he said quietly. She tugged. The line tightened.

William beamed, pride radiating from his eyes. "Set the hook and reel him in."

She swung the rod up like he'd shown her before. Um. The line really strained now, and whatever was under the water wrenched harder. It took everything in her not to drop the stupid thing.

"Crank the reel," he yelled.

"You do it." She tried to hand off the pole.

"Your catch. You reel." He grinned confidently toward her. "You've got this."

She turned the knob thingy frantically. The tight line stiffened further as the pole bent to the pressure. She turned more. The line ended when a massive fish broke the surface of the water. She shrieked, flinging the pole to William. The fish sailed through the air and landed in her lap. She jumped, pushing it off, her mouth open in a silent scream while it flipped and flopped maniacally in front of her. William yelled something she didn't grasp. She leaped back to get away from the flailing fish and lost her balance. The boat rocked.

She fell overboard.

Cold water stole her breath. So cold. Freaking hell cold.

And wet.

She came to the surface for a moment and gasped for air before her head dipped under the water again. Panic seized a tight grip around her. When she opened her mouth, foul lake water filled it.

Her nostrils burned. She refused to give up and breathe in the water.

She failed.

The frenzied movements of her arms and legs seemed detached from reality. They pushed and pulled—reaching for the surface but unable to get there.

The water became a solid force around her. She kicked and pushed against it, her lungs burning. Nearly at the surface she opened her mouth to take in a breath, but it was only more water, and then the pull of the lake drug her down again.

Tightness cinched around her middle, and she shoved against it, using her fingernails to dig into whatever clutched at her. Then, just as quickly as she'd gone under, her head emerged from the depths, and she spit out a mouthful of lake water.

She gasped, but the air was heavy in her abused lungs. Another jagged breath and she prepared to go under again. She fought against the lake. Fought against the solid trap holding her tight around the waist.

The water threatened to engulf her again. She couldn't go under. Not again.

"You're safe." The words were repeated as a mantra against her ear, again and again. "I've got you."

William.

Reality replaced overwhelming panic as she focused on his arm and stopped thrashing. He continued speaking, low and calm, while he swam a lazy one-arm stroke. He held her back against his chest, moving them toward the capsized canoe.

She surveyed the lake, focusing on everything but the water. Her pulse started to even out. She wasn't drowning.

Her gaze caught a bulky man standing on the dock where they had launched. He studied them intently.

Her chest heaved. Recognition slithered through her.

Robbie.

She gripped William's arms harder as a sob ripped straight from her heart.

CHAPTER
FIFTEEN

Lucy clung to William's arm as he held her above the water. He paddled with one arm toward her life jacket floating near the canoe. Her lungs ached, and she pinched her eyes closed against the fear of being watched by the man on the dock. When she blinked them open, the man was gone.

Had he ever been there at all? Maybe her mind had messed with her again, seeing things that didn't exist.

"I won't let you go. Relax with the fingernails, yeah?" William said against her ear.

She instantly loosened her grip and tried not to focus on the imminent threat of drowning.

The neon orange life jacket floated near the boat. He snagged it and turned her to face him. "I'm going to put this on you, hold still."

With one arm around her waist, he slipped the opening over her head. She gripped his shoulders and held on tighter.

His head dipped under the water.

The life jacket kept her afloat, but she didn't release her grip on him.

He bobbed to the surface, his mouth barely above the water. "Let—"

"Will!" she cried out as he slipped under again.

His head barely came out of the water. "Let go—"

"Are you nuts? I'm not letting you go!" She fought to keep her grip on him.

He gripped her fingers in his, holding them in a vise. His head finally emerged above the surface. He coughed and spat out a stream of water.

"Stop trying to save me, or I'm going to drown," he said on a gasp.

Oh.

She stopped trying to save him.

He righted himself and coughed some more. "The other night? When you said drowning was the worst way to go? Yeah. We'll stick with that theory."

Lucy held to the foam life vest as he attached the Velcro on the sides.

"Can you kick your legs?" he asked.

She nodded.

Her legs tangled with his as he guided them toward the shore. The thick muscles of his thigh brushed against hers and, well... damn. Even with everything happening, she still desired him. Her breaths came quickly, and her pulse pounded ruthlessly. It had nothing to do with the water, and everything to do with him.

"Don't be scared. We're almost there. Think of something else." His words were raspy.

Hells bells, he must have misinterpreted her body's inappropriate carnal reaction with panic. *Think of something else.* He didn't have to tell her twice.

She ignored her body's traitorous response. *C'mon. Anything else.* She spit out a mouthful of water after a small wave bobbed up.

William loosened his grip around her. "Put your feet down, you can touch."

She did as she was told. Relief soaked through her as her soggy tennis shoes found the bottom of the lake.

He kept his arm around her shoulders as they stumbled to the rocky beach. "You don't do things halfway, do you?"

She lifted her chin, so their gazes met.

Concern filled his eyes. "You okay?" William slid a hand against her neck and pulled her forehead against his shoulder.

Oh heavens, this was nice. Too nice. "If I say yes, are you gonna let go?"

He chuckled. "Not a chance."

———

Lucy glanced up from the lunch she was unloading off the room service tray when the door to the cabin opened.

William stalked through. He scowled at the floor but didn't say a word.

"You okay?" he finally asked, gruffer than usual. "From the lake."

"I am." Aside from the present hot flash thanks to his abdominal muscles currently on display.

He snagged his sandwich and leaned against the counter, his gaze focused on his bare feet. Five huge bites with very little chewing, and he finished. He tossed the plate in the sink, crossed his arms, and glared into space.

"Hey, if it costs money for the boat thing, I'll pay for—" she started.

He pulled a small box from his pocket. She barely caught it when he tossed it to her. A gasp escaped her lips when she recognized the logo on the box as a prescription medication for erectile dysfunction.

"Why?" she asked.

"That's my question." His eyes were blank.

"What are you talking about?" she asked, breathier than she intended. Damn, but she already knew. Sarah. Rebecca. They got to him.

"Max caught me up at the lodge. Explained he's a special kind of doctor. The kind that works with men who have particular issues." He made air quotes at the last word as Rebecca had in therapy.

Lucy smacked a hand to her mouth.

"Seems his wife told him about our problems in the bedroom and asked him to help us out. Would you like to explain why you gave me syphilis?"

Uh-oh. Lucy took a deep breath and whispered through her fingers. "You weren't supposed to know."

"You give a guy an STD, he's gonna find out." His stony expression added to the shame piling up inside her.

She scooted backward, stopping when her legs hit the dining table. "Hang on. I didn't give you anything."

"Right," he clipped. "You never told Sarah *and our therapist* that I can't get it up?"

"Well, now, the thing is…" She swallowed the lump of regret forming in her throat and licked at her lips. "I did kind of do that. It's not what you think, though."

He rubbed a hand over his hair.

"Ten days." That muscle directly under his jaw twitched. "In ten days, there will be an announcement about my takeover of Crestone. Ten days, and this will be regional news. My face, everywhere. Crestone is nearly a billion dollar company, so it could even be national news. The last thing I need is for some yahoo to want his shot at fifteen minutes and announce that I have venereal disease. Which. I. Do. Not. Have."

"Max is a doctor. He can't say anything."

"Technically, he's not my doctor. Nothing prevents him from blabbing."

Oh.

First, holy mackerel had she screwed up in amazing proportions this time. Second, Crestone was worth that much? Wow.

She opened her mouth to speak but had no idea what to say so she closed it. Then she opened it again and closed it again. "I didn't realize."

He stared at her with raw intensity.

She glanced away. "I'll talk to Sarah, and I'll find Rebecca."

"No. No, you won't. You won't talk to anyone about this. I'll call my attorney and somehow explain to her *why* we may need to issue a statement regarding my sexual health. She'll love that."

If he clenched his teeth together any tighter, they'd probably shatter. He waved a hand. "Not that I have much pride left anyway. It's like the reality show all over again. The media will twist this, spin it, and tear me apart."

"I am so sorry." Acid burned her stomach. "So sorry."

He studied his feet, and his right hand moved to his neck, rubbing the indentation near his back.

"You know what? So am I." The emptiness of his expression when he glanced up didn't only sting. No, it branded her.

"Will, it was an innocent comment. One I regret."

"It wasn't a comment. It was a lie. And it hurts." This time he caught her gaze, and his disappointment colored every bit of his handsome face. "I thought I knew you better than this. But you know what? I don't. I know nothing about you. Not really. I know you don't like water, and I know the little crumbs of information you've tossed my way. What are you so afraid I'm going to find out?"

Where would she even begin? She didn't want him to know so much, didn't want him to remember.

"Lies of omission are still lies," he said when she didn't respond. His words were a direct hit that didn't only burn, they cut.

She always sought out the truth and hated lies. William had paid attention to her in a way she wasn't ready to acknowledge. No one had ever handled her with such care. He was genuinely compassionate toward her.

And she'd ruined it.

"I'm going for a hike." The tone William used was neutral, like he didn't care.

She couldn't let him go alone. Not this upset. Not when it was her fault. Not when he had literally saved her life. "Can I come?"

He shrugged. Then he nodded.

She nipped her bottom lip with her teeth. "I'll grab my shoes."

Clearly, he was done pursuing her. And she could absolutely understand his reasons.

Good. It would be done. *They* would be done.

CHAPTER
SIXTEEN

In hindsight, wearing her Converse tennis shoes on the lake that morning was a bad idea. They were soaked. Unwearable. Which left her orange Hawaiian-print flip-flops. Looked like she was hiking in flip-flops.

She found William on one of the planked cedar benches. He leaned back against the outside wall of the cabin, his ankle crossed over his knee.

Lucy's heart lodged in her throat. "Hey." She took a step forward, unsure what else to say.

William had always treated her warmly, but this time he only gave a sad nod. His gaze didn't meet hers.

"I'll carry the backpack." He took the bag from her shoulder, avoiding any skin on skin contact before he slipped it over the strong muscles of his back.

"Thanks," she mumbled.

She shuffled a few steps behind him in awkward silence, a nagging quiet that tugged at their time together.

William turned left at a fork in the trail.

"Did you get a map?" The words stuck thick in her throat.

He continued forward, as if unfazed by her question. "Don't need one. The trail goes around the lake, looping back to the lodge."

"I know it's against man code to carry a map, but maybe we should turn back and get one before we get too far on the trail." Her big toe snagged on a jagged stone, scuffing the skin so a drop of blood pooled at the nail. It began to throb. Head down, she scanned the ground to avoid rocks.

When he stopped two steps ahead, she stumbled into him. He reached to steady her; his expression unreadable.

"Right, we don't need a map." She gripped the soles of her shoes with her toes to keep herself steady.

His gaze met hers with gentle ease. It lasted only a moment before that expression of indifference she hated so much snapped back into place. This wasn't right at all. From the day at the gas station when her window had broken to the game of *Confessions* at the cabin, he had constantly given bits of himself to her. Now, for the first time in his presence, loneliness crept in. So afraid of sharing too much, she had rationed the information she gave him. He hadn't been wrong when he said she dodged his questions. A lot.

She couldn't unwind the past, but she could push herself.

Trust him.

Columbine flowers sprouted along the thin, steep trail where they hiked in silence.

William marched ahead of her, and she did her best to match the pace he set. As the trail rounded across the edge of a cliff, her entire focus switched to not taking a header onto the jagged rocks. The grip of her flip-flops slipped, and she stumbled to her knees with an *oof*.

William helped her up. She wiped the dirt from her kneecaps.

"Will?" she asked softly.

He paused. His expression had gentled when she fell. It remained kind.

She squeezed his biceps to keep him from turning away. "I confess I like almost all the colors." She had to do this. Give him more. "You asked the night we played *Confessions*. I didn't answer because, well, I didn't want to get too close. But you should know, I don't have a go-to favorite. It depends on the day."

He didn't respond but didn't move either.

"I also confess I didn't get my first kiss until I was almost twenty years old. You asked that, too." In the distance, a low murmur of thunder answered her confession, but nothing from William. "What else do you want to know about me?"

"Everything, Luce," his voice was rough.

A handful of fat raindrops splattered on the rocks around them.

She drew a breath of damp mountain air as more thunder rumbled closer this time. She could do this. *Trust him.*

"M-my given name is Lucille. My parents are Berta and Graham. Before I moved to Confluence, everyone called me Lulu, but I've always preferred Lucy."

Now I prefer when you call me Luce.

Those golden eagle eyes scoured her face as she spoke. She searched his right back to catch the spark of any memory. She was Lulu. He had to remember. She was finally ready for him to remember.

C'mon William.

His eyes remained blank. Nothing.

She blinked against the realization that she had changed so much he truly didn't remember her. Or, perhaps, more likely she hadn't been important enough for him to remember anything about her in the first place. She had been one of many on the production crew. His attention had been...elsewhere that entire time.

Her heart sank. The biting hope she'd held deep inside that who she had been might not matter to him corroded away to nothing. It would matter, he would only see her as who she had been—the person she'd worked so hard to blot out.

William stepped toward her. "Why are you in Confluence? Why here?"

"People aren't nice to me, Will. I used to be such a mess. But I fixed that, and I realized the only thing I have is my career. I want to be a reporter more than anything I've ever wanted in the world." She sucked in a lungful of mountain air. "I came to Confluence because some creep who watched me on the news thought I was his."

More raindrops started to fall. Neither of them moved.

She closed her eyes and pressed her fingers against them.

"Lucy…" William dropped the backpack and reached for her.

"No. You want to know. And I want to tell you." She took a deep breath. "The lights went out in the stairwell of my apartment building that night when he came for me. I thought it was a rolling blackout. Not a big deal. I was almost to my floor when he shoved me against the wall. Pressed a knife against my throat."

A pulse at William's temple pounded hard with each beat of his heart. At the moment, it worked overtime. He stepped forward and tilted her face to his, running his finger against her jaw.

"I thought I was being mugged. But it was him."

The air of the stairway had filled with the scent of her fear, the stale alcohol and tobacco on his breath, and his saccharine sweet cologne.

"He hated that I was on the news. Made plans so he could take me with him. Whether I wanted to go or not, that didn't matter. There was somewhere in the Mojave where he had a place."

William dropped the backpack and reached for her.

"Please, let me finish. I have to," she said.

William nodded.

"He broke my arm when I fought him. Then the door to the stairwell opened, and my neighbor saw us. She turned on the lights. He must've panicked. The knife slipped, and he cut me just under my neck."

William hissed in a breath.

"He tried to carry me out, but I bit his ear, and he dropped me. I hit my head hard enough to get a concussion. Between that, the broken arm, and the blood I lost when he cut me, I passed out. That's all I remember until I was at the hospital."

William's face was anything but gentle. Fury practically poured from him.

"I'm hiding in Confluence because it's safer to disappear into a fake life than it is to live in a real one, never knowing when I'll be watched, when he'll hurt me again. What will the next hospital visit mean? Another slashed throat and broken arm? Or will he manage more this time?"

William stepped forward and tilted her face to his, running his finger against the small scar along her neck she always covered with makeup. The rain pelted them both with droplets.

"He cut you." It was more statement than question. "I'm going to find him. I'm going to see that he's dealt with."

"I didn't tell you, so you'd help me. I told you so you'd understand, so we can still be friends."

The storm opened above them. Raindrops quickly turned to sheets of water slashing across the trail.

He rubbed his hands up her arms before turning her forward on the trail. "Let's get you out of the rain."

She tripped down the hill as her stupid sandals slid against the mud. William gripped her arm to hold her steady while the thunder pounded angrily. They hurried toward the base of the mountain, the evergreen trees providing little cover as they plodded forward, slipping along the soggy gravel of the embankment.

The trail ended at the lake. And, damn, they came out on the opposite side. The lodge was barely visible through the storm. They should've turned right at the fork. It would be at least two more miles around to find shelter.

"This is where that map would have come in handy, huh?" she asked, glancing up at him.

He grunted, but there was a whisper of a smile there. "This way."

She followed blindly. When they turned a corner, a small building sat squat among the trees. Canoes, rowboats, and a motley assortment of oars were stacked haphazardly outside. Lightning flashed nearby, and he pulled her along beside him. He let go of her hand to try the door, but it was locked. He pushed harder with his shoulder.

No luck. The rain continued to drench them.

"Stay here," he yelled over a clap of thunder before he disappeared behind the back of the shack. She wrapped her arms around herself. How smart was it to take cover in a metal shack during a lightning storm, anyway? She was standing there alone, shivering, when the door opened, and William ushered her in.

She stepped inside. "How'd you get in?"

The place was stacked top to bottom with life jackets, a wall of fishing poles, and a small desk.

"The window wasn't locked. I climbed through." He set down the backpack and unzipped it to rummage around. "Don't suppose you packed a towel?"

"No." She shook her head.

"Come here." The softness of his tone was at odds with the storm raging outside. He motioned to her as he sat against the pile of life jackets. She plunked down next to him, and he drew her close. Surely, he did it to warm her.

Oh boy, did it. She practically turned into a cloud of steam as his hands rubbed against her skin. Each stroke echoed in a much more intimate place.

"Why did you finally open up to me?" he asked against her hair. The muscles in his arms held her firm, and *God* that was nice.

"I don't want to lose your friendship, Will." She really, really didn't.

"Lucy, you have to know by now that I don't want to be your friend."

Oh. She glanced up through her eyelashes, and his eyes burned bright, right into her. The atmosphere in the cabin shifted dangerously with the intensity of all that was William.

"You don't want to be my friend?" she asked carefully.

"No." His thumb rubbed across her lower lip, and the electricity between them rivaled the lightning outside. "That's not what I want from you."

"No?" she asked.

He turned her to face him. "I want more."

Her heart tripped faster as his mouth got close to hers, near enough she could smell the raindrops mixed with wet earth on his skin.

"You were so mad at me," she said. In the intimacy of the space, only the two of them existed.

"I'm sorry I got angry." He rubbed his hands along the wet fabric of her shirt, lifting the cloth as his fingers moved. He laid her back and moved above her before he lifted the edge of her drenched shirt, remarkably close to the waistband of her panties.

Her breath caught. Hells freaking bells.

All the reasons they shouldn't be together suddenly seemed trivial.

"I'll bring one next time," he said on a low rumble.

"Bring what?" she asked, unable to concentrate on anything other than the water droplets on his damp lips. Lips that parted close to hers.

Less than a centimeter of space and she could kiss him again.

His eyes glazed over. "A map."

Before she could say anything else, he kissed her. He ran his tongue along the seam of her lips and she moaned.

She slipped her hand into his hair and opened for him. The crackling ozone outside had nothing on the two of them.

His fingertips grazed the edge of her thigh, sending goose pebbles all along her skin. As soon as his mouth met hers she went from chilled to the core to heated beyond comfort.

A groan slid from deep in her throat. Or his. Who could really tell at that point?

Had she ever been this turned on by a kiss? No, definitely not. Given the state of his...twitching rod...he was equally affected.

His lips moved against hers. Pressed harder. His tongue invaded her mouth.

For the first time she got it. *It* being that thing people always talked about as chemistry.

Sure, she'd dated. Even invited a few guys into her bed.

But she'd never experienced anything like this.

So, they weren't going to be friends. Okay. The intensity of his kiss made up for any annoyance of a failed friendship. The weight she'd carried all day disappeared as her body reacted to his touch.

He leaned back, barely breaking the kiss, their mouths only millimeters away from each other. His eyes flared with desire.

They were so, totally, not going to be friends.

Her hands bunched against his wet collar, yanking it impatiently to bring him back to her mouth.

All reason vanished from her synapses when his hands traveled under her shirt along her slick skin to the edge of her bra. He tugged the cloth down, the pad of his thumb brushing across her nipple.

She moaned again. Absolutely, couldn't help it. The storm outside raged.

The door to the shack smacked open and a man, not William, cleared his throat.

Holy hell.

William stilled. Lucy pulled away.

His hand slid from under her shirt, and he turned quickly. Two men wearing raincoats with the Twin Lakes logo stood at the threshold holding fishing gear.

"This is a first," the shorter man said, raising an eyebrow. "Wouldn'ta thought to use a pile of lifejackets for that."

CHAPTER
SEVENTEEN

The men went off to the corner of the shack and the thrum of rain on the metal roof lightened. William reached for Lucy's hand and hauled her beside him, tucking his arm around her shoulders.

"So, that happened," she said under her breath. Her expression had gone distant, but he'd remedy that as soon as they got back to the cabin.

"Yeah, it happened." He leaned to her and kissed her neck, intentionally rubbing his stubble on the soft spot beneath her ear.

She shivered.

The rain finally stopped, and he snagged the backpack.

"Ready?" he asked.

She peeked up at him. "I'm starving. Can we stop at the lodge and grab something quick for dinner?"

No. No time for dinner. He needed her alone. If he calculated correctly, he had approximately eight more seconds before he spontaneously combusted. Yeah, he would die right there on the life jackets.

Her stomach rumbled. She raised her eyebrows in an *I told you* gesture.

"Sure, we can go get dinner." He forced a smile. After they ate, he'd initiate Operation Get Alone and Get Naked.

The men met his goodbye with grunts. "We'll be sure to knock next time," one of them muttered.

William held Lucy's hand when they forged ahead into the post-storm mountain air. Aside from the waterlogged ground and the fresh after-rain scent of the forest, he would never have known the angry storm had blown through. They walked in silence, stopping at the edge of the lake. She squeezed his hand, shooting a pulse of desire into his veins.

"Should we head back to Confluence tonight?" she asked.

"What?" he asked.

"I mean given everything… that's happened. And one more night isn't going to expose anything else with the story." She glanced at him expectantly.

Absolutely not. He only had a few more hours with her before they returned to the real world. No way did he want to willingly give up that time. "Do you… want to stay and pick up where we left off?"

"Are you sure? Sure, we should do this?" she asked without any conviction at all. "Sure that you want to do this? With me?"

He quirked an eyebrow. She hadn't second guessed it when she'd outlined a map of the Twin Lakes resort on the roof of his mouth with her tongue.

"Here's *my* proposal. I'll buy you dinner, and we'll go back to the cabin. When we get there, I'll do this." He dropped his fingertips to her hips.

She held her breath, right on cue.

"Then I'll lean forward and kiss your neck." He illustrated by brushing his lips against her sensitive skin.

She gulped, and her hands gripped his biceps. "That's nice. You could do that some more."

He grinned, letting his lower lip skim her jawline. "When I'm done, I'll put my mouth right about here."

He touched his lips casually to hers.

She shivered. "What's next?"

"Then, I'll slip my hand right here." He demonstrated over the cloth of her shorts, moving his flat palm against the denim. She made a strangled noise and drew closer, her breath coming more quickly to match his own.

"Would you like that?" He said the words against her mouth.

She nodded. "Yes."

He let out a relieved breath. "And, yes, Luce. I'm sure I want to be here with *you*."

He kissed her briefly and wrapped his fingers with hers as they made their way to the lodge.

William would die a slow death at the hands of Lucy. She took her time over dinner—long enough to dry out. She laughed and clearly savored their time together. He should've enjoyed himself, too, but his mind looped their plans for the rest of the evening on replay.

"Let's head back, yeah?" he asked.

"Uh-huh." She stretched her arms over her head, giving him a front row view of her breasts tight against the now dry T-shirt.

He had lost his mind. Poof. Gone.

Given that any semblance of coherence disappeared, he couldn't be sure, but it seemed he dragged her back to the cabin like a caveman.

If he were a cartoon villain, he'd be rubbing his sinister hands together.

She stopped abruptly. "Wait, you didn't use your key?"

"The door wasn't locked." He turned the handle to show her.

"I locked it when we left." She was adamant.

"Luce, we were both upset. It was a mistake. No harm done." All this talk of doors and locks put a serious kink in his evil genius plan.

Her face paled. "No, *you* don't understand. I'm *sure* I locked it."

He gave her a reassuring squeeze. "Wait here. I'll go in and check it out."

"I'm not waiting out here alone." She stuck close behind him.

When he flipped the switch, lights flickered on. Normally, he wouldn't think anything of the way they wavered. But with Lucy freaking out, the subtle dim and flare gave off a seriously creepy vibe. She gripped his back pocket, and subsequently his ass, as she shuffled with him through the cabin. "We were both upset when we went out. I'm sure—"

"I could've sworn I locked it. This is getting ridiculous." She paled and crossed her arms around herself protectively. He preferred where her hands had been before.

"What's ridiculous?" He moved to her.

"I keep seeing things that aren't there. It's part of the traumatic stress stuff. It's getting worse." Her lip trembled. "I thought I saw the guy. The one who hurt me. I thought I saw him at the lake. But I didn't. Just an illusion."

He rested his hands on her shoulders. "Luce, you lived a nightmare. Of course, it affects you. But I won't let anything bad happen."

Her eyes got misty as she nodded.

He kissed her forehead. "Let's see if anything's missing."

They'd planted a few pieces of jewelry and several hundred dollars throughout the room. It didn't take more than a few seconds to realize the cash had been lifted. He shouldn't have been excited, but his instincts clicked on high alert, and he went straight to the cameras.

"Should we call the police?" Lucy asked, checking the lock on the door for the second time.

"Not yet. We'll check the video and then we'll talk to management."

"We should check on Sarah and Max. See if they're missing anything." Lucy crossed her arms across her chest and rubbed at her shoulders.

He gave her his best not-a-chance look.

"Or we could just do it your way." She helped set up the computers to run the video. Three clicks and…

"It's that front desk lady."

Sure enough, the front desk clerk who had checked them in

appeared on the video rummaging through their bags and pocketing the cash he'd left inside the pockets.

"Looks like we got our evidence." Lucy grinned at the woman stealing from them on the screen.

Will's phone beeped from the table where he'd left it behind. He ignored it.

Lucy jerked her chin to the table. "You need to check that?"

"Probably." He reluctantly released her and snagged the phone. He grimaced. Twenty-three missed calls, ten messages. "This might take a minute."

"Don't mind me." She smiled weakly and waved him away.

"It'll just take a second." He winked at her.

While he wanted nothing more than to shut out the world and drown in Lucy, he patiently returned each message.

A second turned into an hour, and an hour into two as he put out fire after fire. Lucy had fallen asleep on the bed ages ago. Given the way she yawned, all that she'd been through, and how quickly she'd fallen asleep, he didn't wake her after his last call—as much as he'd wanted to.

Instead, he poured over the spreadsheets covering the table. They outlined the financial benefit of the upcoming acquisition with the Colorado Springs station. The trouble was that the benefit was all for Crestone. A lot of people in Colorado Springs were about to find themselves out of work. He scrubbed a hand over his hair. His gut told him it wasn't the right thing to do, but the money definitely talked.

"Hey." Lucy dropped her feet over the side of the bed.

He glanced at her and grinned. "Hey."

The ridiculous panda bear nightshirt she wore skimmed her thighs, the cupcake cherry directly over her nipple.

"Thought you were asleep." He kept the words neutral. He wanted to lift the edge of that panda bear. Unwrap her slowly. Taste her.

"I was. What's all this?" She gestured to the papers covering the table.

"This...is my empire." He shook away the corrupt thoughts of what lay underneath the cupcake.

Lucy leaned against the table.

He stared at the cherry on her shirt.

When she crossed her arms, the cherry stretched tight over her breast, taunting him.

He took her in, all of her—her face scrubbed free of makeup, her hair in a messy bun on top of her head, the ludicrous panda that skimmed her bare legs—legs he wanted wrapped around him. She seduced him without even trying. His chair scraped across the wood floor when he stood.

Moving in front of her, he placed his hands on both sides of the table to frame her there.

"What're you doing?" she croaked.

"You." The rough word grated his vocal cords.

"I like that idea."

He felt those words straight in his gut.

"I want this, too, but I worry."

"Worry about what?"

"That you'll regret it. That this is a bad idea."

He kissed her—peppermint toothpaste and desire on her lips. "Sometimes the bad ideas are the best ones."

"You just made that up, didn't you?" She ran her lips along his collarbone, her hands settling on his torso.

"I did."

He cradled her face between his hands. "I confess...the things you do to me, Luce. I want you. Now."

"Why?"

"Because you're everything I'll never deserve."

Her expression softened. "I confess I want you, too. Tonight. But this can't be for forever."

He touched his lips lightly to hers. "Then I guess we'll just have to make our time count, won't we?"

"You're going to be my boss."

"Not tonight. Let's take this day by day, see where it goes?"

"Okay." She pressed her mouth to his. They opened their lips in unison, tongues gradually demanding more until he throbbed with the need for release.

She broke the kiss. "Your rod's twitchy again," she said, breathless.

"Yeah?" He lifted her to the table. "I'd like to say something witty, but I'm busy right now."

"Do you want me to fall on you like that rooster? I can even make a cock joke." The vein in her throat pulsed as her heart pounded. She opened her thighs around him, so his thick erection pressed into the softness of her core.

"Absolutely not." He leaned to suckle the cherry at her breast through the fabric. She pushed her body closer, offering more, claiming everything.

A moan escaped from the back of her throat.

He lifted his head and moved his fingers under her shirt to her nipple to tug the wet flesh. She groaned and pressed harder against his pelvis. The layers of cloth meant nothing as she rubbed against him until he nearly finished right there. Her breath quickened, and he tore his mouth from hers.

"Bed," he said over her harsh gasps.

"Wha—?" Her pupils were totally liquid, confused.

"Let's go to the bed."

———

Lucy tried to focus on William, but she couldn't. The arousal he'd built inside her overwhelmed any sense of reality.

The high of their encounter began to crumble around her. "Drawer."

He pulled her from the table.

As they approached the bed, he abruptly turned and lifted her in his arms. He lowered his mouth to the crest of her breasts, nuzzling her as she moaned. Instinctively, she wrapped her legs around his waist in some kind of primal dance.

Sex had never been such a craving before. Clearly, she'd been doing it wrong.

His mouth crushed against her lips with an intensity she'd never experienced, and he nipped at her lower lip with his teeth. It should have hurt. Strangely, it was…sensual. Heat, pleasure, and sin.

She weighed nothing as his tongue continued searching. She gripped her ankles around his back, hanging on as he explored every inch of her lips and mouth.

Somehow they reached the bed and practically fell to the sheets. His torso aligned with hers. He peppered soft kisses over her face and down her throat, stopping at the curve where her neck met her shoulder.

All those years of practice were certainly coming in handy for him because he crafted her desire with the skill of an expert.

"Will," she said on a gasp.

He kissed her palm and moved it over the slope of her belly, down beneath the waistband of her panties between her legs.

She closed her eyes. They were doing this. He was doing this. With *her* hand. Was that even possible?

Yes, clearly it was because his fingers mingled with hers, against her wetness, in an utterly wanton experience.

He lifted his head from where he'd buried it against her throat. "I have a confession."

"Please don't confess you want to stop." She gasped as he moved his knuckle over the already sensitive flesh of her entrance.

He chuckled. "Not a chance."

"Thank God." She bit against her bottom lip. "Then what's the confession?"

"I've wanted to be inside you since the first moment I saw you." He kissed along the line of her collarbone.

No, that wasn't true. She knew that much. He hadn't wanted her at all in Florida.

"I'll match your confession," she said against his chest.

"Yeah?" He caught her gaze and held it.

"We're wearing too many clothes."

"You forgot to confess." He grinned a you-lost-the-game grin.

Damn.

His mouth never left hers as he grappled with the fly of his jeans. Before she could take a solid breath, the barrier was gone. Holy crap, the Committee for the Furthering of the Covington Name had left him quite the endowment.

He yanked her panties to her thighs. She shimmied out of them while he pulled his shirt over his head to toss it aside.

His erection pressed against the side of her leg when his mouth covered hers again. His hands ran along the curve of her hip, igniting a path along her flesh. She gasped when he rubbed his palm against the heat of her, finding the sweet spot and caressing until little bursts of light flashed in her eyes.

She reveled in the safety of his embrace and the rough fingertips moving intimately against her wetness. "I confess, I really love when you call me Luce," she said.

He pressed his lips against her ear. "Luce."

Her panting turned harsh, in tempo with the rhythm of his fingertips. The intensity of his touch amplified every breath. She groaned as her head fell back, the edge of her release remaining out of reach.

"You're safe with me, Luce."

She was. And somehow on a fundamental level she finally understood what safety meant.

One of his fingers slid inside her, testing, exploring. She gasped.

Then he added another.

She was safe. The little walls she'd built all around herself to protect her emotions crumbled.

Her body throbbed, and the wave of orgasm finally released in the security of his arms. She held onto him as though he'd disappear, taking his fantastic fingers with him. But he wasn't done. He continued to work her up once more until the intensity overtook her again and she came hard against his hand.

Before she could take a solid breath, the warmth of his body was gone. A drawer rolled open and then smacked closed.

"I need you." His voice broke as he returned to her. "Now."

At his words, she stripped her nightgown over her head. He dealt with the condom, and his arousal stretched the damp apex of her thighs. Her legs wrapped around his hips as gradually their boundaries blurred. Together they drowned in each other.

CHAPTER
EIGHTEEN

Lucy woke as Will drew his lips along her neck. She peeked at the alarm clock beside the bed. Two o'clock in the morning was entirely too early.

"Good morning." His breath tickled against her skin. After round two several hours ago, they'd fallen asleep tangled together..

She drew a sharp breath when he paused near the curve of her breast. The hard muscles of his back tensed under her hands.

"Ye—" The word cracked. "Yes."

"We have to leave today." His tongue flicked at her nipple.

Yes, yes, they would. They had the story. Now it was back to reality.

She gripped his hair, holding his mouth in place. "We have right now, though."

His hands got in on the action and every neuron in her brain focused on them. Coherent thoughts stopped coming in that moment.

"Yeah." He smiled against her skin and tucked her hand into his own.

The world came into sharp focus as he trailed kisses across her belly. He freed his hand from hers to spread her knees. He continued to kiss and lick, lower and lower. Her heart hammered in her chest.

No one had ever gone down on her before.

"I've never done…" She grabbed a fistful of his hair. "Oh. That's nice."

Gently, he set her hand aside. He glanced up from his explorations and flashed those damn dimples. "Then I'd say it's about time."

He ran his tongue in a circle over the bundle of nerves at the core of her, flicking and sucking in alternate waves. She couldn't stop the moan that escaped from between her lips, and had no way to suppress her heels as they dug into the bed to lift her hips more firmly against his mouth.

Their yoga mat therapist had been right. There were other things he could do that had nothing to do with—oh dear, his fingertips trailed up her thigh and spread her center apart. Then they went *there*. One and then two dipped inside. He made some kind of feral noise as his tongue continued to do really amazing things.

How did he get it to turn to the side like—oh God, the muscles inside began to contract as he continued his work. He picked her heels up off the bed and wrapped them around his shoulders, his own palms trailing along her lower back to hold her against his mouth. In turn, she gripped the bed sheet in two solid handfuls.

She thought he could kiss before. He'd been holding back. The French had nothing on the way he moved his tongue down there.

She made a sound she was pretty sure wasn't lady like at all, and then everything seemed to spin. The heat between her thighs burned hot for him before releasing her on a wave and pulling her under.

As luck would have it, his idea was a fantastic one.

———

William sat on the bench outside the cabin and wanted to beat his chest like the caveman he'd proven himself to be. He was fairly certain he'd never been a woman's first *anything* before. Even *his* first had been thoroughly experienced when they hooked up in high school. He grinned at the lake in front of him as though he expected it to respond somehow. His night with Lucy had been unbelievable. Yeah, this morning had been incredible, too. Caught up in their activities, neither had gotten much sleep. Although, given the satisfied smile she wore when they tumbled out of the shower, she didn't mind.

He sipped at his cup of coffee. His heart gave a little tug. Damn, he had never fallen for a woman this hard. He was in trouble, and he didn't even care.

"Hey." Lucy emerged from the cabin and tucked her hair behind her ear. "Coffee again? You're the best."

Yeah. He'd proven that around four times in the past ten hours. She smiled, uncertain, and raised her mug to him. Even in the early morning, she was stunning with her hair haphazardly tied up. Her ridiculous nightshirt dipped a little low, showing just enough cleavage to make him want to immediately take it off. With the intimate knowledge of what lay underneath, he squeezed his hand on the handle of his mug to keep from doing just that.

"You're beautiful, Luce."

"You don't have to say that." Her body brushed against his, and she ran her hands along his bare stomach.

"I said it because it's true. Get dressed. Let's go to the lodge and grab breakfast before we head out."

She rolled her eyes. "So demanding."

He lifted her chin with his fingertip. "We established that last night."

A heavy red blush covered her cheeks.

"You're blushing, and I didn't even take out my—"

"Stop." She jabbed her fingertip at his chest.

He caught her around the waist to kiss her thoroughly. "You stop."

"You're smooshing me," she said against his shoulder.

His phone buzzed with a new voicemail. One glance and he

winced. He jabbed the play button, and his father's curt voice echoed through the phone.

"William. No time for attorneys. The Colorado Springs station received another offer. They're entertaining it, and the whole thing doesn't look good for Crestone. Their managers are headed to Confluence, and I'm meeting with them. You're expected to attend. Call me when you get this."

His father's irritating command seriously grated. Of course William would attend, but not because his father commanded. He wouldn't be left out of a meeting that important. Which meant his plans for the day just changed.

He tossed his phone on the bench a bit harder than necessary.

"Everything okay?" Lucy glanced up from under her eyelashes.

He felt her gaze straight in his chest.

"We're headed back." He stomped inside.

He had a feeling that even if the meeting was a success, he'd need to make a few trips over the mountain to ensure the buyout moved forward.

CHAPTER
NINETEEN

A quick wrap-up with the management at Twin Lakes, a chat with the local deputy, one arrest warrant issued, and William and Lucy loaded the truck. They were on the road in record time. Once they saw the video there wasn't much management could say. The desk clerk admitted to the double bookings but held out on the thefts until she realized there was video. The resort had a load of bad publicity coming their way once the story broke. At the moment, that was the least of William's concern.

They turned into the KDVX parking lot, and he glanced across the cab of the truck to Lucy. Her forehead leaned against the glass, her expression tense.

The connection they had started to build would be strong enough to survive reality. William hoped.

Didn't he deserve to be happy? He'd screwed up a lot in his life. He'd also spent years redeeming himself. Enough was enough. He wanted to be with her. Whatever she was willing to give, he was ready to take.

"I have to wrap up a few things here. Stick around, and I'll follow you home?" He threaded his fingers with hers.

She pulled away and shook her head. "I need to get back to Mitzy. Simon didn't make it over this morning."

He climbed out of the truck. "Lucy." Her name lay heavy on his lips. "I'll only be a minute."

Lucy pulled her fake ring off and slipped it into his hand. Heart heavier than warranted, he closed his fingers around the cubic zirconia. She paused. Dropped her hand to his arm. "I'm scared, Will. Because of the way I'm feeling about us. What we have. How it'll work now that we're home."

The fear in her eyes made his gut clench. "Let's go slow then."

She nodded. "Slow."

"You'll stay so I can follow you home?" he asked, tracing her bottom lip with his thumb.

She nodded. "I'll go check my voicemail or something."

He chuckled and walked her to the door. Once she was safely inside the security door of the building he glanced back to his truck, Parker leaned against his tailgate.

"Tell me I didn't see what I just saw." Parker crossed his arms.

"Don't know what you saw, so no comment." William lugged the equipment cases from the truck bed and stacked them beside a tire.

"Despite the fact that I've known you for years, or maybe *because* I've known you for years, I have to put out a big ol' *what the hell are you thinking?* She's staff. You can't fool around with staff."

"I care about her." And it was none of Parker's goddamned business.

Parker cursed under his breath. "Like all the women before her?"

"You're not exactly one to talk with the daily rotation of partners in and out of your bedroom."

"Lucy doesn't need your issues piled on top of everything else she's dealing with at the station. She needs to focus. Do a good job. Not bang the boss." Parker grabbed a box of equipment and added it to the growing pile.

"Do not talk about Lucy."

"This is how you start. When you're done, you toss them aside."

"It's not like that. We're not like that." William had never fought for a woman the way he was prepared to fight for Lucy. That meant something. He grabbed an armload of cases and moved to the building behind Parker.

"Don't drag her through the chaos of your life," Parker said.

"This time it's different." So different. On every level. Parker caught the door to the building for them both.

"This is a mistake."

"My mistake to make." William punched the elevator button.

At KDVX, the television in the control room buzzed low while the master control operator kept tabs on the daytime talk shows.

An extravagant bouquet of exotic flowers sat on the edge of Bridgett's desk. The traditional romance shtick could be key to a long-term relationship with Lucy. William would buy her flowers, take her to dinners, and go gently. They had gotten really serious, really fast. He'd never gone the slow route before. No one he'd ever dated was important enough for time-honored charm with dates and all. Yeah, he could do it.

Parker began unloading the cameras onto the shelves in the small equipment closet. "I'm only watching your back— and hers. Don't screw her around."

"If you're so worried about it, go rat me out to my dad."

This conversation was over.

"Rat who out to me?" His dad leaned against the doorjamb. He stood in his four-thousand-dollar suit, briefcase in hand.

Parker flinched.

William couldn't catch his breath.

They were in the basement of the building, but that didn't stop William's stomach from dropping about ten stories. "No one."

"Glad you made it back in time. I saw your truck in the parking lot. Thought I'd check in with you." Dad shoved a hand into his slacks pocket. "Can't believe you're still driving that old thing."

William continued to unload the equipment, taking his time to organize the shelves as he worked. "Yeah, well, that *old thing's* gotten me where I need to go over the years."

"Parker, how's your sister doing?" Dad asked.

William paused. No one asked about Allie. She was expressly off-limits. Parker always made that clear.

"Same." Parker shifted uncomfortably.

"Glad to hear she's stable." Dad nodded to William. "I trust you've been over all the documents I forwarded?"

"You sent them an hour ago, and I just got back. So, nope, haven't gone through them."

His father's expression was unreadable. "You'll want to do that before morning. Prior proper planning—"

"Prevents piss poor performance," William finished for him and then went back to organizing.

"You got your story?" Apparently, his father was interested in chit-chat. Fantastic.

"Yeah." William folded up the last of the equipment cases they'd taken with them.

"Housekeepers stealing stuff?" Parker snagged the inventory clipboard off the hook on the wall.

William shook his head. "Nope. Front desk lady stealing stuff."

"Sweeps week is coming soon." His father lifted his briefcase and tucked it under his arm. "Hope you found something you can use."

Yeah. William rubbed at his neck. "I've got some ideas."

His father leveled a stare at him. "Stories aren't always organic. Good reporters know when to push boundaries."

William raised an eyebrow at him. "Better reporters know that pushing boundaries doesn't mean testing the waters of journalistic ethics for the sake of ratings."

Yeah, William had been the victim of pushing ethical boundaries on television once. It had cost him years of his life to repair his image because the producer of a stupid reality show wanted better ratings.

"Ratings mean money. Money pays the bills. It's all about the ratings, son."

"Journalism is supposed to be about truth, not ratings, *Dad*."

Dad stared at him for a long beat before he smiled nearly imperceptibly and walked away.

William stared into the blank space his father left behind. What had that whole thing been about anyway?

"So, tell me, how's life in the lion's den with my dad? Sounds like you two are pretty chummy with him asking about Allie. You never talk to anyone about her."

Parker visibly tensed. "It's not like that."

"What is it like then? You're supposed to be my friend, but you kicked me out because he promised you a promotion. A promotion he's no longer in a position to give."

William clenched his teeth against the years of friendship Parker had tossed away over job advancement. "Now—"

"It's my sister." Parker signed the bottom of the form.

William paused. "What about her?"

"There's a rehab program in the Springs that can help with her rehabilitation. I need to get her there. *I* need to get *us* there." Parker hooked the clipboard back on the wall.

William grabbed his suitcase from the floor. "This whole thing is about Allie?"

"You should know by now my life is about taking care of Allie. I'm not being a prick. I'm getting her where she needs to be. It's the least I can do for her." Desperation leaked through the words.

When would the guy give himself a break? Everyone knew the accident wasn't his fault.

Parker started to slip past him.

"I've got money," William said to his back. "I'll set you both up in Colorado Springs. However long you need." What was the use of having money if you couldn't use it to help?

Parker turned. "I'm not taking charity. If you can't make this acquisition happen to get me to Colorado Springs, I'll figure something else out. I always do."

William blew out a breath. Looked like he had to learn everything about the merger in a night so he wouldn't blow the transaction tomorrow.

For Parker's sake.

A heavy pause settled between them.

"How good is the story you got? At Twin Lakes?" Parker asked, finally, clearly ready for a subject change.

William leaned against the shelf. "We got good video, and they double-booked our room. The front desk clerk broke into our stuff and took cash. I've got a load to work with."

Parker thought on that. "Can I see?"

William nodded, led the way to an editing bay, and loaded the video. He explained everything as they watched. But then they watched past when the front desk attendant had left. The door to the cabin opened once more and William's heart dropped.

The newsroom was quieter than normal since there were only a few producers and a couple of reporters around. Lucy sat at her cubicle and her gaze drifted to the dark purple calla lilies sitting on the edge of Bridgett's desk. Once again, she forced her eyes to focus on something else.

She had received a bouquet of flowers like those from Robbie each day for two weeks before he'd come for her. They'd arrived with nearly illegible notes filled with nonsensical promises she hadn't understood at the time.

He wanted her to be his. He hated sharing her with the world. She had to get off camera so she wouldn't be available to everyone. She was his. His woman wasn't a slut. Putting herself on television made her a tramp.

She shook her head. The flowers on Bridgett's desk were only flowers, nothing more. They weren't even for her.

It was officially time to go home so her mind would stop playing tricks on her.

She pushed back from her desk and finally found William in an editing bay with Parker.

"Who is he?" William asked, rewinding the tape with the push of a button.

"No idea." Parker leaned into the screen on one of the monitors to study something. "If he came in after her *and* he didn't take anything. What do you think he wanted?"

"The guy goes through *everything*." William replied, pointing to the other screen.

Lucy cleared her throat. "Hey."

"Hey," they said in unison, oblivious to her.

She stepped into the cramped bay. "What's going on?"

"Luce, is this the guy you thought you saw at the lake?" William rewound the tape and pushed play. He clicked another string of buttons to zoom in on the intruder's face.

She backed into the heavy soundproofing material on the wall.

Those eyes. That familiar face. Oh, God.

Robbie had changed. He'd gained some weight over the past months, hadn't shaved in ages, and had a manic gleam to his eye that slid icicles straight to her core.

"That's Robbie," she said, calmer than she felt.

Neither of them moved.

She lunged for the button at the bottom of the screen to turn it off. The image zipped into a thin line before disappearing.

She closed her eyes and counted, trying to ground herself and find calm again. No luck. Her heart pulsed, and the room shrank. She couldn't breathe. This wasn't real. It couldn't be.

She pressed at her chest, but the air wouldn't come.

"Parker, call the police," William said, eerily calm. "This is the guy that hurt her."

Through the roaring in her ears, he sounded far away, even though he was right there.

"On it." She vaguely heard Parker's reply.

The latch clicked, and her harsh breathing cracked into a sob in the little soundproof room.

"Luce, I'm going to put my arms around you. You're safe here. It's just you and me."

She nodded slightly. At some point, she'd slipped to the painted concrete floor, her knees pressed protectively into her chest. The wheels of a rolling chair squeaked as he shifted it to the side and moved so they sat together.

His arms enveloped her, and his fingers threaded into her hair when she shoved her face against his chest. "Breathe with me. That's it. That's my girl."

Tears burned across her cheeks to seep into his tie.

"He followed me there." She gripped the fabric on his arms. "He's here, Will."

"Parker's getting Jeff." His hand ran over her hair as her breaths evened with his.

"I'm scared." She wasn't sure she spoke loud enough for him to hear.

"I know."

Her fingers clenched his shirt so hard they hurt. "I don't want to let go of you."

"Then don't." His arms squeezed tighter. "Stay here as long as you need."

"How did he find me? I mean, I've done everything right–"

"We'll get this straightened out. Seeing him feels like a bad thing right now, but now we know where he is." He ran a hand along her back.

She didn't have it in her to smile at him or look up, but she did squeeze his arm. He shifted her so her face moved from his chest to his neck. She could spend hours against him, breathing in the fresh scent of his cologne that mingled with fabric softener.

"I'm not a weak person. Please don't tell anyone I broke down like this." She jutted her chin, hoping she appeared dignified.

"This stays between us," he agreed.

Parker stuck his head in the room. "Chief Lawson is on his way."

"You ready for this?" William wiped the remnants of her tears with his thumbs.

Lucy let out a long breath. "No. But I'll be okay."

He stood and pulled her up, wrapping his arm around her as they walked down the hall.

"Lucy," Bridgett called from behind them. "These came for you. I took care of them until you got back."

William and Lucy both turned around. Her world tilted as Bridgett moved to hand her the vase of dark purple lilies.

"They're from him," Lucy whispered. "He's sent them before. Exactly like those."

"Toss them," William said to Bridgett.

"You're kidding, right? These are expensive flowers. Lucy has an admirer." She moved closer with the impressive arrangement.

"They mean death, the flowers. They're also poisonous," Lucy said.

Bridgett froze and glanced at the flowers. "You're serious?"

"Unfortunately." Numbness took over her fear. Lucy welcomed it.

"Why on Earth would someone send you poisonous flowers?" Bridgett did not seem the least bit impressed. But then, did she ever?

"Because he's trying to send me a message."

Bridgett glanced from Lucy to William to Parker. She looked at Lucy kind of strange.

"You're kidding." She sniffed at one, and Lucy nearly fainted.

William snatched the flowers from her and tossed them roughly into a nearby trash.

Bridgett pursed her lips. "Those are *nice* flowers."

"Poisonous death flowers," William growled.

"Bridgett?" Parker asked, devoid of emotion. "Let reception know we're not accepting any unexpected deliveries until I tell them otherwise."

She glanced longingly at the flowers, limp in the trash can.

"Don't test me," Parker said, totally serious.

Bridgett looked to the ceiling as though appealing to a higher power before she sauntered away.

William ushered Lucy into the conference room where the television had been set up to play the video from the cabin. Parker adjusted some cables while William poured her a glass of water. The mundane tasks contrasted sharply with the fact that a man somewhere out there was making plans to kidnap her, or likely worse. And he wasn't searching somewhere in California. He was close. The door to the room cracked open.

Her heart stumbled over itself, only righting when one of the receptionists ushered the Chief of Police into the room.

"Hey, Jeff," Lucy said.

Jeff cleared his throat. "I hear we have a development. Are you doing okay?"

"Not particularly." She tried to smile, but failed.

Jeff asked questions while Parker re-wound, paused, and played the images. William settled behind her chair, his hands resting on her shoulders. Her senses were on high alert, amplified by his touch, each image on the screen, and every sound in the room. She couldn't understand how she could be so numb and so wired at the same time.

"I'll get an officer on those flowers. Find out where he bought them. Any idea how he followed you?" Jeff asked her.

"I don't know."

Jeff shuffled some of the papers in the file folder on the desk. "This guy, whatever his reasons, has made it clear he's willing to do anything to get to you. I would prefer if you'd take extra precautions until he's apprehended. I'll arrange for additional patrols of our neighborhood and around the station. That's what I can do as a cop. As your friend, I'd like you to check in with me a few times a day. Let me know you're okay."

"I'll make sure she's not left alone," William said with authority.

Parker sat on the edge of the conference table. "William can bring her to and from work. She'll be safe as long as she stays in the building. We'll change the security code for KDVX, add extra security, and I'll make sure the other staff understand what's going on."

"I'll pay for a private security guard at each entrance. I want all staff escorted to and from their vehicles. Especially at night," William chimed in.

"Don't you guys think—" Lucy started to say.

"What about when she's at home?" Parker asked.

Still here, guys. Lucy opened her mouth to speak, but they kept talking over her.

"With increased patrols and the Chief of Police living right nearby, she should be safe," Jeff replied.

They weren't listening, not at all. "I really think—"

"She's moving in with me." William used his CEO tone, and the others nodded in agreement.

Okay, no. Whoa. "I am no—"

"That'd be for the best," Parker spoke over her.

"You think you can talk to Dixie? Have her lay off her co-habitation rules for a while?" William asked Jeff, without even a glance toward her.

"Will, seriously—"

"Hang on, we're sorting this out." He squeezed her shoulder again.

She turned to give him her best attempt at an icy stare. "I am not moving in with you."

"Okay, I'll move in with you. That's better anyway. Your walls aren't pink. Jeff, you okay playing interference with your mom?"

No. It wasn't better. Not at all.

Jeff nodded.

Lucy's blood pressure rose. No one was listening to her. "You are not—"

The radio clipped to Jeff's waistband crackled, and he turned a dial at the top to silence it. "Mom'll come around, especially now we know the threat followed Lucy here."

Enough was enough. "Stop it, all of you." Lucy stood abruptly, knocking over her glass of water. The room went silent as the liquid ran a path down the center of the conference table. "I mean it. Stop. Will, if we are staying together it's because we want to, not because you feel like you have to. And I'm not asking for you to pay for extra security. Jeff, extra patrols that don't interfere with your other cases would be great, but I don't need a babysitter. And Parker, can you *please* get me a napkin or something?"

"She'll be all right." Jeff threw a lopsided grin at William before addressing her. "I'm still assigning extra patrols, and William staying with you is a good idea."

"She can move in with me," Parker said as he dug through a cupboard and held up a roll of paper towels.

"Not happening." William put an arm around her waist, clearly staking his claim. She glared at him. She didn't want to appreciate being marked as a possession, but she did. Also, it ticked her off at how comforting his arm was. Ack.

Jeff raised both eyebrows at them. "She can't move in with Simon and me. There's barely enough room for us and the dog. I can ask Mom, though. She might be game as long as you're into *Wheel of Fortune* marathons and willing to eat butter pecan ice cream with her before bed."

Oh hell-to-the-no. She wasn't living with Dixie.

She crossed her arms in defiance.

"Lucy, there's nowhere else I'd rather be than with you," William replied. "Trust me when I say this is not a hardship for me."

Her heart plunked straight to her toes at William's words.

"Can I get a copy of the video?" Jeff turned his radio back on and stood. Apparently, the meeting was over.

"Absolutely," Parker said as he opened the door and stepped outside with Jeff.

"Will?" Lucy scowled at him and gestured around the room. "I feel like this is a dream and I don't even know what just happened."

"You got a roommate, and there's been a big break in your case. Focus on that." He sat across from her so their knees bumped. Her treasonous nerves thrilled at the innocent touch. *Down, girls.*

He threaded her fingers with his, and the nerve endings in her hand sighed. "You're frustrated, but we're going to keep you safe."

Now, what was she supposed to do with that?

CHAPTER
TWENTY-ONE

Lucy really wanted to know how to block the upheaval that had become her life. Running away hadn't helped. The changes she'd made did nothing. This whole thing continued to spin wildly out of control.

Fine. This would be her reality for a while, so she decided to *carpe* her *diem*, whatever that meant.

Another small break in the case, and Jeff found Robbie had been staying at the Pillow Talk Motel under a false name. Paid cash. But he'd left.

As soon as that news came through, William went further than security for the office. He added another necessary ding in her self-reliance when he hired a private bodyguard for her, all the way from Denver. He moved fast, and the bodyguard arrived within hours. The guy stuck to her like peanut butter on jelly—a constant, unspeaking shadow. She understood William took her security seriously, but she'd already lost so much independence.

Bitter anger washed over her whenever Robbie came to mind. Her fear had lessened over the day, replaced by fury.

Another glance in her rearview mirror and yes, Mr. Bodyguard —Neilson—stayed right behind her in his shiny black SUV. She parked in front of her apartment to find Dixie lounging on the porch with a rifle propped against the railing. She wore a neon-pink-floral muumuu dress with matching lipstick that didn't quite make it inside the lines.

"Hey, Dixie," Lucy called as she stepped from her car.

"Glad ta see you're still alive." Dixie grabbed her rifle and hauled it under her arm.

Neilson cleared his throat and stepped in front of Lucy. His aviator glasses covered his eyes so she couldn't study his expression, not that she'd had any luck reading it all day. He achieved the ultimate poker face seemingly without effort. "Rifle, ma'am."

"She's okay," Lucy said, stepping aside so she could talk to Dixie. "She's my landlady."

"Figured I'd stand guard for a bit. Jeff said I don't have to use warnin' shots if your guy shows. Who's this 'un?" Dixie gestured to Neilson.

"My bodyguard," Lucy said with a glance to her take-a-bullet-for-me protector.

"Agreed ta let you take on a roommate. Jeff didn't say nothin' about two men livin' with you." Dixie scowled. "How many men can you take? One was my limit."

Neilson coughed into his hand and shifted.

"No. I'm—*we're* not," Lucy said with as much patience as she could muster. "Can I go inside my house now?"

Dixie gestured to Lucy's bodyguard again. "Is he livin' here, too?"

"No, ma'am," he replied a bit too quickly.

"This keeps up I'll have ta up your rent, missy. Can't have men comin' and goin' all times of the day. This ain't Miss Dixie's House of Tricks and Tiddles."

Lucy flushed with embarrassment.

Dixie harrumphed and hauled herself down the stairs using the shotgun as a cane. "Looks like I'm off duty. Give me a holler if he needs ta leave, and I'll take another shift." Dixie narrowed her eyes and looked him over. "Have you been a bodyguard for celebrities?"

"Yes, ma'am," he replied with a blank face.

She quirked a heavily penciled eyebrow. "Anyone I would know?"

"Likely so."

That got her attention. "We talkin' A-list?"

"Confidentiality, ma'am."

She tilted her head to the side. "Cher or Vanna White?"

"Can't say."

"Do you ever say more than two words at a time?" Dixie asked.

"Depends."

"This'uns a character. He can stay." She smiled what Lucy'd dubbed her best Southern hospitality smile and ambled away, whistling the Tennessee waltz.

Lucy turned to the stairs, but Neilson was in front of her before she could take a step. "Property check. I'll need a key."

Hey there, it turned out he could speak a full sentence…kind of. She handed over the key. His fingertips grazed the pistol at his hip when he pushed open the door.

She'd never witnessed a property sweep before. What a disappointment when it turned out to be just a guy walking around her house. Mitzy hissed half-heartedly when he stepped into the bedroom.

"I have a cat," Lucy said, belatedly. Of course, he saw that now that Mitzy had made herself known. Nonetheless, cat, there she was.

"See that." So, they were back to two-word sentences. "All clear."

Yep, definitely.

"Um, what happens next?" She set her purse on the table. Should she tip him like a bellman?

He removed his aviators, slipped them into the pocket of his black polo shirt, and stood at attention. "Forget I'm here. Do whatever you normally do."

She put a teakettle on the stove and futzed with the burner knob that slipped constantly. Normally after a day like today, she'd eat an entire carton of Cherry Garcia frozen yogurt. But she preferred to binge eat in private, thank you. Of course, she could bake William a cake, but she wasn't a great baker, to say the least.

"You want a cup of tea?" She gestured to the stove.

"No, thanks." How could he stand in one place like that without getting tired of, well, standing there?

"You're welcome to sit, turn on the TV, whatever you'd like. Make yourself comfortable."

"I'm good." He had the no-emotion thing down. Sheesh.

She and William would have a talk later about loosening up the bodyguard. Being followed by Robbie was creepy, but having her life examined by the guy in her living room wasn't great either.

But he clearly wasn't going away anytime soon. Perhaps it was time for her to take back her control. Do the things that were within her power and forget about the rest. William would need space for his things on the bathroom counter. She would even give him his own drawer in the dresser. Yes, taking charge of her life.

Speaking of…

"Neilson, I have a security question," she said. "What if I used myself as bait for Robbie? What if I took back my power and did what I want to do. Go back to being on television?"

Neilson frowned. "It'd make my job harder."

"But, uh, not impossible?" she asked.

He frowned some more. "Nothing's impossible."

Mulling that little nugget, she dangled a tea bag with a tag proclaiming its calming properties into the mug of hot water.

So, what, she didn't have control over everything? *This is me, letting that go. Moving forward.* She stomped purposefully to the hall closet. Barely past the living room, the world did that slow-motion but super-quick thing. The front door opened, her bodyguard pinned her against the dark wood paneling of the wall, and hot, not-so-calming tea water sloshed over the rim to scorch her wrist. "Sonofa—"

"Hey, Luce. What—"

"Hey, Will." She waved a hand feebly. "I think your bodyguard is saving me."

William growled. "You think maybe you could stop saving my girlfriend now?"

CHAPTER
TWENTY-TWO

The last thing William expected was to find Lucy's bodyguard pressed against her. And he definitely didn't expect it to piss him off this badly. He set his hands on his hips and stood firm. "Next time, I guess I'll knock."

What did he expect? The guy was doing his job, but damn he hated another man touching her.

"That's William." Lucy extricated herself from the bodyguard. "If you shoot him, you probably won't get paid. Next time you rescue me, let's discuss removing hot beverages from my hand first." She flinched when she shook away the water dripping from her hand.

"You okay?" the security officer asked her.

She nodded and blew at her wrist.

"James Neilson, All-Pro Security." He flicked the safety back on his gun and reached to shake William's hand. "Wasn't expecting company. Door opened. I acted under perimeter breach protocol."

William clenched his teeth. Since when did "perimeter breach protocol" involve rubbing up against Lucy? "I'll be home the rest of the evening. You can go for the night."

"Tomorrow, three a.m.?" Neilson asked.

William glanced to Lucy. Her eyes were big, and she still blew at her burned wrist, but otherwise she was in one piece.

"Sounds good." William stepped aside so Neilson could pass.

The man stopped at the door, turned, and simply said, "Lucy."

Then he shut the door behind him.

William followed Lucy to the kitchen. "I can request someone else if you want. Someone older with lots of wrinkles who doesn't grope you when I open the door."

"Pssh. You've got nothing to worry about. He's married." She opened the door to the freezer and placed a bag of frozen peas to her arm. "And I prefer men who actually talk."

"Tell me about these men you prefer." He reached for her hand and lifted the bag to check the damage. Not much of a welt, but the small bit of scalded skin looked angry.

"I prefer you, Will Covington," Lucy said with a smile. "Even if he does maybe know Cher."

Damn, she was pretty.

"If he doesn't talk, how do you know he's married?" he asked.

"He's got a ring on his left hand."

Well, then, that was something.

"What're your plans for the evening?" Will asked.

She licked at her lower lip, mesmerizing him, and reminding him there were lots of things they could do together.

"Getting you moved in, I guess. I was going to make room for your stuff when you came in. Will one drawer be enough, or do you need two?"

He studied her mouth with rapt attention. *Every* part of his body was wide awake.

"Earth to Will." She waved a hand in front of his face.

His breath quickened as her mouth ticked into a grin. "Huh?"

"What's with you? Are you still upset your bodyguard tried to save me from you?"

Of course he was upset the guy he paid to protect her had plastered himself against her, but he wasn't going to tell her.

"No. All good. One drawer. Perfect."

"You should know that your story is all stacked for sweeps week. It's gonna be great," Lucy said, seeming to let the normalcy of them together take hold. "I saw the final today."

He smiled and it bought him one right back.

Her grin faltered. "I've also been thinking about something…"

"Okay." But, why did it seem like he wasn't going to like what she had to say?

She seemed to take a mental inventory before speaking. "For eight freaking months, I've taken a back seat in my own life. Eight months of hiding from someone who tracked me anyway. I don't want to be scared anymore. I don't want to continue removing myself from a job I loved. He's found me anyway, so I'm tired of hiding from him."

"What does that mean? You're tired of hiding?"

"I kept myself off camera. Gave him exactly what *he* wanted," she said. The words spilled quickly. "All that got me nowhere. I think it's time to prepare for the future I have always wanted. A future in front of the lens—not behind."

"You want to taunt him?" That seemed like a horrible idea.

"Neilson and I tossed the word bait around a little," she said.

He gritted his teeth. "You are not bait."

"He already knows where I am, what does it matter if I do some time in front of the camera?" she said it, but there was still a flicker of fear in her eyes.

Now it was his turn to take the mental inventory.

"I can't risk you," he said.

She deflated, and he hated that his words had done that.

So he strode to her, placed his hand against her jaw. "We're going to get this guy. And when we do, you will be safe. And when you are safe, you have my full support."

CHAPTER
TWENTY-THREE

"See you tomorrow," Reid said to Lucy as they exited the elevator to the lobby.

She tossed him a grin. "Bright and early."

Neilson caught her arm, stopping her short as a petite Italian woman walked purposefully toward them. Neilson stepped close beside Lucy.

"That's Will's stepmother." She tugged her arm from Neilson's grasp.

He relaxed slightly. Lucy, on the other hand, strung tighter. In no universe was this good.

"You are Lucy?" she asked.

Teresa...yes, her name was Teresa, that's what Will had said.

"William's girlfriend?" Teresa reached to Lucy with a perfectly manicured hand.

Word sure traveled fast in this small town. "Yes." Lucy shook her hand. What was the protocol when one met the estranged step-mother of the man she was sleeping with? "Teresa, right?"

Teresa's frown was nearly imperceptible. "He told you about me?"

"That morning, at the coffee shop when we saw you." And

during some games of *Confessions* that would be uncomfortable to mention. "It's nice to meet you...officially."

Teresa clasped her purse. "My husband, he told me when you are done with your work. I hoped I could buy you lunch?"

"Oh." Lucy froze in place. Will's father kept tabs on her, too? First Robbie. Then Will. Now Neilson. And now Will's father. When did her life get so interesting that everyone memorized when and where she'd be?

"I'm sorry. You already have plans." Teresa glanced uncertainly at Neilson. "Perhaps another time."

A scheduled nap could hardly be considered plans. Yet, she could not have lunch with Teresa. Will's family had hurt him too badly. When it came to parental problems, Lucy was an expert at avoidance.

Teresa glanced to the ground, clearly choosing her next words carefully. Whether it was a language barrier or nerves, Lucy couldn't tell. "Next week is William's birthday. We hoped you could convince him to celebrate with us," she finally said.

Um...no. That would be a bad idea. Bad, bad, bad idea. Horrible. "You'll have to ask him," Lucy said as gently as she could.

"His father and I, we miss him. This separation, we hope to... I'm sorry, the words are hard when I get upset." Teresa drew a deep breath. "We hope to heal. William and his father, they hurt so much when his mother died. You understand this?"

Well, kind of. That still didn't make a birthday celebration with his estranged father a good idea.

"Teresa, I wish I could help," Lucy said. The woman did seem kind, genuine. "But you should talk to Will about this. I can't be in the middle."

"You call him Will?" Teresa's rounded eyes grew sentimental. "His mother and grandmother called him Will. He always insisted everyone else call him William. You are very special to him if he lets you call him this."

Lucy's belly fluttered with nervous uncertainty. *You have special permission to call me Will...* That's what he'd said when they left for

Twin Lakes. Never had she even considered the nickname meant anything.

"You convince him to come for his birthday." Teresa's hope-filled expression almost undid Lucy and her resolve. *Nearly.*

"No, I'm sorry. It's not my place." Lucy glanced to the exit.

"You care for him," Teresa said, earnestly.

"Of course, I care for him. He's wonderful. That's why I can't do something to cause him more pain. He's hurting. A lot. I'm sorry I can't help you." Lucy stepped to leave, but Teresa reached for her.

Neilson cleared his throat in warning. The man didn't need to speak to get his point across. His skill for communication without actually using words never ceased to amaze her. Teresa got the message and withdrew her hand, staring oddly at the bodyguard.

"If you care for him, really care for him, you will help me. He misunderstands. His father and I love him. We want to fix this. Please." The pain in Teresa's eyes eerily matched the distress Lucy had seen in Will. "Bring him back to his family. His father and I are moving away soon. I wish to heal this first."

Damn on a donut. That was a really hard argument to fight.

"Luce, I thought you left?" Will's words echoed in the vast lobby.

She turned to him. "Will, I…"

He stopped mid-stride, a mixture of torment and disbelief flashing in his eyes.

"What is this?" He glanced at her and then Teresa.

This day kept getting better and better.

"*Cucciolo, Mio,*" Teresa said to him. Something passed between them at her words. "*Mi manchi.*"

Will didn't respond to Teresa. He held control of his emotions, but Lucy could tell he was barely tethered.

"Luce?"

Every cell of her body wanted to go to him, comfort him. This wasn't the time. "Teresa asked me to talk to you about your birthday."

"I asked your Lucy if she would convince you to come home for your birthday." *His Lucy…* "Come for supper." Teresa's olive skin paled as she spoke.

He moved beside Lucy and grabbed her hand. "Who will be there?" he asked.

Lucy blinked hard. He hadn't said no.

"Your father and I. Whoever you'd like to invite." Tears pooled in Teresa's eyes, but they didn't spill. "Lucy could come? Perhaps your friend will be coming, too?" Teresa glanced to Neilson.

Will nodded at him. "He's Lucy's bodyguard."

Lucy stood in shock. Will was actually talking to his stepmother. This could be good. He could find some peace with his family. Or this could be very, very bad. It could backfire. He could end up with deeper scars.

"You need a…body—guard?" Teresa's thick accent paused on the last word as though she examined it as she spoke.

"It's a long story. Will here seems to think I do, and Neilson is a barrel of fun, so I don't mind too much." Lucy forced a laugh.

Teresa and Will both stared at her.

"I see," Teresa said, very obviously not seeing.

"Lucy is a news anchor. She was assaulted. Now the man is stalking her. Neilson keeps her safe."

Huh. In four sentences he'd summed up nearly a year of her life.

Teresa reached a hand to her throat. "Oh dear."

"I'll talk to Lucy and let you know about dinner."

He hadn't said no.

"*Grazie*, William." Teresa stepped tentatively toward him. She raised a hand to his cheek, but stopped short of touching him.

He squeezed Lucy's hand so hard it hurt. "C'mon Luce. I'll walk you out."

Teresa locked her gaze on Will. "*Addio mio cucciolo.*"

"Teresa." He gave a polite nod and tugged Lucy behind him to the exit.

He never let go of Lucy as they hurried to Neilson's SUV. Neilson moved behind them at a good distance.

"Do you want to spend your birthday with your family?" Lucy asked.

"No." He swallowed roughly.

"Then let's have dinner. Just us." She reached to brush a lock of hair from his forehead. "I can bake you a cake. I'm a decent baker."

It was really hit or miss, but he didn't need to know that. She'd figure something out if her cake was a bust.

He opened the backseat passenger door for her.

"It'll probably be from a box. The cake, I mean." She climbed inside.

"I can live with that." His dimples flashed.

She buckled her seatbelt. "It'll still be good."

Probably.

"I have no doubt." He leaned down to kiss her a quick goodbye.

"Do you think I should just order you one from a bakery?" she asked when he broke the kiss.

He grinned. "No."

"Okay, but you've been warned."

He chuckled, but it didn't reach his eyes. She could sense him detaching. The exchange with Teresa had done damage, and there was nothing Lucy could do about it.

———

Will was early for his birthday party. Well, it was just her, a cake, and dinner reservations.

That counted as a party, though. She was pretty sure.

Lucy glanced around at the powdered sugar-covered kitchen and back to the cake. She leaned her head a bit to the right. It was almost level.

"Luce?" Will called from the living room.

"Hey, Will." She stuck her head around the corner. Like always, her breath caught at the sight of him. "Happy birthday to you..." she sang, mostly off-key.

He grinned at her. "You've been busy."

"Your cake's finished." She glanced at her frosting-smeared apron. "Had a little bit of a powdered sugar explosion."

"What's all this?" He gestured to the three boxes delivered by courier a few hours ago.

"They came for you. I figured you were expecting them."

He frowned at the packages. "No."

"Mr. Covington, tomorrow?" Neilson had become such a part of her days, Lucy tended to forget he was around.

"Thanks for staying with Lucy." Every day Will and Neilson said exactly the same thing. Afterward, Neilson would leave, Will would kiss her, and she'd do naughty, naughty things to him.

He didn't go straight to her today. Instead, he pulled the tape from the first box and opened it up. He removed a worn football and tossed it in the air before setting it gently on the sofa. "My stuff from when I was a kid."

Lucy came behind him, ran a hand around his waist, and pressed her cheek against his back. "Teresa?"

"I guess so. Probably."

"You okay?"

He moved so his arms were around her. "Yeah. I am."

Together they unpacked the boxes of knickknacks and memories. She laughed at the stories he told about each object, learning more of the enigma of Will, uncovering truths about his past.

Lucy caught sight of a young Will in a stack of photos near the bottom of one of the boxes. She ran her finger along the edge. In the image, a teenage Will with an earsplitting grin stood next to a woman with the same expression. His mother? He had her eyes.

His father stood behind them. Will looked exactly like his father—minus the gray hair and the lines around his eyes. It was like a glimpse into Will's future. His father leaned against Will's truck. It was much newer back then, but still hadn't come straight from the Ford showroom floor.

"Is this your mom?" Lucy asked.

He glanced at the photo, and his expression gentled. "Yeah,

that's Mom, right after Dad and I fixed up the truck. I saved up for it. It was the first thing I ever bought for myself."

Lucy squeezed his hand. He went back to unpacking the box in front of him.

"Your mom's beautiful."

His throat worked. "Yeah."

Lucy set the picture aside with the other photos so they could be framed.

"Whose is this?" She tugged a blue lace bra from under the stack of photos.

He had the decency to blush when he snatched it out of her hand.

"Let's not talk about that." He rose to toss it in the trash bin.

She should've been jealous. Should've gotten angry. Surprising herself, she laughed. "Do you keep trophies from all your conquests?"

"No." He kissed her forehead. "Would you believe me if I told you I have no idea where that came from?"

"No." She giggled again.

Before she could process what happened, his body covered hers.

"I don't want to think about who that belonged to. The only thing I want to think about is this." He ran a hand up her shirt, over the cup of her own lacy bra. Her whole body buzzed with arousal. "And who *it* belongs to." Desire flared in his eyes.

They fooled around on the couch like teenagers, kissing, groping. Everything she'd wanted to do with him when she was seventeen. When things heated past the point of no return, he carried her to the bedroom.

———

This was a spectacular day to turn thirty. William couldn't help the smirk forming on his lips. For the second time that day, he was inside Lucy. Astride him on her knees, she moved, giving him the birthday present she promised.

Her.

Naked.

He ran a hand down her belly to where they were joined. Eyes glassy, she fell to her elbows, panting against his mouth.

If today was any indication of the future, his thirties would be a fantastic decade.

He stroked her hips and buried himself deeper.

She closed her eyes, leaned back, and smiled. He groaned.

In one smooth motion, he twisted her to her back, thoroughly enjoying the little *O* of surprise her mouth made before he drove home. She hitched a leg over his hip, pushing into him farther—moving with him harder, faster.

"So beautiful." He slipped his thumb between them, tracing the line of her belly to the soft spot between her legs.

Her breaths quickened, then her muscles clenched around him, pulsing rhythmically as she arched. He relished the intensity as she finished. And then he followed. He dropped his forehead to the pillow beside her and let himself go.

They were both breathing heavily when he lifted up on an elbow.

"Hey." He ran his fingers through her hair.

"Hey to you, too." She snuggled into him, wrapping her arms around his back and tracing little circles there. "Happy birthday."

He smiled. "Best birthday ever." Sometime during the past week he'd fallen ass over elbow for her. The lens on the camera of his life unexpectedly focused, as though he'd been seeing the world through a filter. Now, with her there, he didn't need the filter any longer. Sharp reality wasn't quite so cutting with her around.

She hadn't stopped harassing him about putting her on camera. He hadn't budged. No, he refused to put her at risk.

"I didn't even give you your gift," she murmured.

"Thought you just did."

Between the bedroom activities and the lopsided cake in the kitchen, she had her bases covered. Speaking of bases... He ran a hand over her breast. She swatted his hand and leaned across the bed to the nightstand. He ran a hand over her ass. If she showed it off, the least he could do was appreciate it.

She tossed him a small box and grinned huge. "Here it is."

"You got me a box."

"Open it." She snuggled against his chest.

How could he say no to that?

The brown ribbon slipped off easily.

She nudged him with her elbow. "Keep going." She bit at her lip the way he adored so much. "They're kind of from Mitzy, too, but mostly from me because I paid for them and shopped for them. Well, Neilson shopped with me. But he didn't say anything or pay for anything, so he doesn't count." She leaned in, her full attention on the box as he lifted the lid.

Settled in the box were two gunmetal silver cufflinks, embellished with smiling cats. They had yellow gemstone eyes.

He chuckled. "You bought me cufflinks…shaped like cats. You shouldn't have."

She punched his shoulder. "They're sentimental."

"Yeah?" He raised an eyebrow at her.

"Okay, clearly you don't get it," she said, deflated.

Nope. He was pretty certain he didn't. He shook his head.

"That night when we found Mitzy? I thought these would be a reminder of that first night. How we started."

He stared at her, his beautiful Lucy. A woman who bought him cat cufflinks for his birthday because they were sentimental. His heart thudded against his chest. He hadn't only fallen for her. He'd fallen *in love* with her.

"Forget it. I thought they were fun. I'll get you something else." She reached for the box, but he grabbed her hand, tangling his fingers with hers.

"They're perfect. Absolutely perfect." He kissed each fingertip on her hand, loving how her mouth fell open and her breath hitched.

"You don't have to wear them. They're silly. I just tho—"

He held a thumb to her lips. "They're you. Totally you, Princess.

I love them." *And I love you.* He swallowed the words, unsure if she was ready to hear them. Uncertain if he was ready to say them.

"We should go," she finally said, breaking whatever spell he'd been under. "Reservations and all that."

"After I get dressed and put on my brand new cat-inspired cufflinks. Then we can go." He winked at her. "Do they light up or anything? Because if they did, that would be amazing."

"I'm never buying you anything again." She sat up in a huff, grabbing the top sheet to her breasts, but he snagged her around her waist and pulled her back to him. She fell against him with a small *oof*.

"Every year for my birthday, I'm expecting something as perfect as these. Cat cufflinks are going to be hard to beat, though." He kissed her intently. The best birthday present he'd ever received.

"You ready for the big day?" Lucy came to the kitchen to find Will absorbed in a pile of files; his forehead creased in concentration. The sun wasn't even up yet.

He frowned and slid his thumb across the screen of his phone. "I am."

Will's birthday the day before was fun. The entire night had been amazing. Somehow they'd even managed to make it to the restaurant for dinner. Today, well, today was back to reality.

Warmth settled in her chest. He was so handsome, and he was hers.

For now.

Her fingers itched to smooth the lines along his forehead. "Did you sleep at all last night?"

Around one that morning he'd left the bed and hadn't returned.

"No. Too much on my mind." He had made a pot of coffee sometime in the night. He'd been taking care of little things like that all week. She melted into a puddle of caffeinated gratitude each time she found her favorite mug set out.

She glanced longingly at a slice of chocolate birthday cake for breakfast, but poured herself some coffee instead. "Things all ready for the press conference?"

Today's public announcement of him as the new owner of Crestone was, in his words, *a big deal*. Executives from the dozens of stations he now owned would attend along with the regional press.

She leaned a hip against the table.

His scowl deepened. "Yeah."

"Everything okay?" She tapped his shin with her toe. "You're kind of lost over there."

"Another problem with Colorado Springs. Think I'll need to leave tonight for a day or so. How do you feel about a trip over the mountain?" He glanced up. His concerned expression thawed when he caught her gaze.

"I have to work tomorrow." She had already found a replacement for her morning show today so she could help out at the press conference. Two days would be pushing it.

He tugged her to his lap, another small intimacy she loved.

She traced her fingers along the curve of his cheek and stopped at the dimple. Anticipation flashed in his eyes when she leaned her mouth to his, initiating make-out session three of the morning.

"You taste well caffeinated." He jerked at the tie on her robe and ran a hand along her waist. She smiled against his lips as he trailed his fingertips up under her *Keep Calm and Rub Some Bacon on It* T-shirt.

"You're trying to distract me, so I'll agree to come on your trip, aren't you?" She adjusted her position on his thighs.

"I happen to know your boss won't mind if you take the day off." He winked and ran his hand around her back to bring her closer.

"I can't. As long as I work at the station, you're not my boss. You're my boss's boss. Or whatever." She snuggled into him. "It's also inappropriate for us to discuss work when your hand is up my shirt."

He chuckled. "This is the best time to discuss anything. Your temperament is so much sweeter when my hands are on you."

She couldn't argue with that. Still, this was important. He got the message because he slipped his hand away.

"No special girlfriend treatment at work," she said, seriously.

He tucked a hunk of hair behind her ear. "Now who's the one that isn't fun?"

"I've got to stay here tomorrow, do my job. All that." She stood. "You won't be gone long."

He waited for a beat. "I'm not comfortable being so far away from you with that guy out there."

"This is going to be our reality for a while, right? You'll have meetings all over, and I can't go with you every time. Besides, Robbie hasn't even tried to contact me. I think he gave up."

Will hesitated, but the truth remained—Robbie had never gone this long without contact. After the flowers, she'd expected he would find ways to communicate, like before. It had been over a week with nothing.

Will's gaze held hers. "Then Neilson will stay the night with you. Please."

Even if she didn't want Neilson there, arguing was futile. If Will wanted Neilson to stick around, he would hire Neilson. Lucy had grown to like the guy, so he might as well hang out and not talk with her instead of freezing on the porch where Will would likely have him stand guard if she balked.

"'Kay."

Will tapped out a message on his phone. "I'm also visiting our friend Max, so he'll understand I don't need those little blue pills he gave me. Not looking forward to that one."

"Why?" she asked.

"My attorney's idea. I'll explain why we were really at Twin Lakes. If that doesn't work, at least I'll officially be a patient. Then he can't legally say anything about my health. One quick, uncomfortable visit, and that's done."

Hell. What would a visit like that entail?

"I'm so sorry. I totally screwed up with that whole mess."

He tossed his phone on the table and stood, stretching his arms over his head. "It's working out. Don't be sorry anymore."

"I can totally vouch there are no problems in that department." Her cheeks heated.

He kissed her forehead and moved to the sink to rinse his plate.

"What's this?" He raised a thick manila envelope of pictures they hadn't gone through yet from the counter.

"The last of the stuff from your boxes."

"Huh." He ripped open the envelope and flipped through them.

Her mug barely made it to her lips when he stilled, peering closer at one of the photos. He stared at a photo in his hand, not looking up.

"What's wrong, Will?" She set her cup back on the table.

He raised his gaze to her, squinted, and then glanced at the photo again.

"This is impossible." His eyebrows pinched when he frowned.

"What?" she asked.

He didn't respond, only ran a hand over his neck.

"Will, what's not possible?" she tried again.

He glanced at her, then back to the photo.

"You're starting to scare me." The rubber-covered feet of her chair squeaked against the linoleum as she scooted away from the table.

A vein in his forehead started to throb.

"Wi—"

"*Lulu.*"

The emphasis on her childhood name stopped her short. What was he so pissed about?

"Wi—"

"Is there something you should've told me, *LuluBelle*?" He dropped the stack of photos on the table beside her plate and pointed to the one on top—a cast and crew photo from the reality show in Florida.

Hurt played across his face, the tick in his jaw working as he clenched his teeth.

Oh, God.

"W-what're you talking about?" She rushed to her feet, bumping her toe on the leg of the table.

"That's you. On the left." His eyes flamed with determination.

It was. He knew.

"All the games of *Confessions*, all the times we talked, you never said a word," he accused.

She reached for the image, and everything inside her crumbled to pieces.

The photo from that summer burned her fingertips. The picture had been taken a few days before he left, a week or so before they wrapped filming. He was handsome and fun-loving with his arm around a blonde. Jealousy pooled inside Lucy as it had all those years ago. The blonde woman was flashing him a knowing smile, and he had his head thrown back, laughing.

Lucy stood alone on the other side of the image. Unwanted. Invisible.

"Will... I..."

"You're the caterpillar," he said in disbelief.

Caterpillar? The word pierced straight through her heart, and the little bits of herself she'd held together over the years crushed the breath from her lungs.

Will had never used that awful nickname before—not once— even when it had followed her that summer to Florida. She'd been ridiculous enough to keep a diary, and she'd written about the name. Her roommate in Florida had been another bully in her life and shared that tidbit with the rest of the crew. The stupid nickname had been a part of who she was until she met Katie. She'd burned the diary and built a new life. But all the years Lucy had spent knitting together her self-confidence turned to ash right there in the tiny kitchen in Camelot.

"I can't believe you lied to me." His tone was careful, controlled.

She raised a hand to her mouth. They stood there, staring, saying nothing, her heart breaking.

"I need a minute," he said. Then he turned on his heel and stalked out of the room, leaving her alone with the photo.

Lulu...Caterpillar.

Her eyes fixed on the disastrous picture that spelled the end of who they'd become together. She swallowed the fear rising in her throat as anxiety she hadn't experienced in weeks wrapped around her.

The tight vise around her insides gripped harder. Tears pricked the edges of her eyes, but she refused to let them fall. He was the one who hadn't recognized *her*.

Lucy pressed her fingers against her eyelids as the shock drained away, leaving only pain.

She walked calmly toward the bedroom, the slow movement at odds with the raging emotion inside. He leaned against the wall in the hallway, arms crossed, his gaze on his socks, in a posture of intense reflection.

"I'm not a caterpillar."

At her monotone words, he glanced up. She studied him for a moment, unable to find any trace of warmth. Once more, reality had invaded her cocoon of happiness.

Of course, he wouldn't want her anymore. No one ever wanted a stupid caterpillar. Now that he remembered, he would never look at her the same.

"Don't ever call me that again." She tore the image in half and threw it on the floor at his feet.

The pain reflected in his eyes matched her own.

"How do you think it felt that you didn't remember me? I even told you my name, and you still didn't get it. You wanted this." She pointed to herself. "You only wanted the improved version. Not the awkward girl I used to be."

The anger coming from him began to fall away. "Luc—"

She waved a hand in front of him. "Oh no. You don't get to 'Luce' your way out of this. I guess you're right about people. Change your appearance, and they only see what they want to see. You didn't want to see *that*." She shoved a finger toward the ripped photo at his feet. "So you didn't."

"Lu—"

"And it stung. But I realized we were both people we didn't

want to be back then, so we should just move forward."

He rested his hands against his hips. "I never pretended to be something I'm not."

A film of sweat formed under her arms, and her heart raced. He could not be for real.

"No? You sure about that? You've done the exact same thing. Pretending to be a consumer reporter at KDVX when you're about to be everyone's boss." She kept going, the words flowing with anger. "Looks like in eight years neither of us has really changed."

He sucked in a breath. "That's pretty low."

"You've got places to be. Places that aren't here." She tried to slip past him.

He stepped in front of her, blocking the small hallway. "Why didn't you tell me?"

She crossed her arms across her chest. "It doesn't matter now."

"Why, Luce?" he practically growled the words.

"You should go."

He moved toward her. "Lucy, *why*?"

They'd finish this now—then he would go. She took a breath. "I didn't want you to remember because I was hiding. I didn't want my past to follow me here." The word *caterpillar* echoed through her brain, taunting her. "Then, when we got close and you didn't remember, it stung. I knew if you remembered, you'd only see that girl when you look at me."

He cussed and glanced away.

She ground her heel into the disastrous image, slammed the door to the bedroom, and stripped off her robe. A sob desperately tried to escape from the depths inside her. She swallowed it down. *Caterpillar.* Never, *never* would she have expected him to join the crowd of bullies who spent years tormenting her. Like Robbie…like everyone she'd ever known. Their only purpose remained to hurt her any way they could. Robbie broke her arm. Bones healed, though. Will broke her heart. The fracture wouldn't mend.

Tears are a luxury girls aren't afforded. Her mother's words echoed in her mind.

She crossed her arms over her breasts, embarrassed. Ashamed. The bathroom door stood ajar. She snatched a handful of clothes from the dresser and turned the lock behind her.

She.

Would.

Not.

Cry.

With nowhere to go, she turned on the shower, ready to wash away Will's scent. Wash away her pain. Wash away the world.

"Luce?" he called through the thin door.

She refused to answer him.

A firm knock against the door.

No.

She gripped her fingers tight to keep her hands from shaking.

The shower warmed, and she climbed in, raising her face into the stream. It dissolved any semblance of armor remaining. Like cotton candy dropped in a lake, the dam around her emotions disintegrated and every unshed tear she'd ever held inside released.

She stood there, unmoving, until the hot water ran out and a cold, angry stream spiked against her skin. She didn't turn it off. The freezing water rinsed away her warm tears.

Another knock sounded against the door—this time louder than before.

"I have to go, Lucy." Will rattled the doorknob. "Neilson's here. I... It's almost time for the press conference." He paused. "I have to go."

She didn't answer.

"Lucy, say something. I can't leave like this."

She finally shut off the water, wrapped a towel around herself, and cracked the door.

"The woman I realized that I love kept something from me and I didn't take that well," he said. "I'm sorry."

The woman I love... The words were an anchor holding her in place. People didn't love her. She wasn't built for that.

"You love me?" she asked, opening the door.

He crossed his arms and blew out a breath. "Yeah, Luce. I love you."

"You can't," she said, disbelieving. "No one loves me. I'm not that kind of person."

"What kind of person's that?" His expression turned serious. Well, more serious.

She opened her mouth but the words wouldn't come. She cleared her throat and tried again. "The kind people love."

"Didn't get that memo." He searched her face, but she had no idea what he could possibly be seeking.

No, he couldn't love her. "You only think you love me. It's just an illusion. I don't... I don't think I can do this, Will."

He tried to open the door. "Can't do what?"

She held the door firm, so there was only a sliver of opening. "This. Us. Love. I... I don't know how."

"We'll work through it. Just... keep Neilson with you today. So I know you're okay." He didn't say anything more when he tugged the door shut.

She took her time, rubbing a towel against her chilled skin, combing her frozen hair.

They were done. It was time to leave Confluence. She'd send out her resume tape immediately. It was old, but it would have to be her ticket out of here.

Stupid caterpillar...

She firmed her resolve, held the pieces together, and stepped from the bathroom. The room was quiet.

Good. She wiped at her cheeks.

He'd gone.

She needed a plan.

Robbie could follow her wherever she went. She didn't care. She wouldn't live in fear of him anymore, and she definitely wouldn't stay here. She clenched her fists with determination.

She'd make some calls and ask for favors. If she took precautions, there was absolutely no reason she couldn't be onscreen again to do the job she loved so much.

CHAPTER
TWENTY-FIVE

Lucy stuck around the newsroom with Reid, both of them the only staff left at the station. Everyone else had either gone off on various assignments or disappeared upstairs to rub elbows with the network executives.

The time for the press conference to start came and went.

Lucy didn't attend.

Will needed to focus, and the last thing he needed was Lucy distracting him. That's what she'd told herself anyway.

After the announcement and questions, they would have a big VIP party for the Crestone executives. Lucy wouldn't be there, either. She would hang out in the newsroom and help the night producer once the stories came in. Perhaps she and Reid could order a pizza. He'd taken it personally upon himself to teach her inappropriate jokes. Maybe she'd even laugh today. It beat sulking at home.

Neilson stood guard at the KDVX entrance, he disappeared into his surroundings better than anyone she'd ever known. And back in the day, she'd been pretty darn good at disappearing into the wallpaper.

She rose to grab the scripts off of the printer. The phone rang. Reid grabbed the receiver.

The police scanner crackled. She turned it up. "Car two five.

195

Dispatch. Car two five. Attend six-five-four Rivers Drive for multiple reports of animal—"

"Lucy?" Reid called from across the newsroom.

Lucy clicked off the scanner and rolled the chair away from her desk so she could see him. "What's up?"

"We've got a situation." Reid placed the phone back in the cradle. "An alligator's loose in the river."

Lucy shook her head dramatically. "I'm sorry. For a second I thought you said there was an alligator in the river."

Reid didn't laugh. "That's what I said."

"Quit joking around." She rolled back to her desk.

"It's not a joke."

Okay, so he was being totally serious.

"How would an alligator get in the Confluence River? Don't they need salt water?" She stood and propped an arm against the side of her cubicle.

"No idea. But a guy apparently lost an alligator—some kind of zoo transport. We just got a tip that it's in the river."

"Am I being punked?" She glanced around the empty room. Stranger things had happened on slow days in the newsroom.

"If you are, then I am. All the media is at your boyfriend's press conference, so we could get the exclusive if we hustle."

Her heart dropped at the mention of her "boyfriend."

"We could totally scoop them. Who do you want to send?" Reid asked.

"No one." She didn't want to call down a reporter. It would raise eyebrows if she pulled any of them away. The other news outlets in Confluence might start sniffing around.

She could do the job, and she didn't exactly have many options here, desperate times and all that. Besides, this was a plan—get on camera and get out of Confluence.

"How long since you practiced your photog skills?" She tossed a notepad in her purse and zipped it closed.

Mischief flashed across Reid's face. "You're going to scoop this, aren't you?"

Yes, she was. An alligator in the freaking river meant she was absolutely going to scoop it. If they got some video, a few interviews, this would be a great story. The kind a reporter would add to a demo reel.

"What do you say? You want to go rogue with me?" She hitched her purse over her shoulder.

"Been a while, but I think I can remember how to turn on a camera." Reid grabbed one of the camera bags and a tripod by the exit. "They said it went in near the Market at the trailhead. You driving or am I?"

Lucy grinned and snatched her press pass from her desk. "You're driving. Let's go find our gator."

"Hey Lucy, what's the difference between a crocodile and an alligator?"

"What?" She played along.

"No idea, but we're about to find out." He winked at her.

Lucy barely made it out the door when Neilson stepped in front of her. How the hell did he do that?

"No." He set his feet wider. "Not without me." He slid his aviators from the pocket of his polo shirt and propped them on the bridge of his nose.

"Fine." She jerked her thumb to her bodyguard. "We've got a third wheel."

"Better than a third nipple," Reid replied, deadpan.

When they arrived at the river, a small crowd had gathered around the edge of the water. A couple of uniformed police officers stood guard. Lucy distracted them with reporter questions while Reid slipped past.

He didn't waste any time. The camera was on his shoulder, rolling video immediately. It may have been a while since he lugged one around, but no one would ever guess.

The huge, muscled gator sat near the edge of the water ripping apart what appeared to be a giant chuck roast. Several police officers and three handlers in khaki shirts inched toward the escaped reptile. Reid kept a step behind them with the camera.

Neilson caught her arm as she moved to follow. "No," he muttered.

She had no time for this. "You're supposed to protect me from psychopaths, not reptiles."

He stood firm. "Negative."

Lucy glanced at the scuffle taking place by the water. An older man with white hair, dressed in head-to-toe khaki, looped a hook around the distracted gator's head. Then he hopped on the back of the six-footish reptile like a cowboy and held the beast tight. It took two more of them to straddle the head, hold the mouth closed, and wrap black electrical tape around the snout.

Reid remained only a breath away, getting the whole thing on film. Lucy gave mad props to him for not balking as the heavy tail thrashed near his feet. That video was going to be fantastic.

With the gator secured and placed back in its metal cage, Lucy clicked into reporter mode and collected sound bites.

"How did the gator escape from your vehicle?" she asked the lead handler.

The gator wrestler who had some kind of animal teeth strung on a necklace appeared ready to conquer the depths of the deepest jungle in camouflage cargo pants, brown work boots, and a khaki bush shirt.

"Weeeell, this isn't the first time ol' Jack here's made a break for it. First time he's ever made it outside the trailer. I figure we'll take 'em back to Florida. His travelin' days are through."

"What would you say to the people worried about Jack's well-being on the road?"

"I'd say if they're worried about 'em, then they don't know Jack." He smirked.

And there you had it. They didn't know Jack.

She wrapped up the interview, and the gator-wrestlers let her get close to the now-resigned-to-his-fate beast.

Neilson stood beside her, barely out of the shot. He took seriously a six-hundred-pound reptile with nature's version of body armor.

Lucy loved her job. This little adventure would move her forward, out of Confluence.

This was right, moving on. She played those words on repeat in her head—and would until she believed them.

She adjusted her collar and buttoned up her suit jacket before the green light of the camera turned on. Reid cued her, and she smiled her best I-know-what-I'm-talking-about grin into the lens. "It's a jungle out there, Confluence, but this big guy is on his way back to Florida tonight. Thanks to Jack's handlers and a few first responders, the Confluence River is safe once more. To Jack the alligator, all we have left to say is, 'Later Gator.'"

Intoxicated on adrenaline, they hurried back to the station to get the story ready for the evening news.

The station buzzed with preparation for the upcoming broadcast. She didn't have much time to put together the segment, so she plunked herself in an editing bay to clip the snippets of sound and video together. Her image filled the screens, and she lost herself in the little room. Everything in her hummed with elation when she added the final voiceovers. She tapped a few buttons, sending the story to be stacked into the show—just in time.

"Lucy, don't go crazy, but I posted some of our video online." Reid shifted from foot-to-foot just outside the editing room.

She glanced up at him. "What'd you post?"

"The gator wrestling and then your stand-up afterward when he kind of did the alligator I'll-be-back smile behind you, and you said, 'Later Gator.'"

She laughed. The beast had done a decent impression of Schwarzenegger—for an alligator.

The full story would be on the news in under an hour anyway.

"The thing is—" Reid shuffled uncomfortably again. "I have a bit of a following online and well…now the video is trending. There are already memes, too."

Lucy felt her eyes go wide.

"Only a few of them gave it a thumbs down. Totally impressive for a viral video like this." Reid waved a hand toward the monitor.

That was *so* not her concern right now because William moved behind Reid, and every muscle in Lucy's body went rigid.

His gaze went to the screen behind her.

He told her to assign the stories, not do them herself. She got that. But this wasn't exactly a situation that could wait.

Still, his eyes flared. A little vein in his forehead throbbed.

She didn't need to look to know her image was still there, where she'd paused it on the screen, the alligator smiling like a maniac in the background.

The blood in Lucy's head thrummed. At that moment she wanted to run. Wanted to hide. Wanted to scream into the nearest pillow. *Deep breaths*. This was work. Only work, even if it hurt like a million needles under her fingernails.

The wheels on her chair squeaked as she shoved away from the desk.

"Reid, give us a minute." Will jerked his head toward the hallway.

Reid, not an idiot, excused himself with a questioning glance at Lucy.

The heavy soundproofing on the walls of the editing bay seemed to close in on her. His voice and the word *caterpillar* echoed in her head. She shook it off. This was work. Not home. This was work and she'd done a damn good job for the station that afternoon.

She rallied her courage. "We got a tip and didn't want the other stations or the newspaper to get the scoop. If I called a reporter from upstairs, they would've noticed. Reid and I got the story. The end."

Kind of.

He pressed his lips together and gestured to the monitor. "Show me."

Lucy scooted her chair closer, pushed a few buttons, and played the video for him. He didn't relax, didn't show any expression. Exactly one minute later, the story finished on the alligator's funky smile.

Sheesh, not even a lip twitch.

"You had no alternative but to go behind my back?" he asked without expression.

Well, sure, of course she had other options. None of them were good ones. "This was the best choice."

He remained silent.

She should probably lay it all out. Break all the news at once. Tear off the bandage in a single sweep. "There's more."

"You said 'the end' before. I'm understanding 'the end' is not 'the end'?"

"Reid posted some of the video online, and it's gone viral." She spit the words out as fast as she could.

He rubbed at his forehead. "How viral?"

"I'm not sure there are levels of viral. I found out right before you came in. That's all I know." She nearly added, "Forgive me, Father, for I have sinned." She wasn't particularly religious, but right now, a bit of divine intervention would be good.

"To be clear, I said not to do this exact thing because I don't want anything to happen to you. And the video is now being viewed all over the world?"

She gnawed at her lip. "It would seem so."

Eyes fixed on the monitor, William didn't say a word. Like he was on the precipice of deciding if he was angry because she hadn't listened, or pleased because his station got the scoop on a big story.

She continued, "Look, things happened today that ended up with me reporting a story. The video and the reporting, they're good. I'm not saying that because I was involved. I'm saying it because the end result is amazing. I didn't mean for my face to be all over the internet. I didn't mean to upset you. I didn't mean to have my picture turned into a meme."

"What kind of meme?" Will broke his stare from the monitor back to her.

She grabbed her phone and brought up a browser. A few keywords entered into the search engine and yup— reporter Lucy, standing in front of the smiling Arnold Schwarzenegger alligator. This one said, "They told me I could be anything, so I became an... Investi*gator*." She handed the phone to him.

He studied the screen, tapping through the variations of what the internet was currently finding hilarious. "You're kidding me."

"I wish."

He puffed his cheeks and let out a long breath. "What's a 'Shenanigator'?"

"No idea. The 'Later Gator' one is kind of funny, though. That's a pun on what I said in my stand-up."

No response.

"I was only trying to get the story, Will." She took her phone back and slipped it in her pocket.

"You wanted to be bait." His words were raw with intensity.

"Oh, my God. Seriously? No. I didn't want to be *bait*. I don't *want* a lunatic following me. I don't want any of that. What I *want* is to do what I was born to do."

He flinched, his expression turning lax.

"Maybe we just need a little space to process everything," she suggested.

"You'll get it while I'm in the Springs." His frustration vibrated in the air around them. "All the space."

Parker's voice cut through the air. "William, we've got a situation."

Will closed his eyes and counted to three under his breath. "This day is just full of those. What now?"

Parker walked toward them with intent. "News was short on content today, so Lucy's story ran at the top. National picked it up as the kicker to the evening news."

Oh.

She stilled.

William squeezed her shoulder. "You don't do things halfway, do you?"

She couldn't move with the rushing in her ears overwhelming all thought.

Her story had hit the national evening news.

———

The funny thing about living your dreams is that afterward life still goes on. She made the national evening news. Will wasn't happy about it, but he still had to leave for Colorado Springs.

Will had left his mother's letter propped on her kitchen counter. Lucy glanced at it again. The edges of her anger frayed further into forgiveness.

It made no sense. He had told her he kept it with him always, that it kept him centered, grounded. Why would he leave it behind as some cryptic message for her to decode?

"Do you have any eights?" Neilson asked from across the small Formica table.

"Go fish. Any twos?" Lucy replied, absently.

He handed her the two of clubs. She added the card to make a stack of twos and tossed them on the table. "You're a guy, right?"

"That depends," Neilson replied. "Any aces?"

"Go fish." Lucy scowled. "What does it depend on?"

"Your question," he replied, deadpan.

"I figured you might have some insight into the male mind." She organized the cards in her hand, rearranging them by number. "Any queens?"

His poker face remained in place. "Go fish."

"What do you think it means when a guy tells you he loves you?"

"That depends."

"On what?"

"He want in your pants?"

"No, for the purposes of our conversation, he's already in... Okay, you know what? Never mind." Lucy held up a hand.

Neilson grinned. "William?"

Yes, of course it was Will. "Maybe."

"Inappropriate for me to comment then."

"Okay, it's not him. It's a…I don't know…a guy named Ernie."

Neilson folded his cards in his hand and leaned back in his chair, tapping the edge of the cards on the table. "Hypothetically, a guy doesn't toss around the L-word without meaning it. *Unless* he wants in your pants. He's already in? Nothing to gain."

Lucy dropped her fist to the table in mock drama. "You *can* communicate with words."

"On occasion." Neilson waved a hand over the table. "Any kings?"

"Go fish," she mumbled.

"Still irritated at him?" he asked.

"It's subsiding. I'm tired, though. Think I'll call it a night." She yawned and tossed the rest of her cards down. "Thanks for keeping me company."

She rose to clear their dishes to the sink while he put the cards back in the box.

"Lucy."

She raised her head to look at him.

He smiled at her, a real, honest to goodness with teeth and everything smile. "Ernie's lucky."

He must've meant it. Neilson didn't use many words, but when he did, they counted.

"That might be the nicest thing anyone's ever said to me."

Her phone rang from the counter next to Will's mother's letter.

"That's probably Ernie," she said, glancing to the display. Yep.

"Answer it?" Neilson nodded to the phone as it rang again.

She took a fractured breath and wandered from the room. Some things hadn't changed. She would still be leaving soon, but tatters were all that remained of her anger. He was right. They needed to talk when he got back without her temper making an appearance.

Lucy clicked it on and put it to her ear. "Will."

"I know you probably don't want to talk to me, but I had to see if you were okay."

"I'm okay," she replied.

He paused. "I didn't expect you to answer."

"I chatted with Katie. Then Neilson and I had a talk—it helped."

"Yeah?"

"Neilson's a surprisingly good listener."

"I'm glad," he said softly.

She climbed onto the bed and picked at a stray string on the orange comforter. Neither of them said anything.

"Your mom's letter is here. I thought you might be missing it, but it's on the counter."

"Keep it safe for me, yeah?" His voice muffled a little.

"I can do that." The thread she pulled on the blanket unraveled.

Normally, aside from her angry tirade this morning, things had been easy between them. Tonight everything was…stilted.

"I checked in with Jeff," he said. She could practically see him running his hand over his head, like he did when he talked about anything to do with Robbie.

"Any news?"

"Apparently, you beat out grumpy cat and that guy from the beer commercial for top new memes tonight. Jeff's been following your online fame."

"Will—"

"No break in the case, but Jeff's hopeful, given your exposure, it'll attract Robbie from wherever he's been the last weeks."

She didn't respond. What could she say to that? There was no joy in the idea that Robbie would show up again. She wanted him caught, sure, but not because he would come for her again.

"Do you have meetings tomorrow?" she asked, changing the subject.

"Mmm hmm." He sounded distracted. Papers rustled in the background over the line.

"I'll let you get to that then." She shifted the phone to her other ear.

"Princess?" he asked.

"Hm?"

"See you later alligator."

She grinned. "After a while, crocodile."

He chuckled. "I love you."

Nothing to gain.

Another long interval passed, neither of them saying more. She could tell he was still with her by his breath in the receiver and the subtle background sounds in his hotel room. Could she love him? It didn't seem possible. No. She'd never opened herself up that way before and she had no idea how to do it now.

"I'm so sorry," she finally whispered.

She really, really was.

CHAPTER
TWENTY-SEVEN

William had managed to condense days of lengthy executive meetings in Colorado Springs down to hours. He still hadn't quite solved the puzzle of how to keep the merger without putting a bunch of people out of work.

For now, things were stable with the acquisition, and he'd figure it out. But he needed to get home. Sort out the mess with Lucy. He hadn't handled things well. He'd been pissed. They could sort it out. He knew they could.

Fine, so he messed up when he found the photo. There was time to fix everything. Admitting anything else wasn't an option—even if she wouldn't answer her phone.

Being away, even for only a day, had shown him he had fallen hard for her.

Now he just had to tell her.

Leather briefcase slung over his shoulder, he hurried to his truck parked across the lot at what would soon be the flagship station for Crestone.

"William!"

He glanced up as one of the Colorado Springs executives he had met with rushed toward him.

"Jim." William nodded as the older man came closer. "Everything okay?"

"It is." Jim clapped him on the back. "Wanted to catch you before you left town."

Jim had been the lead troublemaker on the buyout, waffling back and forth. They had made headway today, though.

"Looks like it'll be a tough road on this merger." William glanced around the lot again.

Sadness played across Jim's face. He jerked his head toward the building behind him. "This station's been in my family for three generations. A lot of good people have worked here for years."

William waited, understanding that Jim needed to say whatever he came to say. He had to let Jim come to the conclusion the rest of the executives had already arrived at—Crestone was the best answer for everyone. Jim, unfortunately, was still holding firmly onto the past.

His Adam's apple bobbed in his wrinkled throat. "Think it might be time to let her go. You're a stand-up guy. I can see that now."

Damn, it was hard to witness a leader make the decision to give up everything his family had built. "I'll take good care of your company," William assured him.

"Wouldn't sign it away if I didn't believe that." Jim shifted slightly. "I hope you'll give our employees a chance to prove themselves."

"I can't promise anything. You know how these things go."

"Son, when you've been around as long as I have you'll find out there's always a different way. Usually a better way. Especially when you're talking about laying off good people. Brenda in accounting's got a sick husband. Tony, our master control operator, has six kids and shows up to work every morning at seven. On the dot. Twenty years. These are the people your merger puts out of work."

That was a knife to the heart. Jim was right. There had to be a solution that didn't leave all these people without jobs. William had been over it and over it, but there was no way he could keep them on once Crestone took over. The extra overhead made no sense and would drain the company.

And then it hit him like a brick over the head.

"What if you had an individual investor? This person comes in and infuses enough operating cash to get the station back on its feet. Can you convince the board to go for that?"

Jim's expression changed. "No investor's going to bet on a race horse that's losing."

"He will if the horse can win. And the people are worth it." William walked back to the building with Jim at his side. "This horse is a winner. I'm willing to bet my personal money on it. I'll need to have one of my guys here to watch over things. Make sure everything's on track."

"Fine." Jim clapped him on the back. "That'd be fine."

"You'll get me the votes?" William put his hand out.

This handshake agreement would mean more to Jim than any ink and paper ever would.

"I'll get those votes. There'll be a lot of relief all around." Jim squeezed his hand. "You've turned out well. Patricia did good with you."

"You knew my mom?"

If he wasn't mistaken, Jim's eyes misted over.

"That I did. Used to spend quite a lot of time with her and your dad, back before you were born."

William's parents had never mentioned Jim. "No kidding? I had no idea."

"Patricia was a good woman. Missed by many."

"She was…is." William cleared his throat.

"Know things haven't been easy since she died, but she'd be proud of you." Jim squeezed William's shoulder.

He swallowed a punch of emotion. Those words, spoken in that fatherly tone, meant everything. He had given up, long ago, hearing them from his own father. But this…well, strangely, it brought him peace.

"Thank you. I've ah…" William gestured to his truck. "Got some personal business."

"A special someone, eh?" Jim winked. "I'd know that look anywhere."

William jerked his chin to the building. "Let's get this done so I can get back to her."

———

Disbelief. Total shock. Lucy stopped the message, clicked replay, and listened again. She nearly had it memorized.

"Lucy, it's Carlos. Carlos from California. You remember me. Of course you do. Long time no talk. Hey, I saw your alligator spot. I was hoping I could convince you to come work with me again. I'm managing a station here in Ohio. I have a couple of positions available right now…a morning anchor position and a general assignment reporter. I'm hoping one of these might interest you. Would love to work together again. Call me."

She took a huge breath. Leaving Confluence would be her reality.

Numb, she started making a list of all she'd need to do before she made the move.

Stupid Caterpillar.

It was too late to return Carlos's call. She'd do it first thing in the morning, and start packing immediately.

In the meantime, she'd keep her chin up. Keep living her life. Which, at the moment, included taking out the trash.

She hefted the overfull bag from the plastic bin, turning her head away from the smell of three-day-old yogurt containers and the chicken she had never gotten around to cooking.

"No."

She jumped at the word and glanced up.

Neilson crossed his arms across his chest.

She glowered at him. "Stop doing that."

"Doing what?"

"Surprising me. Is it that hard to announce yourself?"

He raised an eyebrow at her. With his freaky ability to fade into the background of her life, he had probably been there the entire time.

"Trash day's tomorrow." She grunted as she heaved the heavy bag.

"No," he said again.

"Uh. Yes." She started past him, but he put his hand out to stop her.

"It's late. It's dark. No."

She set the bag down. "Don't care. It stinks. Yes."

No response.

"Look. If you won't let me, could you be a gentleman and take it out?"

Sheesh. She couldn't even take her trash out.

He glanced at the bag, made a bit of a face, and gestured for her to hand it over.

"You're the best bodyguard ever."

He lifted the bag and grabbed the box of recycling. "Anything else?"

"Nope. I'll get the door." She moved ahead of him and turned the lock. "Thanks for this. I'll bake you a cake or something."

"Lopsided cake." He smirked. "Mmm."

"Fine. No cake for you." She laughed as she swung open the door.

Neilson's expression went cold. He cursed and lunged for the gun at his side, dropping the trash and recycling so newspapers and milk jugs flew everywhere. He raised it, but two loud pops sounded, and he stepped backward on his heel, dropping his gun on the carpet.

"Neil—" Lucy stopped, her feet suddenly glued to that little strip of riveted metal separating the entryway linoleum and living room carpet.

The heavy scent of spent gunpowder overwhelmed the small room as two red splotches spread across Neilson's abdomen.

Neilson lurched forward at the man in the doorway. The thud of Neilson's fists connecting with soft tissue broke the quiet of the night, and a strange reality took hold.

The porch light illuminated a face she could never forget, and her breath caught. Robbie had shot Neilson. Oh, God. Another pop from the gun in Robbie's hand and Neilson grunted, but continued his assault.

The rushing in her ears overwhelmed all sense. The men tussled into the room, and the lamp on the end table toppled to the ground with a thump. The bulb snapped, and after a brief flash, it went out. Only the faint light from the kitchen and the porch remained, casting a bizarre glow onto the men.

She opened her mouth to scream, but sound wouldn't come. Her feet wouldn't budge. She wanted them to move, but they wouldn't go.

Neilson clutched his stomach, the shocking crimson liquid staining his hand.

"Run." He gurgled as blood trickled from his mouth down his chin. He didn't look at her, his focus on Robbie. Neilson stumbled forward using the force of his momentum to push Robbie backward, toward the kitchen, away from Lucy.

Lucy willed her legs to move, praying they would obey.

They did. But she didn't run away. She refused to leave Neilson alone with a maniac. Not after he took two bullets for her.

A piece of broken light bulb sliced her foot. Ignoring the pain, she grabbed the lamp base. Holding it high over her head, she brought it down hard against Robbie's skull, knocking him back. A trail of deep red blood ran along his temple.

He tossed an arm out and threw her against the wall. It cracked behind her. His meaty hand wrapped around her neck. Air wouldn't come. Her mouth opened and closed in a silent attempt to speak. Her grip on the lamp failed. It fell to the floor.

"I am not the enemy." He ground out the words and squeezed his thick fingers tighter. His vile breath played across her face—a sadistic combination of chewing tobacco, whiskey, and burned plastic. "Stop making me your enemy."

Bright stars danced in her vision. Neilson grunted, stood unsteadily, and reached for a pistol tucked in his boot. She turned her face away, unwilling to watch what came next. But Robbie dropped his hold and whirled on Neilson.

She collapsed to the ground, rough gasps escaping her throat. Another crack echoed through the room. Neilson fell backward, blood seeping into the carpet around him. He didn't move. Not even a twitch.

She choked on the stench of fresh blood, sulfur, and putrid chicken as she crawled the rest of the way to the doorway, desperate to get help.

Nearly there, her fingertips grazed the cold threshold.

She cried out when Robbie's arm came around her, lifting her and hauling her to his doughy chest.

"I wouldn't leave you," he rasped against her ear. "Could never leave you."

Bile rose in her throat as the pool of blood around Neilson grew. She kicked and bucked against the arm clenched around her middle.

"He needs an ambulance." Hot tears pooled in her eyes.

"We'll go somewhere I can take care of you. Where it'll just be you and me." Robbie dragged her to the kitchen and threw her against a chair. He grasped her hands together and secured them with a zip tie. "This is all for you Lulu. Don't fight me. I'm the good guy here." He ran his thumb along her lower lip and slid his finger under her chin, raising it to him.

The deranged glow in his eyes softened, and he ran his thumb along her lips again. "Shhhh. We'll be together."

She yanked at her hands. The ties were loose, but not enough for her to slip free.

"Please. Help him." Her desperate words fell on psychotically deaf ears.

He got intimately close to her face and rubbed his lips back and forth against hers until she turned her head away. He moved his mouth to her ear. "No."

Frantic, she searched for something, anything, to use as a weapon. Nothing.

Movement near the sink caught her attention.

Mitzy.

She wrenched her hands again. They had covered this in the self-defense class she took months ago. She pressed her wrists to face each other, like the instructor had demonstrated, and tried to force her hands free.

Nothing.

Lucy gulped back a sob as Mitzy snarled at Robbie and jumped on him from the counter, teeth bared.

He grappled with the cat and threw her against the window above the stove. Mitzy clutched the curtain with her claws, and it tumbled to the stovetop on top of her. She screeched a long wail and scampered from the counter. Lucy gasped in horror when Mitzy's back leg struck the loose knob, and it turned with a click. Fire erupted from the gas burner, melting the polyester curtain.

Robbie wiped blood from his head with the end of his T-shirt. He set his gun next to the sink and removed a large knife from the block on the counter.

She nodded to the stove and tried to keep herself calm. "The cupboards are on fire. Cut me loose. I'll put it out."

He ignored her.

She pressed her wrists together harder. The tie scraped over her knuckles. Frenzied, she wriggled her wrists to move the plastic farther. One hand barely slipped through, and then they were free. She tucked them against her legs so he wouldn't notice.

The saddest excuse for a smoke alarm chirped weakly as the smoke increased.

"Why do you fight me?" He turned the knife to the side, examining it. He ran the blade against his thumb, drawing blood. "I'm here to help you. Always here to help you. Now we can have everything together. You'll see."

Lucy gulped.

"You're mine now, and you're very…touchable." He moved his gaze purposefully along her body.

She held her hands together, hating how he stopped at her breasts and pursed his lips.

"Shouldn't have gone on television again. You know how that makes me feel."

"You're right. I made a mistake." Her gaze flitted to the curtains turning to flames on the stove. Hysteria tried to overtake her, but no way would she let Neilson bleed out in the other room because of her.

Robbie barked a crazed laugh. "That's why I have to teach you. You have so much to learn from me."

She rubbed at the raw skin on her wrist. "Don't make this worse. Please."

He lowered the knife a bit, and the way he looked at her, like he could see right through her, slashed her open, exposing every vulnerability she ever had. "Should've been mine. Everything's ruined now that the police are involved. Should've listened the first time I told you to stop sharing yourself with the world. I don't share."

"I-I'm sorry. I can still be yours."

"No. Not like I wanted. But we'll still be together. This time forever. No more people. No more running. I'll send you first. It'll be quick. Then I'll follow." Flames licked across the counter, rising up along the wall to the cabinets. Robbie didn't seem to notice. He kept his eyes fixed on her. "I'll be quick. Together forever. Like it always should have been." He raised the knife once more, his pupils huge and his face disturbingly blank.

Lucy glanced to the living room. "Please. Let me help Neilson. He's a good person. This doesn't have to end this way." Her heart hammered against her chest. She had to get to Neilson.

Neilson.

She blinked against reality. Neilson was bleeding. Damn if she would go out without fighting.

Robbie moved closer. "Hold still. I'll be fast. You won't feel much. Wait for me on the other side. I'll be right behind you. Promise you'll wait for me on the other side."

He was going to kill her. She couldn't let that happen.

One chance. She would only get one.

She focused on the knife.

Just a bit closer.

She'd do what Neilson did, take him by surprise and use his own momentum against him.

"It'll be okay. I promise." His eyes glazed, and he smiled.

He got close enough for her to smell his rancid breath. She clenched her eyes closed and shot out of the chair, ramming her shoulder into his chest. He fell toward the stove, screaming when his back hit the flames. The knife clattered to the ground. Her feet braced wide, she shoved him into the fire again.

"Lulu." He screamed her name, over and over.

She slammed her knee into the softness of his groin. He squealed a demented sound and dropped to the linoleum.

A sob ripped from her throat. She scrambled, grabbed the gun from the counter, and aimed at his chest. He writhed on the floor. The acrid scent of burning flesh, blood, and smoke filled the room. Her hands trembled. She shook her head and positioned the gun as her self-defense instructor had illustrated in class.

She steadied her aim. Flames danced in front of her as her finger twitched against the trigger.

CHAPTER
TWENTY-EIGHT

Sirens wailed in the distance. William broke into a full run to Lucy's apartment, trying to ignore the rising tide of panic in his chest. The door stood wide open, but no one was around. Something was very wrong.

He rushed across the entryway, and his heart stopped.

Smoke burned his nostrils. Neilson was mid-military crawl across the carpet, leaving an unmistakably gruesome red trail behind him. The light chirp of a smoke detector beeped in the kitchen.

William rushed to Neilson. Blood gurgled down his chin as he tried to speak. William turned him to his back, yanked off his own suit coat and held it against the man's seeping chest. "Where's Lucy?"

Neilson mouthed her name, pointing to the kitchen.

No.

William bolted to the kitchen. Plumes of filmy soot made it impossible to see more than a few feet ahead of him. He moved farther into the room, coughing into his hand as flames licked along the cupboards. Thick gray smoke tumbled from the burning wood. He nearly came apart when he found her holding a gun trained on Robbie.

William moved behind her, and she jerked away at his touch against her shoulder. He steadied her arm as the beefy guy squirmed on the ground, shrill, indiscernible sounds bubbling from his throat. Angry burns festered where his clothing fused with skin along his back.

"Lucy, give me the gun." William kept the words as even as he could.

"No. This has to end. He can't keep doing this to me." She coughed, and her finger shook dangerously against the trigger.

If she pulled that trigger, it would shred her.

"This isn't you. You aren't a killer." He moved his hand over hers. "It's time to give me the gun."

Her grip on the handle relaxed enough so he could slide it into his hand. He flipped on the safety and tucked it in the back of his waistband with a silent prayer of thanks that she hadn't followed through. Robbie continued to writhe on the ground, hideous sounds of pain and rage coming from deep in his throat.

His heart stopped beating. He couldn't lose her.

Smoke continued to fill the kitchen, the heat from the flames intense. She started to collapse against him. He wrapped his arm around her to hoist her against his chest. She sobbed. Cruel, wrenching sounds escaped from her small frame. He carried her from the apartment.

Lucy wheezed against his chest. A slippery, wet warmth oozed from her arm.

Adrenaline seared through him, and every muscle in his body clenched.

He had arrived too late. She was hurt.

Bitter guilt multiplied as he hurried down the steps to the little patch of lawn beside Dixie's apartment.

Dixie barked orders at some of the neighbors who had appeared while he was inside. They sprayed garden hoses at the burning building. Flames burst higher through the roof, unresponsive to their efforts.

"She's hurt." He laid Lucy on the grass next to where Dixie stood.

Dixie's eyes got huge, and she raised a hand to her mouth. "Lord in heaven."

He leaned close to her. "Luce, I have to go back for Neilson."

"M-m-itzy's in the house." Agonized tears in Lucy's eyes reflected the fire behind him.

"I'll get her," he promised.

"Will, no. You can't go back inside."

He wouldn't let her lose anything more. "I said, I'll get her."

"Her arm," William said to Dixie.

Dixie knelt beside her. "Ambulance is comin'."

"What? I'm not…" Lucy glanced down. "Damn. W-when did that happen?"

Robbie apparently got closer with the knife than she'd realized. Dixie tugged off her purple cardigan and held it against the gash. Lucy hissed. William went rigid, ready to finish off the guy he had left writhing in the kitchen.

The jarring bleat of a fire engine got louder.

Dixie smoothed Lucy's matted hair and jerked her chin at William with a glance to the burning building.

"I'll hurry," he whispered to Lucy.

It took everything in him to leave her there and bolt back inside. One of the men with a hose hollered at him to stop. But he didn't listen.

Soupy, black smoke met him at the entry. Stumbling into the room and squinting against the filmy soot nearly brought William to his knees.

A sizzling explosion from the kitchen shifted the foundation. William coughed against a surge of smoke. Another crash rained debris around him. His heart ricocheted against his ribs. The kitchen ceiling had caved in.

He pulled Neilson to the door where three firemen in full gear met them at the porch. William handed over Neilson and headed back into the house for the damn cat.

A gloved hand tried to stop him, but he shoved it away. "A guy in the kitchen needs help," he yelled over the sirens.

They could get Robbie.

He would find Mitzy and get out.

Lucy loved her. He loved Lucy. The thought shifted the foundation of more than the apartment. It shifted the foundation of his life.

He loved her.

So by some convoluted formula, it was his responsibility to ensure the cat survived.

Heat scorched his lungs as he made his way by memory through the house, avoiding the collapsed section near the kitchen. He lifted the bottom of his shirt to cover his mouth. The biting metallic scent of Lucy's blood met his nostrils. His shirt was covered with it. He shook his head, unwilling to process anything other than Mitzy.

Save the fucking cat.

She generally hid under Lucy's bed. He hoped to hell she stayed true to form as he crawled through the bedroom, his lungs convulsing against the smoke.

"Here kit-ty kit—" A violent cough erupted from his chest. He squatted to run a hand under the bed.

Nothing.

"Mitzy, come on." He hissed every curse word he could come up with. "Lucy needs you."

He fell against the overheated wall. Once more he swiped his arm under the bed. Soft fur and sharp claws met his hand.

There. He had her.

He grasped a leg and pulled her from under the bed. She hissed and spit, sinking her teeth into the soft pad of his hand.

And then, because he was clearly in the Twilight zone of burning hell, she glared at him with pissed-off yellow cat eyes until something close to understanding passed over her mangled, furry face. Despite the fact that flames seared the walls around them, or maybe because of it, she nuzzled into him.

Yes, she was definitely the Devil's spawn.

"You owe me for this." He held her tight against his bloodied shirt.

The foundation rocked and groaned. Flames licked around the corner into the room, smoke billowing around the doorframe. Stifling heat seized his lungs when he stood, and he was pretty sure he inhaled a few sparks. He wasn't getting back out through the door. His lungs screamed for oxygen.

Damn. He could not pass out.

He glanced at the window—his only option.

Holding the cat, he kicked the window as hard as he could. The thin pane of glass shattered.

"Here!" someone outside shouted.

The cat secured in one hand, he grabbed the comforter and wrapped it around his other before he punched against the remaining glass fragments. Mitzy did not like this apparently cruel treatment. She dug her claws into the muscles of his chest and attempted to launch herself away.

Despite her persistent abuse, he passed her through the opening to waiting hands outside.

Mitzy was pissed. He didn't care. She was alive.

"Lucy," he rasped as the flames licked the walls around him.

———

Where was Will? Goose bumps popped up along Lucy's arm as she shivered and searched the unfolding scene for him.

"They're running over hell's half-acre over there." Dixie tucked another blanket around Lucy's shoulders.

"Will hasn't come out yet," Lucy whispered.

"He will. Mitzy's readin' him the riot act, I figure."

The paramedics and a fireman loaded Neilson into an ambulance. The lights flashed, and with a brief lonely wail of the siren, it drove away. No Will.

He'd gone for the cat. Her cat.

She fought against the stinging pain in her arm—it hurt like a *sonofabitch*. A medic had transferred her to a gurney outside the second ambulance and now examined the slash.

Dixie squeezed her hand and murmured low. Lucy couldn't make out what she said because nothing mattered but Will in that burning building.

Flames had spread to Will's apartment. Huge hoses attached to the fire hydrant near the road sprayed torrents of water over everything. The fire was winning, burning it all into a heap of metal and wood.

"Get Chief Lawson over here," a fireman called out the door to another near the truck. "We've got a body."

Lucy's breath seized, and she tried to get off of the stretcher.

"Keep her still," the medic said to Dixie.

Dixie pressed her against the pillow, holding firm while he attached white gauze to the wound. Lucy jerked and bit her lip against the sharp pain. "Will's dead."

Dixie gripped her hand tight. "Hush your mouth."

Lucy closed her eyes to the silent tears. An unfamiliar hurt unleashed a flood of torment and remorse within her. This couldn't be real. She opened her eyes and stared blankly into the night.

"Butter my butt and call me a biscuit," Dixie murmured.

Lucy turned her head. It took a moment to focus against the flurry of activity all around the building. Will walked toward her, covered in soot.

Her breath caught. A ticked-off Mitzy struggled in his arms. Their eyes met, and she didn't move her gaze from his until he was close enough so she could stroke Mitzy's head. The cat snuggled against her hand, purring softly.

The medic glanced up from taping her bandage and raised his eyebrows at the cat.

Lucy ignored him.

"You scared me," she whispered to Will.

He glanced at the bandage on her arm. "Could say the same. You okay?"

She followed his gaze there. Red splotches already seeped through the gauze.

"Just a scratch," she replied.

Dixie harrumphed. "Pfft. She needs a doctor. I'll take the cat. Hospitals get touchy if you show up with 'em."

She plucked Mitzy from Lucy's grasp and looked to Will, jerking her head in Lucy's direction. "Scared yer girl. Glad ya made it out."

Dixie turned, barked an order at one of the neighbors, and disappeared with Mitzy.

"Robbie's gone," Will squeezed her hand. "The roof collapsed. He didn't make it out."

He was gone. Robbie was really gone. She swallowed the lump in her throat. Relief or regret? She couldn't be entirely sure.

Will's whole body convulsed as he coughed.

"Will..." Lucy started, her blood pressure rising each time his lungs spasmed.

"She's ready to move," the medic yelled, and Lucy's stretcher lurched as someone pulled her to the ambulance.

Will's breaths were shallow, a horrible scraping sound on each inhale.

"Oxygen tank," the medic barked.

No. He was really hurt.

"I'm fi—" Will doubled over as a new round of spasms racked his lungs. Lucy tried to pry herself off the stretcher to help him.

One of the paramedics put a hand against her shoulder. "Let them take care of him."

They loaded Lucy into the back of the ambulance, and Will climbed in behind her. He sat across from her, holding an oxygen mask to his face.

"Will—"

"It's all right, Luce. Everything's fine." The oxygen mask muffled the words. His breath clouded the plastic, partially obscuring his serious expression.

He was wrong. Everything was not fine. Not fine at all.

CHAPTER
TWENTY-NINE

Sunshine radiated through the blinds into the sterile hospital room. Lucy blinked her eyes open and squinted against the light. She checked the clock on the wall at the foot of her bed. Nearly noon.

She was leaving Confluence. She rubbed her palms over her cheeks and blew out a breath.

She'd tell Will. Her path was somewhere else. The road she paved went a different direction.

When she sank back into her pillows, the one propped against the bandage on her arm shifted. She mashed her lips together at the tugging pressure. To her surprise, the emergency room doctors hadn't treated her immediately. They waited for the plastic surgeon to arrive. Everyone seemed put out about the delay, so she was fairly certain it wasn't protocol.

She had a suspicion it was Will's credit card that pulled Confluence's one and only plastic surgeon from his bed at midnight to fix her up.

A light tap at the door, and her nurse popped her head in. "Oh good, you're awake. You have a visitor. Feel up to it?"

"Who—"

"She's awake? Then of course she's up to it." Katie's voice came from the hallway.

"Katie?" Lucy raised herself up, grimaced, and lay back on the bed.

Katie slipped past the nurse into the room.

"Hey," Lucy called before the nurse could leave. "Is there any news? About Neilson?"

"I checked an hour ago, and he was still critical, can't say anything else without a release."

"Keep me posted if"—Lucy swallowed the lump in her throat and glanced down at the partially exposed bandage across her arm —"it changes?"

If he dies…

"I can do that," the nurse said softly before she left.

He had to make it. She couldn't process the alternative.

"How'd you get here?" Lucy tapped a button to raise the head of the bed a little.

"It's called a car. Nifty things. You get in them, turn the key, and they take you where you want to go." Katie leaned to give her a hug. The scent of gumdrops and cinnamon perfumed the air around her.

She took a long look at Lucy, pausing at the large swath of gauze and tape. "Jeff called me in the middle of the night to tell me what happened."

Jeff. After things calmed down at Camelot, he had visited with Lucy at the hospital to take her statement.

"Is he all right?" Lucy asked.

"He's beating himself up for not catching Robbie." Katie bit at her lower lip. "Listen. Between that whole alligator thing and your house burning down, I figured your family would be worried, so I called your parents last night when I heard."

Lucy sucked in a breath. "They aren't coming, are they?"

Katie scooted one of the metal guest chairs closer to the bed. "I told them not to, that you'd call later."

"My cell phone is presently a molten mess of plastic and metal somewhere in Camelot."

Katie flopped to the chair. "You can use mine when you're ready. Where's William?"

"Down the hall. Smoke inhalation. They're keeping him for observation."

Will did not appreciate being confined to a bed. The nurse informed her of this fact because, apparently, he was not being a model patient. As soon as they were separated in the emergency room, he insisted he needed to keep checking on Lucy. He finally agreed on a note passing system through the nurses—a flashback to the era before cell phones. The messages had stopped a few hours ago when the nurse told her they had taken him for a chest x-ray.

"Did you guys figure out your caterpillar problem?" Katie asked, a bit too casually.

"No." Lucy studied little bits of dust that danced in the light. "But then I got offered a job in Ohio. Reporter, anchor, they're giving me my pick. I'm taking the job. Will doesn't know yet."

Katie tilted her head, contemplative. "This is what you really want?"

What a person wanted seemed to shift, didn't it?

"When are you going to tell him?" Katie asked.

"Well, I guess as soon as we're alone. They say I'll be released this afternoon. I have no idea where I'm going to go though. Where are you staying while you're here?"

"At a hotel…with Jeff."

Um. Say again? "With Jeff?"

Katie's cheeks turned red. "The kid's staying with Dixie's at one of her other houses for a few nights."

"Is there something you never mentioned?" Lucy asked.

"We had a thing when I lived here."

Lucy's mouth dropped open. Then she lifted her hand to theatrically press it closed.

Katie fussed with the edge of Lucy's blanket. "It's not a big deal or anything. Nothing serious."

"I can't believe you held out on me with this," Lucy said low. "I mean, Jeff's totally adorable, but you never said anything about him."

"It's complicated."

Lucy gestured around the room. "I've got time."

"Is she in here?" The door muted the sound coming from the hallway, but Lucy recognized her mother's high-pitched voice immediately.

"She's got to be. They said she's in two-oh-four. This is two-oh-four," her father replied.

Lucy gritted her teeth. "Katie, is there an oxygen tank under the bed?"

Katie leaned down. "Yeah, do you want me to get a nurse?"

"No. Just, uh, hit me over the head with it until I'm in a coma. That'd be great."

"Lu—"

The door creaked open.

"Lulu, are you awake?" Her mother entered the room, and Lucy promptly pretended to be asleep. Or dead. Either would work.

Katie shook her arm. "Wake up, sleepy head. Your mom's here."

Lucy glowered at Katie and gave a little wave in her mother's direction. "Hey, Mom."

"There's my Luluroni." Her father barreled over her mother to get to the bed. He wrapped her in a huge hug.

Ugh. She hated that nickname. She gasped. "Dad. Bandages."

He reluctantly let go.

"Hi, Mr. Campbell. I thought we agreed you'd wait for Lucy to call?" Katie quirked her head to the side.

"Girl keeps getting herself in trouble. Figured I'd have to come sort this out."

Was he for real? "Sort what out, exactly?" Lucy asked.

"First that whole fiasco in California, now here. You need to quit winding up in the hospital."

Lucy scrunched her eyebrows together and opened her mouth to respond.

Her mother made a face at her. "Darling, you look atrocious. Do they not have combs at this hospital? We can pop out and get you one."

Lucy scowled. "Good to see you, too, Mom."

She pressed her eyes into slits and attempted to make Katie's head explode with only her mind.

It didn't work.

"Thank God I don't have to plan your funeral, Lulu. Can you even imagine?" Her mother flicked something from her fingers and wrinkled her nose as though the place smelled awful. At the moment, it was scented with industrial strength cleaner, gumdrops, and extreme irritation.

"I try not to, Mom."

Katie made big eyes at Lucy and mouthed, "I'm so sorry."

"She doesn't want to talk about death, Berta. She's in the hospital, for Pete's sake." Her father crossed his arms over his argyle sweater vest.

"Here we go," Lucy said under her breath.

"This is kind of fun to watch," Katie whispered.

Lucy disagreed. And she'd finally had enough.

"Mom. Dad. I had a really rough night. And you know what? It's actually been a really rough ten years. So, if you don't mind, I'd appreciate it if you'd go." Lucy gestured to the hallway. "Like. Now. Now would be great."

"That's very rude." Her mother dug through her Louis Vuitton purse. "Have you eaten? I thought I had some crackers from the plane. Darn, where'd they go?"

"You ate them while we waited for our bags." Her dad gave his condescending look he'd practiced to perfection.

"Right, well we can order something up. That'll make things better." She leaned to Katie. "She always had the strangest moods. Food's the best way to calm her down."

Lucy seethed, and the monitor at the side of the bed started to chime.

"Out. I mean it." Lucy pointed to the door. "You march in here uninvited telling me all the things that are wrong with me. If you want to come and support me, great. But you've been here less than three minutes, and you've insulted me, criticized my hair...and...I don't need you here for *that*."

"Is she on drugs?" her father asked Katie in total seriousness.

Lucy exaggerated a strangling noise.

"Luce." Will's hoarse voice came from the entry.

Her dark knight had come to her rescue again. Where had he found jeans and a T-shirt? And when did he have time to shower? He dropped a bag from the nearby café known for their breakfast burritos on the tray table next to her bed.

"You brought me food." Lucy's stomach rumbled at the thought.

Her mother raised an eyebrow at Katie.

"Who'd you have to bribe to sneak it in?" Lucy asked.

"No bribes, just some well-placed phone calls." He gestured to her parents and Katie. "Who are all these people?"

"My family."

"Hello, Lucy's family." He shrugged off his jacket.

Apparently, he planned to stick around awhile. She shouldn't have been relieved, but even with everything else, she felt better when he walked through the door.

She rummaged through the napkins and sauce packets. "Do you have any vodka?"

He chuckled. "No. They frown on mixing alcohol with your pain meds."

"*Lucy?*" her father asked. "Lulu, who calls you Lucy?"

"Everyone," she said, her focus attuned to the emotional eating frenzy in front of her.

"How'd you get out?" Katie asked Will.

"My x-rays and oxygen levels are fine, but I'll sound like I inhaled a bonfire for a while." He propped a hip to sit on the edge of her bed. "Hoped you'd be resting, so I stepped out to get you non-hospital-grade food. Looks like I missed the party."

"Where'd you get clothes? I thought your clothes all burned at my place?"

He stared at her a beat too long. "I have my ways."

"Lulu, why were his clothes at your house?" her father asked.

"You two are *living* together?" Her mother stared at Lucy as though she had suddenly sprouted a parasitic twin out of her neck.

"William Covington." Will cleared his throat and offered her mother his hand. She shook it and gave Lucy an accusing look.

"You're dating our girl?" her father asked.

Holy moly, they were acting like they got to have an opinion about this.

Will squeezed Lucy's knee. "Seems that way."

"What do you do, William?" Her father shot his patented witness-on-the-stand, take-em-down-death-ray stare at him.

This wasn't happening.

Will glanced to her and stopped abruptly, raising an eyebrow. "I...uh...own several television stations across the region."

Lucy snorted. "He owns dozens of them."

"Oh my." Her mother's nasally words pitched higher. "Why's he with you, dear?"

Katie gaped at her. Will tensed.

Lucy squeezed the burrito, and a chunk of chorizo plopped out.

"Why wouldn't I be?" Will had clicked into his get-it-done CEO tone.

Her mother paled. "She's...well...Lulu."

As though that explained exactly why he wouldn't want to be with her. The burrito landed, *thump*, a solid mass into Lucy's stomach.

"Berta." Her father's tone held warning.

Lucy was beyond over this little meeting. They were as impossible as they had always been.

"Could you both leave?" Lucy stared straight at her parents, vaguely aware of Will's hand moving to her leg. "I mean it. Don't come again. You've made your choices. Now I'm making mine. Please...go."

"She's kicking us out." Her mother glanced to her father. "Graham, she can't just kick us out."

"Lucille, apologize to your mother," he barked at her.

"No," Lucy replied, shocking even herself with the unyielding tone of the word.

Will stared her father down and spoke low. "You cannot show up here and take over. Lucy, Lulu, whatever you want to call her... she's not disposable. You can't toss her aside and come back later."

Whoa. What?

He wasn't done.

"I'm not sure what you see when you look at her, but the rest of us see the kind of person who takes in a cat because its owner died." He held a professional note of respect despite the boldness of his words. He rose and efficiently lifted Lucy's mother's coat, shook it out, and offered it to her. She reflexively slid an arm into the sleeve. "Lucy's the person who can't cook but bakes you a birthday cake anyway because she knows you're having a rough time." Her mother had a deer in the headlights expression painted across her face as he unceremoniously hung her purse on her rigid shoulder and guided her toward the door.

"What do you think you're doing?" her father sputtered. Will took a step back to pull shut the privacy curtain, separating them from Lucy. But she could still hear his words.

"She's the kind of woman who makes you smile by simply being in the same room. She asked you to leave. It's time for you to go."

Lucy stared in shock at the pastel-blue divider.

"You're out of line," her father said.

"I said she's not disposable," Will rasped.

"Holy shit," Katie whispered.

"This is a mistake, Lulu," her father called.

"Think she already asked you to leave." Will's words were granite.

More mutterings came from the doorway as they evacuated. But she knew her father was, how would he say it? Displeased. Very displeased. Will didn't seem thrilled either. For once, her mother remained silent.

Will emerged from behind the curtain.

"That explains so much." He wrapped up her abandoned burrito, as though he understood her appetite had vanished.

"I should…um…go. You need privacy." Katie stood and moved to the edge of the curtain. Then she turned and gave her a dazzling smile. "Lulu, can I have him when you're done? Or could you order me one just like him for Christmas?"

Will flashed the dimples at Katie, and she left.

The two of them were alone. And she had something to say.

Except, she couldn't remember what it was anymore.

CHAPTER
THIRTY

Lucy's pale face nearly matched the bleached white sheets of the hospital bed where she lay. But even after her parents' ambush, she seemed okay. William sat with her in the chair next to her bed and curled his fingers around hers. Her smile hit him straight in the gut. He wanted to wrap himself around her and never let go.

He had a lot of time to think last night.

He didn't want to be her boss. A partner made more sense. The way he'd been looking at the whole situation between them was wrong. With him as her boss, it couldn't work. But he wanted to be with her, not just temporary. He wanted her to be his partner.

In business and life.

He'd get her a real ring this time. His mother's engagement ring.

Selfishly unwilling to think about what his mother would have said about how badly he'd screwed up with Lucy, he'd left her letter on the counter. Now, the last words his mother had written to him were ashes in Camelot, opening nearly a decade of regret so deep it could swallow him whole.

But he had Lucy.

She had worn a ring once for him. He'd ask her to wear one again. This time there would be candlelight and roses and promises he would keep forever.

"No one's ever stood up to my parents like that." She twisted the pillow behind her and flinched.

"Do you need something for the pain?"

"I'm good." She bit her lip between her teeth.

He didn't buy it. This must've reflected in his face because her expression hardened.

"Will, serious." She untangled her fingers and patted the edge of the bed. "I'm fine."

He still wasn't buying it. She couldn't be fine.

He stood and leaned a hip against the bed.

The expression that passed across her face punched him in the gut.

"Luce. I'm so sorry. About what happened with the picture, and the name, and the story. I am so, so sorry."

God, he could suffocate in her and not even care. The woman was in a hospital bed, had been through hell, and he wanted nothing more than to ravage her senseless.

She fidgeted with the blanket covering her legs, unable or unwilling to meet his gaze.

He gestured to her arm. "Does it hurt?"

Stupid question. Of course it hurt.

She shook her head and scrunched her nose. "Stings mostly."

His throat worked against the convulsions of a cough building in his chest. The coughing fit overwhelmed him.

"Will?"

"I'm okay." His vocal cords felt like they'd been scoured with nails.

Her gaze finally caught his. "I never told you thank you. Last night. For everything you did."

He would throw himself in front of a train for her, just to have her look at him like she did before he'd found the photo. Used the horrible nickname.

He was so far gone for her. "I'd do it all again for you. But I'd do it better." Hello, cheesy. A dash of carbon monoxide poisoning clearly fried his brain.

"You shouldn't be sweet to me," she whispered.

"Why's that?"

"We need to talk." She glanced at her hands on the bed.

He tensed. Four words that held a promise that he absolutely wouldn't like what came next. "About what?"

"Before you got home, before the fire…" Her hands shook. Not a good sign. "I got a call from an affiliate in Ohio…" She moved her gaze to meet his. "They have a job opening, and they want me. I… I'm going to take it."

A weight pressed against his chest, and it had nothing to do with the smoke from the night before.

"You know this thing between us can't be permanent," she whispered. All the fight seemed to drain out of her.

He could not accept that.

Arms crossed, he blew out a breath. "It started to feel pretty permanent when I fell in love with you."

When I fell in love with you… The words were an anchor holding them in place. Hanging in the oxygen. Ready to devastate.

"People don't love me, Will. I'm not that kind of person." She glanced away because apparently the floor tiles were suddenly interesting.

"What kind of person is that?" He ruffled a hand through his hair.

She opened her mouth and closed it again. Cleared her throat and tried again. "The kind people love."

"Didn't get that memo." He searched her face but couldn't find the sliver of a future he'd hoped to find there. "I do love you."

Her expression softened slightly. "You only think you love me. It's just an illusion."

She said the words, but her eyes didn't match them.

He cleared the smoke from his throat. "I want to be with you."

She moved her hands away. "Will, it won't work."

He stared at her, unable to speak. She was leaving.

He tore his eyes from hers and rose from the bed, pacing to the window to put space between them. Distance, so he could think straight. He wasn't enough.

"Will," she said, "please say something."

The door creaked open.

"Vitals check," the nurse called from behind the curtain. She yanked it open and wheeled in the little cart.

"I should, ah, go. Check in on Neilson." William did what he did best, put on the mask, shut down emotion, and left without a backward glance.

"Will…" he thought he heard her say softly. He couldn't be sure.

————

William's world crumbled around him, but at least Neilson would be okay. Three gut shots and a bullet that grazed his lung. Dude had a guardian angel because he shouldn't have survived. But he had, and the doctors held out hope for a full recovery.

William left the intensive care unit and slipped past a doctor into the elevator. His head throbbed like someone had dropped-kicked it into a professional soccer match.

He was losing Lucy.

He'd said he loved her, but it wasn't enough. What he experienced last night was a trip through purgatory. Now he was officially in hell. A cough racked his lungs as the elevator chimed.

The doors slid open, and he moved to exit when Teresa stepped in. She glanced up and jerked to a stop.

"William." Her eyes glistened with unshed tears, and she wrapped her arms around him.

He let her. If he was in hell, he might as well embrace it. Seemingly on their own, his arms wrapped around her as she squeezed tighter.

"So worried. I call, and you are not here. No one knows where you are. We hear you are in the fire and nothing else." Her accent was heavier than normal. She leaned back and tapped his cheeks with her soft hands.

The doors slid closed again, cocooning them in the small cab of the elevator.

"I got out okay." His attempt at a reassuring smile clearly failed. "I'm fine."

She studied him. "You are not fine," she announced. "We will have tea. Talk."

"I—"

"Enough." She raised her palm to him. Teresa was apparently done with his avoidance. "We are family. Families have communication."

Yes, she was through with his dodging. She had used the tone she'd perfected when he was a child, and she was his nanny. That tone she'd used when he'd gotten caught stealing extra peanut butter cookies in the middle of the night. They'd had talks then, too.

But that was before his mother died. Before Teresa married his father, thrusting their betrayal into light.

She pushed the button for the first floor and gripped his hand as though he were a five-year-old again, ready to bolt. "Your father, he is at the police station asking for information about you. He worries." She dialed numbers on her cell phone and pressed it to her ear. "Hello? Yes, he is here. No...I don't know... Yes, of course I will." Her face softened. "*Ti amo anch'io.*"

Of course she loved his father. They'd been married for years. Still, hearing her say the words grated against his loyalty to his mother. He stuffed his hands in the pockets of his jeans. She clicked off the phone and shoved it in her purse as the elevator opened at the first floor.

"Where are we going?" He really should get back upstairs. Then again, if he were going upstairs so Lucy could put the final detail on her breakup with him, he might as well take his time.

"To talk." She jerked her chin toward the hospital cafeteria. He followed. When they arrived, she ordered tea for herself. He ordered nothing, so she ordered coffee for him.

They sat in a corner booth. He stared at the black sludge in his cup.

"How could you do it to her?" he whispered to the sludge.

Teresa lifted his chin with her fingers, so their eyes met. "Do what? To who?"

"You and dad, together. How could you do that to my mom?"

She shook her head, her thick black curls bouncing with the movement. "I'm sorry, I don't understand. Do what to Patricia?"

"The messing around." He glanced down again.

She leaned forward, her elbows on the table. "Mess around? I don't understand this?"

"Your affair with my father." There, it was out.

Teresa gasped. "*Affare.*" Her face gentled. "This is what you think? This is why you do not come home? William, look at me." He did, and she continued. "We did not. Never. Your mother was my friend. The best one. I would never…"

They were silent for a moment.

"We were with her when she died. Your father, he struggled with this, and he worked all the time. It is a hard thing to let someone go. I know this. From my first husband when he passed. It took time, but your father, he came home, and we were both there in the big house. We found comfort in each other. Comfort turned to love." Her dense accent thickened.

"You were with Mom? While she was dying?" He had to know she wasn't alone in those hours.

Teresa's eyes misted again, and she squeezed his hand across the table. "With her when she died." She had been there.

William swallowed the perpetual guilt at his absence when his mom had needed him most. "Tried to get back. I didn't have enough time."

"She knew. Your mother was very smart. She understand. That's why she wrote the letter for you, so you know she understand."

William cleared his throat from emotion and residual ozone. "Didn't read it. I was finally ready, and then it burned. Last night in the fire."

Teresa removed her hand from his and rested it on her cheek. She spoke under her breath in rapid-fire Italian. He couldn't keep up with it all, but she did use the term *"idiota"* along with his name multiple times, so he got the idea.

Finally, she closed her eyes and pressed her fingers against them. When she blinked them open, she spoke English again. "She was too weak, your mother. So, I write the letter for her. She told me what to say."

William couldn't breathe for a moment. "You know what it said?"

Teresa leaned forward against the table. "She is sorry for the words the last time you talk, and she is proud of the man you become. She say, she leaves you time to prepare before you run her company. Your father, he never wants to be in broadcasting. This is her family company, her dream. She hopes when you are ready you could be successful with Crestone, and your father, he can do the things he wants to do. He loves the boats with the sails. What do you call them?"

"Sailboats?" William asked.

"No, the other, the cat-a-something?"

"Catamaran?"

She gave a quick nod. "Yes. He loves them. We move to the ocean so he can sail. Your mother, she made a plan so he can do this."

William scooted his cup away, unable to speak. The years of worry that had rotted inside were now exposed. "Why did he fight so hard against me?"

"Your father, he is a hard man. You miss her funeral, our wedding. He loves you, but worries you aren't ready. He sees now. You are. Your mother, she trusted you. She loved you. Your father sees this, too, and he lets go now." Teresa wiped her tears on a handkerchief embroidered with poppies.

"Thank you," he rasped, and another round of coughing started.

"Something else is wrong," Teresa announced when he caught his breath.

Lucy.

Teresa didn't miss much. He had forgotten that about her.

"Lucy's leaving."

"That girl I met? Where is she going?"

"Yeah. She has another job offer. She's taking it. I messed up. It's done between us." He gripped the handle on the mug.

"You love her. I see this when you are together."

"She's still leaving."

"When you love someone, you come back to them. She is young, you are young…you don't know this about life yet."

"That's not how the world works, Teresa." His head started to throb in earnest, and not from the fire.

"He turns thirty, thinks he knows everything," she said to no one in particular. Then she said directly to him, "You trust me before. When you were a child. Trust me on this. You apologize, and you prove your love. If she loves you back, you'll find a way." Teresa raised an eyebrow at him. "Come to dinner with your father and me. No more excuses."

She stood and raised her arms with a little wave for him to hug her. He did. And he didn't let go.

"Thank you," he whispered into her hair.

"You need red wine for that cough." She gripped his shoulders and looked up at him. "And soak some sage leaves in the hot water, add some honey. It helps, too."

"Wine and sage. Got it."

"And dinner. You come to dinner."

"Wine, sage, and dinner. Okay." He squeezed her hand.

When she smiled, it hit him straight at his heart. He'd missed her. Missed that smile.

"Now, walk me out. You're a gentleman."

"I'm a gentleman," he parroted.

"This one"—she jerked her thumb at him—"always so smart."

He hugged her against him, and then he walked her to her car.

CHAPTER
THIRTY-ONE

Three weeks later…

William was sweating. The bright lights of the *Beach Nights Reunion* studio warmed the set past comfortable levels.

He tapped his foot against the blue carpeting and stared ahead into the array of cameras and screens, production crew and directors. His blood pressure rose higher than the ratings haul the producers assured him this show was sure to carry.

Lucy had to understand how he felt. She didn't believe he loved her, but he did. And he was willing to put his reputation on the line again to prove it to her.

Now he only hoped to hell she'd watch the show—and they wouldn't flay him again on national television.

"William?" Mason Hale, the host of the show, stuck his hand out to William.

He shook it. "Hale."

"Long time, huh?" Hale flopped in the seat across from William. "Heard you were a hold out to this whole thing." He gestured across the set.

William nodded. "Took a little convincing."

Cameras weren't rolling, but his mic was already attached to his collar, so he knew better than to say anything that could be edited into something it wasn't in post-production.

"What do you say we get this party started?" Hale took the cue cards a production assistant slipped to him.

"Sounds good." William stilled his tapping foot.

He was a journalist. He had spent years in front of the cameras. He shouldn't be terrified of what these assholes were about to do. And yet, he couldn't stop sweating— literally and figuratively.

Makeup powdered his face, and a cameraman wearing a headset held his fingers out beside camera two in a silent countdown from ten…nine…

He could do this. Eight…seven… For Lucy.

Six…five…

Because he loved her. Four…three…

And she needed to know how much. Two…one…

Camera two's red light flashed to green. The camera guy pointed to Hale in an exaggerated motion.

They were on. Hale blabbed an intro, the rushing in William's ears amplified, he plastered on a smile and waited for Hale to ask him something.

"We've got one of our most popular *Beach Nights* alumni with us today, but first let's take a look back." Hale smirked and the light on camera two flicked to red once more.

William stared at the monitor on the floor beside the camera. They put together a montage of William and his time on the show. He pressed his lips together. This was expected—the rehashing of the women, his idiocy, bringing the past back to the present. It's what he had to get through— the price he had to pay—for the chance to get through to Lucy.

"Next please," his younger self said from the monitor.

This is where Hale would pounce. The camera clicked to green without warning. Hale turned to William.

"So, inquiring minds want to know who *is* your latest *next, please*?" The Hollywood smile Hale flashed looked like a shark circling a bucket of chum.

The chum being William.

They were about to be disappointed.

"There's not a new, next please. Hasn't been for a long time." William glanced down and then looked straight into the camera. "Things changed for me. I'm not that guy anymore."

Ever the professional, Hale's expression didn't change, but William saw the way his eyes dilated briefly in annoyance.

"No one at all?" Hale probed.

"No. There's not another next, please."

"I'm sure our audience is disappoint—"

"Now, I'm in love with an *only one*," William cut him off. He wasn't the least bit sorry about it. "She doesn't believe that. So I'm here, in front of everyone, to make that point. So she'll believe me. Did you ever meet someone who just makes you happy, Hale?"

Hale's expression faltered. "I guess that's the question we're asking you."

"Yeah. I met her. She means everything, and I'd do anything so she understands how much I love her. Even come here and talk to you."

———

One Week Later …

"You did *not*." Katie slammed her hands on the table in not-so-mock shock.

Lucy gripped the flimsy table at the diner to steady it. "Yep. I kinda did."

She had done it. Quit her job. Again.

After watching Will on television, how could she not?

The few belongings she still owned were loaded up, and with only the cat for company, she spent two days driving the fifteen hundred miles to Denver for lunch with Katie, and then in a few hundred more miles, she would be home.

Home. Confluence.

Katie made a circle with her French fry in the air. "So I'm clear. He went on national television, said there isn't another 'next please,' so you decided that meant quit your job, drive across the country, surprise him, and hope he's still interested?"

Well...yeah. Lucy glanced at the hot dog she couldn't bring herself to eat because her nerves were shot. "This is quite possibly the stupidest thing I've ever done."

"Or the most romantic." Katie sighed.

"Maybe both?" Lucy shifted her elbows on the table and dropped her forehead to her palms.

Katie laughed. "Are you sticking around in Denver for a bit or headed straight through?"

"Lunch with you and then on to Will," Lucy said to the table.

He had called her a few times since the interview. She'd tried to pick up the phone, but couldn't bring herself to do it. Heck, she'd even attempted to call him a few times, but once his name was on the screen she couldn't press the button.

What she had to say needed to be said in person. "When are you thinking for the wedding?" Katie asked, casually.

"One thing at a time. I need to get to him first, find out if he even still wants me."

"He made a whole scene about how you aren't disposable to your parents." Katie made a face. "He still wants you."

Lucy hoped she was right.

Katie beamed. "Only one way to find out."

Yes, indeed. "Guess so." Lucy pushed the hot dog away. "I'm thinking I'd like red for the wedding."

"You could do a whole red and black theme. Or is that too Dracula?"

Lucy grunted. "One thing at a time, Katie."

"Don't put me too close to Jeff for the festivities. I'm not speaking to him."

"Why not?"

"That boy has mommy issues, kid issues, job issues, you-name-it issues. Let's just say, if it's an issue, he's probably got it." She paused, thoughtful. "Except bedroom issues."

"I'll never be able to look at him the same."

Katie raised an eyebrow, put her index finger at the edge of the bun, and then melodramatically pulled it out about a foot. She tossed Lucy a knowing look. "Not even kidding."

"You did not just tell me that."

"Nope, I believe I illustrated it. Now, either you eat that"—Katie gestured to the untouched hot dog—"or you hop in the car so I can go buy a bridesmaid dress. What's it gonna be?"

Lucy gagged. "I think you just ruined hot dogs for me forever."

———

Lucy gripped the pink plastic pet carrier as the elevator door opened to the plush lobby of the Crestone corporate offices. She could do this.

Mitzy scratched at the air holes and bawled.

"Stop it, Mitzy. We're almost there."

Will's receptionist wasn't around, and neither was anyone else. Lucy scooted past the reception area to where he sat, leaned over a stack of papers, the end of a ball-point pen between his lips. She wanted to be that pen.

His forehead creased, and his lips ticked down, but he still looked amazing. Two days of driving, and her appearance reflected it. She wore jeans and a purple, striped crewneck sweater liberally sprinkled with the remnants of potato chips and a few splashes of her orange soda.

He, on the other hand, looked like he just wrapped up a photo shoot for Eddie Bauer. It must have been a casual day at the Crestone offices because he wore jeans and a gray pullover with a little zipper at the neck. It was unzipped, revealing a lighter gray shirt underneath.

He poked at the buttons of the phone propped on his desk.

Lucy's own phone suddenly blared an Adele song from in her purse. She fumbled to silence it, and he snapped his head to the door.

"Hey." She waved to him.

His jaw went slack.

Mitzy gave a disgruntled howl from her carrier.

"Luce." He dropped the phone back into the cradle and stood. "I've been calling. What're you—"

"We need to talk." So much to say.

His expression went dark. Right. Last time she said those words to him, it hadn't gone so well.

"No, it's not bad or anything." Lucy grimaced. This wasn't going the way she planned. At all.

Mitzy slammed herself against the metal door of the carrier, apparently through with her temporary confinement.

Will's gaze dropped to her cage. "Is she okay?"

"She's grumpy from the drive." Lucy held the carrier up to her eye level. "Stop it, Mitzy."

The cat hissed.

"Should we let her out?" he asked.

"Probably." Neither of them moved to let Mitzy out of her confinement.

If a cat could huff, Mitzy did.

"I confess I needed to see you," Lucy said.

"We're confessing?" His eyebrows drew together, and his hands drifted to his hips. "What are you putting on the line?"

Oh.

She dug through her purse and patted her pockets.

Nothing.

The only thing she had was a furious cat. She bit at her lower lip and set Mitzy's carrier on his desk.

His lips twitched.

"I'll match that." He reached into his desk drawer and removed a blue Tiffany pouch. A brilliant diamond ring slipped into his hand. He set it beside Mitzy. "It was my mother's."

Lucy's lips parted slightly. Holy crap.

The ring. The cat.

"You first." He tucked his hands in his pockets and jerked his chin to her.

"I confess that I came to tell you…" She stumbled over the words. "I came to tell you that I quit my job. I know. It's totally crazy. But I messed up, I didn't listen, and new roads should be paved…and my future is here. It's…you."

"Roads should be paved?" he asked.

"Well, yeah. And you can change them, pave new ones." She pressed a hand to her forehead. "I didn't say that right. What I mean is I want to be with you."

He ran a hand over the back of his neck and studied the carpet.

"Here's the thing. I fell in love with you, too."

His face gentled further. "Come here, Lucy."

"Will? Wh—"

He walked purposely to her, and she couldn't say anything more because suddenly his arm was around her waist, and she was *there*. Then her bottom was on his desk, his hips were between her legs, and his mouth moved to take hers.

"Will, you didn't confess. That means you lose."

His face dipped lower. "You take that ring, Princess, and I'm pretty sure I just won."

She blinked. "You threw the game."

"Maybe."

"We're engaged?"

"Looks that way."

"Yeah," she said on a breath.

"Four kids," he said against her lips.

She made a face and pushed him back. "No."

"No to any kids, or no to four?"

"We've been over this. Two. And that's my final offer."

He unpinned her hair, running it through his fingers. "Works for me."

She curled her fingers around his arms. "I'm going to need a job."

"Crestone has some openings. Whatever you want to do."

"I was thinking I might try print journalism. See what they have available over at The River's Edge." She glanced up at him from under her eyelashes.

"You want to work for my competition?"

"Well, I can't work here. You're the boss. It'd be totally inappropriate. Or I could always become a breeder for hypoallergenic poodles."

"Yeah, Mitzy would *love* that."

"I'll figure something out. I've got time. But where are we gonna live?"

"I bought a house a few weeks after I moved to Confluence. It's not huge, but the neighborhood is good, and the decorator I hired has been working on it for a while, so there's some furniture."

"I don't understand. If you had a house, why'd you stay in Camelot?"

His eyes got soft, and he ran a thumb along her jaw. "You."

"Me?"

"I couldn't be away from you."

Her pulse skipped, and she nestled her cheek against his chest. He held her head against him, and they stood that way for a long, long time.

"Can I kiss you now?" he asked, tilting her chin so she looked at him.

"Wait." She held up a finger to his lips. "I almost forgot. I brought you something."

She leaned back and rummaged through her purse, digging out the letter she wrote him and the little package.

"What's this for?" He shook the package.

"For waiting for me."

The lines around his eyes relaxed.

"Open it," she urged.

He tore off the shiny brown wrapping paper. "A cat-shaped letter opener?"

"It goes with this." She slipped the thick envelope into his hand. "I know you have a thing about opening letters, so I figured I'd help out with that."

He flashed his dimples at her and slid the opener along the top of the envelope, breaking the seal and reading the first page. "Luce," he whispered.

"I couldn't remember exactly when I fell in love with you, so I wrote down all the times I knew I loved you."

His gentle expression was unreadable as he shuffled through the pages. "Some of these are from things from when we were in Florida?"

"Well, yeah. I was kind of in love with you back then, too."

The Adam's apple in his throat worked. "Most of the pages are blank?"

She rolled her eyes dramatically. "Well, I didn't actually expect you to open it."

He tossed her a bland look.

"Kidding." She trailed a finger along the edge of the papers. "Figured I'd need lots of pages so I could fill them in for the rest of our lives."

He searched her face, his golden eyes probing, consuming her. She moved her hands up along his sweater, along the ridges of his chest to his neck.

He kissed her then. Thoroughly.

When he broke the connection, the hope of a lifetime together reflected in his eyes. "I won."

"No, I think I did." She stroked the tender spot under his ear.

"Are we getting married?"

"Yeah," she replied.

"Then I won."

With those words, the pieces of herself she'd spent so much time barely holding together finally bound tight. Whatever he might think, clear to her bones she held the knowledge that *she* had won.

EPILOGUE

The KDVX live news van was parked in the dirt lot at the Miracle Mike Festival. A crowd had gathered to watch the interview as it broadcast on the five-thirty news. The rooster actually spoke this time. William grinned from his perch on the van's step. Lucy had insisted on taking the headless chicken interview. Turned out she had a bit of a competitive streak and wanted to prove the rooster would talk to her. He hadn't believed it could be done. She was proving him wrong.

With the sun tucked behind a large cloud, the dry heat of summer in Confluence took a break. It didn't matter, though. Lucy was oblivious to the world around her when on the job. In the summer heat or a winter blizzard, she didn't care once the camera rolled. His wife was funny like that.

Yeah, he had married her. It'd been almost a year now with no signs of the honeymoon being over yet. About two-point-five seconds after she'd accepted his proposal, he dragged her to the courthouse, and in front of God and a judge, they vowed to love each other as long as they lived. That was a lie, though. If any kind of afterlife existed, he'd love her then, too.

She now owned half of everything that was his, including KDVX. Apparently, that made it okay that she worked there sometimes. She didn't hang out at the station often, but every once in a while she'd tackle a story "to keep her skills sharp." That wasn't the whole truth, but he understood she got off on the high of being on camera, and he loved that about her.

These days, The Butterfly House Foundation she'd dreamed up took most of her attention. The foundation created anti-bullying agendas for kids through after-school programs. At the moment, the programs were full with a waiting list, and that was unacceptable to Lucy. She worked overtime to figure out how to expand their capacity. That was unacceptable to William because it bit into their time together. He was working on hiring an assistant for her. She hadn't agreed yet, but she would.

"Guess who got a rooster to talk?" Lucy sauntered toward him, her skirt molded to the curves of her hips.

He stood and dusted the dirt from his jeans. "You certainly have a way with cock."

She snorted. "C'mon, I've been saving my calories all week for a funnel cake. There's a place that puts whipped cream and those sugar-covered marshmallow chicken things on top."

"Peeps?" he asked.

Her eyes danced. "I heard they even lop off the heads before they serve them. Isn't that awesome?"

Yeah, she fit right in here at Confluence.

She grabbed his hand and made her way through the crowd. "If there's a food truck filled with marshmallow chicken heads, I wonder if they'd let me buy just the heads?"

"Anything you want, Princess."

"Have you talked to Parker, lately?" she asked.

Parker continued to keep track of William's investments in Colorado Springs. He'd turned that station around in only a few months. They'd been in the black for months, and everyone had kept their jobs.

"Yesterday."

"Allie?"

"Same."

Lucy glanced away. "I'm sorry."

He threaded her fingers with his and squeezed.

"Holy crap, is that Neilson?" She stopped abruptly. "Neilson!"

Her former bodyguard paused and turned around, the crowd parting to move around him. He nodded at William before his gaze fell on Lucy. "Lucy."

She scuttled to him and tossed her arms around his shoulders. Neilson glanced uncertainly at William.

He shrugged. "She's a hugger. What can I say?"

Neilson patted her back awkwardly until she stepped back.

"What're you doing here?" she asked.

"Festival security," Neilson replied, deadpan.

"I just got a chicken to talk. Well, it was a guy in a rooster suit, but I got him to talk." She beamed at Neilson.

"Nice work," he replied, a smile tugging at the edges of his lips.

"Actually, we need your help. Lucy's got a project, and we could use your expertise to install security." William put his hand out for Neilson.

The newest project of The Butterfly House was a safe haven for women—a secure place to live while they got back on their feet. His father had donated William's old family home to the Foundation when he and Teresa moved to Tortola. Turned out his dad had a heart after all. Lucy immediately went to work to change the zoning and renovate the property into apartments. Point two of why she needed an assistant.

Neilson shook William's hand. "Involve chickens?"

Lucy scowled at him and punched his shoulder. "No. Although...that's not a bad idea. Build a chicken coop. Maybe even get some horses."

William couldn't help the laugh that escaped his lips. "Whatever you want, Luce." He ran a hand over the small of her back. "Neilson, we'll be in touch to discuss the security of the livestock. We're off to find the funnel cake guy."

"Sounds good." Neilson squeezed Lucy's shoulder as he passed. "Have fun."

Lucy smiled at him before he disappeared into the crowd.

Turned out there really was a booth that sold funnel cakes with headless chicken Peeps on top.

"How much for a bag of the marshmallow heads?" William asked the concession guy.

"No one's ever asked that before," he replied. "Twenty dollars, I guess?"

"We'll take them. And whatever Lucy wants." William tugged out his wallet.

Lucy's eyes lit up, and the way her face went soft for William when the concession guy handed over the huge bag of marshmallows made it worth every dollar.

They stopped at a table near the kid's play area where toddlers climbed on oversize plastic farm animals. The bluegrass band on the stage warmed up for their set, and Lucy dusted the powdered sugar from a chunk of funnel cake. Yeah, life was pretty amazing these days.

"I confess I've been thinking." Lucy sat beside him and leaned her shoulder against his arm.

"We're confessing? What're you putting on the line?" He breathed in the scent of coconut on her hair. Heaven.

She held up the bag of marshmallow heads.

"Must be serious if you're willing to put your heads on the line." He reached into his pocket. "I've got keys to the truck and my last stick of gum. You go first."

She flicked at the powdered sugar on the side of her plate. "I confess I've been thinking that maybe we should start planning our family."

Warmth that had nothing to do with the summer filled his gut. He turned her to him and ran the pad of his thumb along her jaw, studying the freckles on her nose. There were eight of them. He'd counted.

"Are you ready for that?" he asked seriously.

"Yes," she said.

He swallowed. Hard. "That's amazing, Luce. That's—"

And then she kissed him, and she was his.
And he could breathe.

Don't miss out on future Christina Hovland releases!
Sign up for the newsletter at
christinahovland.com/newsletter.

ACKNOWLEDGMENTS

Thank you to my husband, Steve, who supported, encouraged, and held my hand through this dream of mine to write a book. My kids —all four of them—for being patient as I, "Just finished this chapter." Over and over and over.

My mom, Shirley, and my sister, Sereneti. You both are such a huge part of why I'm able to do what I do.

My best friend, Karie, who knows me better than I know myself and doesn't hesitate to come rescue me at midnight whenever I need it.

Kiele, thank you for always keeping me grounded. You are my person.

The C-Mommas for teaching me a game called *Confessions*. Blythe, Courtney, Dallas, Leeann, Jillian, Lindsay, Sarah, Shasta, Stephanie—for the support and always being my focus group. I love you ladies.

Courtney, thank you for being one of my first beta readers and my reading buddy.

Shasta, you are Queen of the Comma. Thank you for always being willing to answer my grammar questions.

Sarah, thank you for helping me unravel plot tangles and encouraging me.

Lindsay, I'm so blessed to have you as my cheerleader.

Jackie, thanks for the kickass line about being ass up on GMA.

And all the others I've lost touch with as our babies grew and life took over, thank you for being my friends.

Thank you to Amanda Heger, Alice Yu, Cheryl Pitones Rider,

Sara Dahmen, Kate Forest, Deb Julienne, Wendi Sotis, and Shannon Patterson for your advice and notes.

Victoria for answering my questions about hospital protocol and medical treatment for fictional characters.

Todd for answering random questions about the legal needs of fictional characters.

L.A. Mitchell for making me believe this dream is possible.

Corinne DeMaagd for all you taught me.

Tera Cuskaden, who championed this book like a boss!

The team at Prospect Agency. Very specifically, Emily Sylvan Kim.

Diane Holiday for being my first line critique partner on this story and for always being available to help me.

C.R. Grissom for always being there for me with a ready ear and a shot of infused vodka.

Deb Smolha, LeAnne Bristow, Miguella T. Twosias, Anne Morgan, and Claire Marti for the critiques, beta reads, and friendship.

And, finally, the Romance Chicks.

Dylann Crush.

Jody Holford.

Renee Ann Miller.

There are no words for the gratitude I feel daily for a random Twitter message that turned into life-long friendships with you ladies.

ABOUT THE AUTHOR

Christina Hovland lives her own version of a fairy tale—an artisan chocolatier by day and romance writer by night. Born in Colorado, Christina received a degree in journalism from Colorado State University. Before opening her chocolate company, Christina's career spanned from the television newsroom to managing an award-winning public relations firm. She's a recovering over-achiever and perfectionist with a love of cupcakes and dinner she doesn't have to cook herself. A 2017 Golden Heart® finalist, she lives in Colorado with her first-boyfriend-turned-husband, four children, and the sweetest dog around.

ChristinaHovland.com

facebook.com/HovlandWrites

x.com/HovlandWrites

instagram.com/HovlandWrites

goodreads.com/HovlandWrites

tiktok.com/@hovlandwrites

patreon.com/hovlandwrites

The Mile High Matched Series

Rock Hard Cowboy, Mile High Matched, Book .5

Going Down on One Knee, Mile High Matched, Book 1

Blow Me Away, Mile High Matched, Book 2

Take It Off the Menu, Mile High Matched, Book 3

Do Me a Favor, Mile High Matched, Book 4

Ball Sacked, Mile High Matched, Book 4.5

The Mile High Rocked Series

Played by the Rockstar, Mile High Rocked, Book 1

Knocked Up by the Rockstar, Mile High Rocked, Book 2

Married to the Rockstar, Mile High Rocked, Book 3

Tapped by the Rockstar, Mile High Rocked, Book 4

Reckless with the Rockstar, Mile High Rocked, Book 5

Standalone Novel(s)

The Honeymoon Trap

It Doesn't Have to Be This Hard

On the Map

The Mommy Wars Series

Rachel, Out of Office

There's Something About Molly

April May Fall

GOING DOWN ON ONE KNEE

**Turn the page for chapter one of
Going Down on One Knee!**

**He's a Rocker.
He's a Biker.
He's the wedding planner.**

Number-crunching Velma Johnson's perfectly planned life is right on course.

That's a lie. Sure, she's got the lucrative job. She's got the posh apartment. But her sister nabbed Velma's Mr. Right. There has to be a man out there for Velma. Hopefully, one who's hunky, wears pressed suits, and has a diversified financial portfolio. He'll be exactly like, well... her sister's new fiancé.

Badass biker Brek Montgomery blazes a trail across the country, managing Dimefront, one of the biggest rock bands of his generation. With the band on hiatus, Brek rolls into Denver to pay a quick visit to his family and friends. But when Brek's sister suddenly gets put on bed rest, she convinces Brek to take over her wedding planning business for the duration of her pregnancy.

Staying in Denver and dealing with bridezillas was not what Brek had in mind when he passed through town, but there is one particular maid-of-honor who might make his stay worthwhile.

Velma finds herself strangely attracted to the man planning her sister's wedding. Problem is, he ticks none of the boxes on her well-crafted list. Brek is rough around the edges, he cusses, and doesn't even have a 401(k). But trying something crazy might get her out of the rut of her dating life--so long as she lays down boundaries up front and sticks to her plan...

CHAPTER ONE

THE COUNTDOWN BEGINS

Three words. Three. Little. Words. Nothing important.

Okay, so the three words were important. Massive, really.

"Congratulations, you two," Velma Johnson rehearsed aloud to the vase of a dozen yellow roses gripped in her arms. With a reaffirming gulp of Denver's crisp spring air, she hustled through the open-air parking garage to the security door of her apartment building.

Her sister, Claire, had big news. To be exact, Claire and her boyfriend, Dean, had big news. Velma had a feeling she knew exactly what their news would be—they were moving in together. The next step in their relationship. Tension in Velma's neck strung tight at the thought.

A successful career and a posh apartment she could eventually rent out as an investment were steps one and two of Velma's elaborate five-year plan. She had ticked both those boxes. Dean, three kids, and moving to a two-story house just outside of Denver had been steps three through seven.

Not anymore. Now, her sister was moving in with the man Velma had crushed on for years. The one Velma measured all others against. The one she sang Prince and Madonna songs with at the office.

Yes, they were moving in together. That's why Claire had called yesterday and asked to take her to dinner. Velma had insisted they meet at her place instead. Her invitation had nothing to do with the fact she liked having Dean visit her apartment—even if he was with her sister. She'd offered because it made sense they'd want a private location for their big reveal. And when the announcement came that they'd be embracing that next relationship milestone...well, being on her home turf sounded pretty darn appealing.

Just as she reached the security door, the sound of a motorcycle that clearly had no muffler cut through her thoughts. She turned. The bike pulled up next to her car—into the parking spot meant for her guests. A super-muscled, badass-mother-trucker of a biker swung his leg over the side of the motorcycle and stood.

Her heart stopped with a *thunk*.

Vin-Diesel-biker-dude pulled off his helmet and—sweet mother of Mary, had the temperature jumped by ten degrees? She got the picture: he rode a motorcycle, hit the gym twice a day. The type she avoided because she did not do badass. She preferred the suspenders-and-slacks kind of man. Except, at that moment, she debated how important that preference really was to her.

Focus, Velma. Head held high, she approached him. "Excuse me? Sir? You can't park there."

He frowned at the number marking the spot.

Normally she wouldn't mind sharing the space, but with Claire, Dean, and his friend Brek coming to dinner, she needed both of her parking spaces.

This man was obviously not Dean's friend. Dean's friends were all buttoned-up, suit-wearing, Wednesday-afternoon golfers. She was nearly certain.

The black leather jacket and jeans ripped at this guy's knees looked horribly out of place next to her Prius. His longish, rock-'n'-roll blond hair was nicer than hers (although his could use a trim). She didn't even mind the dragon tattoo creeping around the side of his neck or the layer of mud coating his motorcycle boots. Everything about the man screamed masculine.

Velma shifted the heavy vase in her grip. *Fudge.* Which of her neighbors was letting their guests use her spot this time?

"No, see, that's the spot for my apartment." Oh, how she wanted to rub at the headache pulsing at her forehead. She didn't have time for this. Not today. "I'm sorry, it's just that my sister and her boyfriend and his friend are coming for dinner because my sister has big news. And while I have no idea what that news is, it's important to her. So that makes it important to me. Which is why I put on a pork roast, bought roses, and got out my crystal wine goblets. That's what you do when your sister has big news, you know? Never mind she's practically living my five-year plan without even trying, and I'm over here without even a boyfriend. *That* was not part of my plan. At this point, I should be at least six months into dating my future husband."

Oh God. She was rambling. And he was staring at her with a half grin that made her skin flush. Seriously, the way the man smiled should be outlawed.

She ducked her head. "Anyway, I have company coming and I kind of need my spot."

"Five-year plan?" he asked. As though that was the important part of what she'd just spit out.

This is how one makes an absolute idiot of oneself. "You know what? It's fine. You can stay right there. Don't worry about it." She shifted the flowers again and turned on her heel.

See? People said she was inflexible, but here she was, absolutely rolling with it. She smiled at her flexibility.

"One sec," Motorcycle Dude called. "This is the number they gave me."

She paused midstride and turned around.

He ticked his head to the side. "Velvet?"

Oh dear. She could easily be swayed by the gravelly way he said her name. Well, the nickname her family called her—despite her repeated cease-and-desist requests.

"Um, yes?" She gripped the glass vase harder with her clammy hands.

"Brek." He looked at her like she should know him and pointed to his chest. "Dean's friend."

Velma stared.

Oh.

This was Brek? She'd expected him to wear khaki pants and drive a Camry. He reached into one of his saddlebags and held up a six-pack of Coors and a four-pack of Bartles & Jaymes fuzzy-navel-flavored wine coolers. "Claire asked me to bring the beer and wine, since I'm crashing your party."

Wine coolers? She stared some more. *Be flexible*, she reminded herself. *Flexible. Flexible. Flexible.*

"Great. Fuzzy navel pairs perfectly with pork roast." Cheeks burning and arms full, she managed to open the security door.

"So, you're Claire's sister?" His lazy gaze trailed over her.

"The one and only."

His deep-blue eyes rivaled the color of the razzleberry lollipops she loved. The kind that made her mouth water just thinking about them and... *Focus, Velma.*

"Can I come up, Velvet?" His deep voice held a subtle hint of roughness.

"Velma," she corrected. "You're a little early. I'm so behind. Normally, I'm much more together."

"I can come back later." Brek's eyes softened, totally contrary to his outer badassery.

"No. I am officially the queen of flexibility. It's not a problem."

He did the darn grin thing again. She silently instructed her body to ignore it.

"Queen of flexibility. That ought to be interesting," he mumbled mostly to himself but loud enough for her to hear. He stepped next to her, balanced the beer and "wine" against the impressive muscles of one arm, and slid the vase she carried into the crook of his other arm.

"Thanks." This time it was her turn to mumble.

Without looking back, she led him up the stairs to her apartment. Another glance his way, and she'd probably trip face-first into the wall or something equally embarrassing. To prevent herself from taking another peek, she focused on sticking the key in the keyhole of her apartment door as though it took every ounce of her concentration.

There. The door swung open. He stepped through the doorframe, close enough for her to catch the scent of leather and Irish Spring soap. Close enough for her to reach out and touch the stubble running over his jawline. Close enough for her to—she shook her head to dislodge the abrupt light-headedness.

"This place is huge." With a long whistle, he set everything down on her dining room table.

Vaulted ceilings, open concept, white walls and sofa, with pops of jewel tones in her carefully selected décor; it must all appear so unnecessary to a guy like him. But these were her things, proof of everything she had worked so hard to achieve.

Brek walked into the kitchen and glanced to the slow cooker on the counter. "This smells amazing, Velvet. You a chef?"

"Velma," she corrected him again, slipping on an apron with the words *Domestic Diva* embroidered on the front. "And no, I just like to cook."

Velma took in the dinner she'd spent the afternoon planning and preparing. Vegetables had been roasted in the oven, and a chocolate cream pie was setting in the fridge. Not the pudding kind, either. A real, honest-to-goodness, made-from-whipping-cream-and-two-kinds-of-chocolate pie. She hoped she could eat those leftovers while she binge-watched Rodgers and Hammerstein musicals later.

"Then what do you do, Vel*ma*?" His emphasis on the last syllable made her wish her name wasn't so frumpy.

"For employment?" she asked.

"Yeah…or pleasure."

The expression on his face and the way he drew out the word "pleasure" made her toes curl in her sandals.

Right, employment. He'd asked about her work.

"I'm a financial planner," she replied.

Brek rubbed his hands together. "Like Dean?"

"Yup." She and Dean had worked together for years. "Our offices are across the hall from each other. That's how Dean met Claire." Claire had come to visit Velma at work and had wandered into Dean's office by accident.

That was the day Velma's dream of becoming Mrs. Dean Stuart died—all because she had waited too long to make her move and lost her chance.

Mr. Right had met her sister and they'd ended up together, making kissy faces during Thanksgiving dinner.

Actually, they never made kissy faces. The two of them were much too classy for that.

Brek leaned his hip against her granite countertop and crossed his leather-covered arms. "No idea what Dean does at his job, either, but I'm sure you're both fantastic at it."

"We help people with their financial portfolios. Annuities, estate plans, investment management, things like that. What about you?"

"I'm in the music industry." He snagged one of the crystal wine goblets she'd put out earlier and swaggered toward her.

Her stomach did a loop the loop. The swagger affected her more than expected. "You play in a band?"

"Nah. I play guitar, but not professionally. I manage a band." He popped the top off a wine cooler and poured it all the way to the tippy top of the glass. Then he edged inside her personal-space bubble and handed her the glass.

"Thanks." Normally, she didn't drink much—especially on Sundays. Monday marked the start of the week, with new chances and opportunities. She preferred to start it at her best, not hung over with a headache.

Then again, tonight was the night of change. Big-news change. My-sister's-moving-in-with-my-dream-man change. So Velma would have a wine cooler—no use in wasting it when Brek had already poured it—and ignore her attraction to Dean. Steps to a new life filled with…finding a new man who was as perfect for her as Dean was. Baby steps and all that.

Brek slipped off his jacket and tossed it over one of the island barstools. Tattoos ran from the short sleeves of his black T-shirt to his wrists. They looked tribal, mostly wild, and super-hot. If one liked tattoos. Which, she reminded herself, she did not.

"Claire says you two are twins?" Brek asked.

"Uh-huh," she muttered around a gulp of carbonated peach drink.

"You and Claire don't look like twins," Brek said.

Velma pulled a stack of small, hand-painted dessert plates from her for-company-only dish cupboard. "We're not identical."

"No kidding," he replied, serious. "It's the eyes."

Ha. Hardly just the eyes. Velma's eyes were muted gray, like a painter had finished painting for the day and just didn't feel like adding more cyan to the palette. Claire's were a rich brown. More than that, Claire was thin and Velma, well...she was Velma. All curves, like her mother. No matter how many calories she counted or steps the app on her phone registered, the curves stayed put. Velma's hair was dirty blonde. Not the attractive kind, either. In-desperate-need-of-highlights blonde was more like it. Claire's hair was a beautiful deep-chestnut color.

"Why does Claire call you Velvet?" Brek asked.

She sighed and paused, plate in hand. "Family nickname. No matter how many times I ask them to stop."

"Velma." He seemed to be testing the name, letting it melt on his tongue like warm chocolate on a vanilla sundae.

"Not a name I'd lie about." She set out the last of the plates on the table.

"I like it. It's original." The low, rumbly words made her lungs constrict in a warm way she refused to acknowledge.

"Unfortunately, it's not even original." She pulled a cutting board from the pantry. "Claire was born first, so she got the cool name. I was born three minutes later and got Velma."

"It's an interesting name."

"Velma was my grandmother's name. But there couldn't be two of us in the same family, so they all call me Velvet."

"I like Velvet," he said.

She scrunched up her nose. "I don't."

When she was a child, everyone bought her clothes with cheap velvet fabric. They itched. She hated them. As far as she was concerned, velvet was scratchy and uncomfortable.

"This news. Any idea what it is?" Velma asked.

"You don't know?" Brek replied.

"No idea." Except she was absolutely certain they were taking the next step in their relationship by moving in together, and maybe getting a puppy.

Brek popped the top on a Coors. "I figured you and Claire shared everything."

"Nope." Not this time. "Claire just said she has big news."

"Maybe she's knocked up," Brek suggested.

Velma's heart skipped five beats. She grabbed a knife and sliced into an onion with renewed energy. "No way."

"I don't know." He ran a palm over the back of his neck. "Seems reasonable to me."

"Then you don't know Claire. She's way too involved in her career to get pregnant right now." Velma set the onions aside and went to work on chopping carrots to top the salad.

Brek motioned to the cutting board. "Can I help you with anything?"

"Do you know how to julienne carrots?" Velma replied.

"Nope." He shrugged. "But I know how to cook a steak."

She laughed. "Well, tonight it's pork roast, so I'll have to take a rain check on your culinary skills."

"Absolutely. Next time I'm in town, I'll grill you up a steak." He raised his beer to her.

She stared at him. He couldn't actually be serious.

He was serious.

"Maybe they called us here because Dean needs a kidney?" he asked.

"He doesn't need a kidney." Although, Velma would probably give him one if needed. She had a remarkably hard time telling him no. "They're probably just…" *Say it out loud, Velma.* She sighed. "Just moving in together."

"Nah. They wouldn't have dragged me here for that. Maybe their big news is they're gonna try to hook us up."

"You and me?" Velma pointed the knife at Brek, then back to herself.

Of all the options, that one was the most reasonable. And, yet, totally unreasonable. No way would Claire pair the two of them together.

"You said you don't have a guy." Brek's tone turned serious.

Her body irrationally responded to his apparent interest with tingles.

"No." Of course she didn't have a guy.

She'd had lots of first dates lately.

"I get the feeling you need some help loosening up. Enjoy some time away from your five-year-husband-seeking plan. There's a club downtown with a great band playing later. We should go." Brek's gaze raked over her.

His pointed interest was actually…nice. Still, there was no way she would go clubbing later. Brek wasn't her type. Not only because of the tattoos or the extreme need for a licensed barber or his ripped jeans. No, it was more the general sense of unease he stirred within her. Also, it was Sunday. What kind of a club was open on a Sunday night? Definitely not one she should visit.

"You stressed about the dinner?" he asked.

"No," she lied through her teeth.

"You're stressed about the dinner," he declared. "I get that, but there's nothing to worry about."

For a half second, she believed there was nothing to worry about. Truth was, there was always something to worry about. Starting with her clothes. She needed to change into something that wasn't yoga pants before her sister arrived in what would undoubtedly be a perfect sundress.

"I'm only in town for a few days anyway," he continued. "We'll get through the part where Claire and Dean do the awkward you-two-should-get-to-know-each-other schtick. We'll eat and then we'll send them on their way. You don't want to go to a club? That's fine. I'll stick around. What do you say, Velma?"

The way he said her name felt like silk against her skin. Silk was so much nicer than velvet.

She tried to tug off her apron, but her hair was stuck in the tie at the back of her neck. Crud. Another tug. Her hair was really stuck. "You want to go clubbing on a Sunday night?"

"Absolutely." He nodded to where her hair was caught. "Need some help?"

"Yes, please." She pressed her eyes closed.

He looped a finger under the little bow tying the apron at the back of her neck. His calloused fingertip traced the ribbon along her shoulder to the collar of her sweater, unraveling the knot of hair and sending little shivers along his path of exploration.

Maybe she could get away to the club for a little while. It wasn't like she had better things to do. "Where is this cl—"

"Hey, Velvet." Her sister, Claire, shoved open the front door. "Hi, Brek. You made it. Dean's so excited you're here."

"Did you lose him?" Brek squeezed Velma's shoulder.

A hit of sizzle deep in her belly echoed the motion of his touch.

"He's parking the car." Claire closed the door and sauntered to the kitchen with her svelte build and Audrey Hepburn grace. "Okay, I know I've made you wait. But…" Claire bit at the light-pink lipstick on her bottom lip. "Surprise!" She held out her fingers with a little jazz hand motion.

An *engagement* ring perched on the fourth finger of Claire's left hand.

Velma's heart skidded to her toes. She blinked hard. No, it couldn't be.

A ring.

A wedding.

Satin and lace, champagne toasts and flower girls.

This wasn't a puppy. And it was so much more than an apartment.

Velma reached for Claire's hand, her throat constricting. "Oh my gosh."

"I know, right?" Claire squeezed Velma's fingers. "I had to tell you in person."

"Oh. My. Gosh." Velma said again, this time more slowly. She looked straight into Claire's eyes and saw it—excitement and love for Dean. Happiness. Velma glued a grin onto her face. Her sister was happy. That was all that mattered. "Claire. It's perfect."

"I'm gonna go find Dean." Brek caught Velma's gaze and winked. "Now that the cat's out of the bag."

"Wait, you knew about this?" Velma asked.

"Hell yeah, I knew." Brek opened the door. "Didn't want to ruin Claire's surprise, though."

"So you asked me out instead?" Velma asked.

Claire scrunched up her forehead. "Brek asked you out? Like on a date?"

"Oh look, it's Dean." Brek feigned innocence as he held the door wide. "I'm officially saved by the groom."

"She finally told her?" Dean strode inside and glanced to where Velma stood in a swirling vortex of time.

"Uh-huh." Claire nodded, her eyes misted over.

A suit. Dean wore a tailored suit complete with shined cap-toed shoes and gold cuff links. Each black hair on his head lay precisely where it should. He was absolute perfection.

Velma swallowed the heaviness in her throat and tried to pretend it was from excitement for her sister.

"Well, then—hey, sis." Dean strutted toward Velma and wrapped her in a hug. "Claire made me keep my mouth shut for a whole week."

Velma's insides did a little flutter that was totally unacceptable. Time moved at the speed of a sloth. Like watching a car accident happen in real time, when everything went slow and then fast again all at once. "You've been engaged for a week and didn't say anything?"

They'd sat through a load of sales meetings. Two client lunches where he'd driven them both to the restaurant. He'd never given any indication he'd freaking proposed to her sister. They'd discussed retirement plans and supplemental income sources. He hadn't mentioned anything that would've even whispered of proposal news.

"Believe me, it was hard keeping my mouth shut. Can you believe you're going to be my little sister?" His breath brushed against the top of her head.

"Uh…nope," Velma said through gritted teeth.

"It's great, isn't it?" Dean leaned back and scanned her face.

Her knees went weak, like a cheesy movie heroine.

"It is great. Totally. Great. I'm so excited." Velma stepped away from him, refusing to show anything but happiness for her sister's sake. Any feelings from now on would be purely of the appropriate sisterly kind.

Claire and Dean were engaged.

Yup, Velma's Mr. Right was going to marry her sister.